THE
WITCHES OF
EAST MAILING

STEVE HIGGS

VINCI
BOOKS

Vinci Books

vinci-books.com

Published by Vinci Books Ltd in 2025

1

A CIP catalogue record for this book is available from the British Library.

Paperback ISBN: 9781036708573

The EU GPSR authorised representative is Logos Europe, 9 rue Nicolas Poussion, 17000 La Rochelle, France contact@logoseurope.eu

By Steve Higgs

Blue Moon Investigations

Paranormal Nonsense

The Phantom of Barker Mill

Amanda Harper Paranormal Detective

The Klowns of Kent

Dead Pirates of Cawsand

In the Doodoo with Voodoo

The Witches of East Malling

Crop Circles, Cows and Crazy Aliens

Whispers in the Rigging

Paws of the Yeti

Under a Blue Moon

Night Work

Lord Hale's Monster

Herne Bay Howlers

Undead Incorporated

The Ghoul of Christmas Past

The Sandman

Jailhouse Golem

Sparks in the Darkness

Shadow in the Mine

Ghost Writer

Monsters Everywhere

Modern Fairy Tale
No Such Thing as Magic

Albert Smith Culinary Capers

Pork Pie Pandemonium
Bakewell Tart Bludgeoning
Stilton Slaughter
Bedfordshire Clanger Calamity
Death of a Yorkshire Pudding
Cumberland Sausage Shocker
Arbroath Smokie Slaying
Dundee Cake Deception
Lancashire Hotpot Peril
Blackpool Rock Bloodshed
Kent Coast Oyster Obliteration
Eton Mess Massacre
Cornish Pasty Conspiracy
The Gastrothief
Lyme Regis Layover
Majestic Mystery

Car Chase

I watched my knuckles turn white where they gripped the dashboard. I had both legs braced against the forward bulkhead of the car, the bit that separates the cockpit from the engine bay, knowing even as I did, that doing so meant I would most likely break them both if we did crash.

'Hang on!' yelled Jagjit as he flung the steering wheel around. The car was right on the edge of its ability, the tyres screeching their complaint as they struggled for grip amid competing forces, some trying to propel the car forward, some trying to send it barrelling sideways. A spray of gravel was spat from the right rear tyre as he fought for control, but we were through the turn and picking up speed once more as he straightened out and smashed the pedal again.

I relaxed my grip on the roof handle above my head and risked a glance in the door mirror.

'Are they still behind us?' Jagjit asked, his voice betraying his nervousness.

I peered into the mirror once more. The road behind us

1

was clear but I could only see as far back as the corner we had just come around. I watched, counting seconds in my head. One, two, three… Then the huge black car shot into view, its blocky nose looking like a threat bearing down on us.

'Yup. And gaining fast.' I settled back into my chair, but I was hardly relaxed.

'There's no way we are going to make it,' Jagjit whined.

'Just keep going, mate.' I needed to keep him calm, keep his thoughts on the road. At the speed he was driving, it could all go wrong so quickly if he took his attention away from the next bend, the next obstacle.

We were on Drythorn road, heading out of Maidstone, doing over eighty miles per hour where the limit was fifty. It was anything but safe, but we had no option but to keep going. We had a long stretch of straight now, maybe a mile where he could push his speed.

I glanced over my shoulder at the car behind us, it was gaining. The driver less concerned for his safety than Jagjit. I saw Jagjit glance in his rear-view mirror also, then utter a loud expletive. I was thrown forward against the seatbelt as he slammed on the brakes.

Less than one hundred yards ahead of us, a tractor had pulled onto the road, emerging from a field with a loaded trailer on the back. Jagjit's tyres were skipping over the road surface, once again fighting for grip as he tried to avoid hitting the slow-moving object unexpectedly in front of him.

Quite how the black four by four behind us hadn't hit Jagjit's back end was beyond comprehension. There was no way Jagjit could slow down in time, our speed was too great.

The tractor though was driving with one enormous wheel against the hedgerow. The other was in the middle of the road and the gap to the hedgerow on the other side was maybe just big enough for us to slip through. Jagjit had seen it too.

'Dammit,' he swore as he flicked the steering wheel. With no choice but to try it, he lifted his foot from the brakes and, still doing forty miles per hour, he shot by the surprised farmer.

The driver's door mirror caught something solid in the hedge and smacked against the glass of his window, the sound loud in the quiet confines of his car. Then he was fishtailing back onto the road ahead of the tractor. I swung around to see if the larger black car would make it through.

'I think we lost them,' I told Jagjit.

His face grim, he didn't answer. He just pushed the pedal closer to the carpet and picked up speed again.

'We are going to make it, mate. Don't worry.'

He glanced across at me. He was sweating with worry.

'It's only a fitting,' I pointed out.

'Tempest, you would not believe the strings my father had to pull to get us an appointment here at all. When I enquired, they said they couldn't fit me in until March. I mean, March! I'm getting married in four weeks. So, when this cancellation popped up, I knew it was my only chance. What's the time?'

I shot my cuff to check my watch. '1723hrs.'

'Dammit.'

'We are going to make it. They said they would stay open as long as you got there before they close. You have seven minutes and it's only three or four minutes away.'

'They got through,' he announced excitedly.

I looked behind to see Big Ben's huge Ford Ranger bearing down on us again. In it were Big Ben, Hilary, and

Basic. The four of us were to be Jagjit's groomsmen. I only found out this morning that he had proposed. He had only been dating the lady for a few weeks but apparently, that is all it took in their case.

After the battle with the Klowns, which seemed like a lifetime ago but was, in fact, only two weeks ago today, he had considered his options and popped the question. She had been present when they attacked and had been distraught when he sent her to safety so he could come back to fight the Klowns with Big Ben and me. It had been a dangerous situation and could have gone far less positively than it had.

Anyway, Jagjit and Alice fell into the category of whirl-wind romance, and they had set a date of November the 26th and now had to get a lot done in a short space of time. Jagjit thought he already filled me in, but his email had never reached me in Cornwall. It was of no consequence now.

He had left work early today to organise his grooms-men, and we were at his parent's house chatting about what he needed us to do, where the wedding was going to be and a million other details when the call had come through to say Anton Ricoh, famed wedding outfitter, could see us. In a blind panic, we had dived into our cars to blast our way cross-country to Meopham where his boutique bordered the village green. I had heard of the man but knew nothing about him and would never consider spending the insane amounts he was going to charge.

I mused though that chances were most grooms just did as their bride instructed. I was curious to hear if his Indian parents, with their extended Indian family were happy about their youngest son marrying a Caucasian girl. I would not bring the subject up though, so would only find out if he volunteered the information. He had been married once before, a distant cousin that had been pushed into the arrangement as much as he had, I think.

It had lasted only a few months, but I got the impression he gave it an honest try. Now he was in love it seemed, and desperate to please the lady now firmly rooted at the centre of his life.

He slowed his pace as we came to Meopham village outskirts. It was not a big village, the green was directly ahead of us, so with four minutes to spare we were pulling up outside the double fronted shop.

Inside the windows were immaculate suits, hats, gowns, dinner jackets and wedding suits displayed on mannequins. In quite small gold writing it boasted that the proprietor served at the Queen's appointment.

The doors swished open, being held by two well-dressed young gentlemen and we were welcomed inside.

Pub O'Clock

The fitting had eaten up only an hour. For the most part, it had been entertaining as the tailors had struggled with the dimensions of both Big Ben and Basic. I will admit the five of us look like a study in genetics when put in a line. Big Ben stands six feet and seven inches tall and has wide, muscular shoulders tapering to a thin waist because he's lean like a professional fitness model. I carry enough muscle to be called athletic and spend a reasonable amount of time in the gym, but I also have a covering of body fat masking my abs because unlike Big Ben, I cannot drink beer and maintain a perfect figure. Hilary is as skinny as a rake. No matter what he wears, he looks like it's two sizes too big and hanging from his bony frame. Jagjit is slight but is arguably the most generic or normal looking one of us and then there is Basic. Basic is blocky, Basic is above average height and Basic is wide. If a witch turned a fruit machine into a human and gave it flesh, then Basic is what it would look like. He was maybe a couple of inches taller than me, but one couldn't tell because he was permanently slouched. I estimated that he weighed fifty percent more than me and it was almost all muscle.

When the fitting was done, Jagjit had come away happy. The suits would be made up in time for the big ceremony in four weeks, so we had thanked the gentlemen and left them to close up. It was the first time I had been fitted for clothes since I left the Army. Back then, there were appointed tailors that provided ceremonial uniforms and did a great side business in hand-fitted suits.

The drive back to Finchampstead had been at a more leisurely pace, the panic of missing out on something thankfully gone. It was now Friday evening so, as practice dictates, it was time to frequent the local alehouse and sink a few cold beverages.

The village only had one pub, the Dirty Habit, so named for the Friary just outside the village to the south. Our visits there had become a regular Friday night event. Big Ben had ditched his car at my place, and I had hopped out of Jagjit's car next to an alleyway that connected where his parents lived with the street my house was on. I needed to go home and collect my dogs. The two pesky dachshunds were popular at the pub. There they would be given affection and attention by eighty percent of the patrons.

I pushed open my front door as the two dopey sausages tried to force their way out of the widening crack.

'Hey, chaps,' I greeted them as they climbed my legs for attention. I came down to their level so they could lick my hands as I scratched their ears and necks. 'Ready for a trip to the pub?' I asked as I took their collars and leads from the wicker basket I kept on a shelf next to the front door. They buzzed around my feet in excitement.

Whether they understood what I asked them I couldn't tell, but I knew they would drag me into the pub if I took them in that direction and they were generally happy to go out for a walk despite their natural inclination toward laziness.

No more than ten minutes later, having circumnavigated one half of the village in a circuitous route that exercised the dogs, I entered the pub car park with them both straining at their leads as they dragged me to the door and into the warm.

The alcohol-scented walls of the Dirty Habit were familiar and comforting. It was a place where I had spent many hours talking nonsense and drinking beer. To my left, an open fire was kicking out not only heat but the wonderful smell of a real fire. The accompanying crackling, popping noises a joy to hear. To my right, was a roundtable with the four chaps sitting around it, already halfway down their first drink as they hadn't wasted precious drinking time fetching their dogs as I had. Whoever had bought the first round had been thoughtful enough to get a pint in for me. It was sitting untouched in front of an empty chair, condensation running down it to wet the cardboard mat it was sitting on.

In front of me, was the bar. I had no reason to approach it as I already had a drink, but for the first time in a few weeks, Natasha was serving. Now that I thought about it, it was I that had been missing recently. The last two Fridays in a row I had been absent so she might have been here after all. Whether she had or not, it seemed like a long time since I had seen her.

I debated waving a hello in her direction. I wasn't sure what our current relationship status was though. About a month ago she had kissed me and placed the ball in my court. I was probably supposed to have used the ball to score a goal if that is not extending the analogy too far. Instead, I had lost the damned ball or in actuality, her number, so I hadn't called and by the time I tracked her down she had decided that I wasn't worth the effort. I worried that she might be right.

She noticed me standing near the pub entrance though and smiled in my direction. She had been quite short with me the last time we spoke, so this was a marked improvement. Buoyed by that, I smiled back at her, gave a little wave of greeting and took my seat.

'Evening, chaps. Did I miss anything?'

'Only Big Ben telling us about his latest shag. It seems he finally broke his once only rule,' said Hilary.

'And he thinks he might have got a girl pregnant,' added Jagjit.

'Oh? Occupational hazard I should think, Ben. We can circle back to that bit of information. I want to hear about Patience. How did that come about?' I snagged my pint from the table and gulped down a third of it in two swallows. It had started to warm already but was still pleasantly cold.

'It was mostly your fault,' Big Ben replied accusingly.

I set my pint down, my brow ruffled. 'I don't follow, dear boy. Do explain.'

'I ended up spending half of last week with Hotstuff. With you away, she was getting herself into bother. Did she tell you about the spiders and the snakes?'

'She did.'

'What about spiders and snakes?' Jagjit wanted to know.

'I'll tell you later, mate,' said Big Ben before turning his attention back to me. 'So, I rescued her from a gang of kids on the Magdalene Estate, then went with her to rescue a client that was being stalked by the voodoo priest dick and ended up staying at her place because the client said she felt safer with me around.'

I thought about it for a second, 'You mean you shagged her.'

'Well, obviously, but I prefer to think of it as *really* close protection. Anyway, that was Monday night and after that the whole week slipped by without me getting another shag.'

'I still don't see how that is my fault,' I stated, taking another sip of my drink.

'Because to start with, I figured that it was only fair to give you the time you needed to finally pluck up some gumption and give Amanda a seeing to. I know how much you like her. You have been a mooney-eyed kid since she turned up last month.'

I opened my mouth to protest, but around the table, all the others were nodding their agreement. I stayed silent.

Big Ben continued, 'Then I discover she has a boyfriend. Some rich butthole, but she let it slip that she hadn't got around to sleeping with him yet. So where does that leave me? She isn't interested in you because she's dating someone else, she isn't sleeping with her boyfriend because of goodness only knows what reason. So, I figure I might as well remove all the charm suppressors that have been stopping her from throwing herself at me, vagina first, like any sensible woman would, but having done so, nothing happened. I swear that girl is broken. I thought it might have been shark week, but then she stayed a night at my place when the spiders were rampaging hers and she didn't bring any feminine products with her, so it wasn't that either.'

He lapsed into silence. I gave him a minute.

'I still don't get it. What does Amanda's ability to see what a scumbag you are, have to do with you sleeping with Patience for the second time?'

'Oh yeah. Lost track of what I was saying there a bit.

So, Tuesday night no action because I'm with Amanda. Wednesday night no action because I'm with Amanda again but this time she's dressed as a man and all the girls stay away because they assume I'm gay. Thursday night I spent getting tortured and beaten. By the time today had rolled around I had gone three days without sex. When was the last time you went three days without sex?' he asked me, then indicated the question was open to the rest of the table.

'Right now, actually,' I replied.

'I'm married,' replied Hilary. When we looked at him to clarify his answer he said, 'I hardly ever have sex.'

Basic had no answer and Jagjit was grinning because he now had a girlfriend, and I was willing to bet they celebrated the sun going up and going down by visiting each other's private places.

'Weak. Just weak,' Big Ben said shaking his head. 'In contrast to you shandy-sniffing, lightweight excuses for men, I last went three days when I was fourteen. By last night I was starting to get the shakes.'

'You can't get the shakes from having no sex,' I replied.

'How would you know? You can't go cold turkey if you never get any turkey to start with. Patience offered me no-holes-barred action, and I took the deal.'

'Wait. The expression is no-holds-barred,' pointed out Hilary. 'It comes from wrestling where, in some bouts, there are certain holds that one cannot apply to an opponent ...' He saw our expressions and realised he'd misunderstood the premise.

Jagjit leaned over and whispered in his ear.

Big Ben grinned.

Hilary caught on. 'Oh,' he said quietly, his cheeks flushing.

'Anyone want to go to see the fireworks at Leeds Castle tomorrow night?' Big Ben wanted to know.

'Maybe. Let's get back to the bit about you getting a girl pregnant first though, shall we? How did you even find out? I thought you always sanitised their phones to remove your number before you left?'

'I do. Remember the Big Ben business cards?'

'Yeah. For all your vaginal needs. Isn't that the marketing strapline you use?'

'Yeah. Works like a charm,' he boasted, then remembered his plight and looked unhappy again. 'Well, I hadn't thought that thing all the way through and it had my number on it.'

'Making you easy to find.'

'Yeah.'

'Do you even remember her?' Hilary asked.

'Of course. I keep a journal. She was the super-hot redhead on September 9th. I met her in the coffee shop on Fremlin Walk.'

'You don't know her name, do you?' Jagjit said.

'It's Bethany,' he replied, exasperation creeping into his voice.

It was my turn to ask a question, 'Did you know her name before she told you what it was today?'

'Nope,' he said proudly. 'That's why she's listed as the super-hot redhead.' Just then his phone pinged. It often did that and usually, it was a woman looking for sex. He often left the pub on a Friday night with a woman waiting outside his apartment for him to get there. As he looked at the screen his expression changed from one of mild curiosity, wondering what the message might be, to one of dread. 'I don't believe it.'

He put the phone on the table face up so we could see

it. Hilary, Jagjit and I all leaned in to read the screen. Basic leaned in as well, but I think he only did it because everyone else was. I wasn't sure if he could read.

'Hi Ben, It's Britney. I need to meet with you. I think I'm pregnant.'

'Oops,' said Hilary.

'They say problems come in threes ...' Jagjit smirked.

Big Ben locked eyes with him. He wasn't seeing the funny side.

'Soooo. How about the fireworks then, buddy?' I interjected to break the tension.

'I'm going to the gents,' he announced, standing up.

'And I'm going to the bar.' I collected the empties as Big Ben wandered away. 'Same again all around?' I confirmed. There were nods in reply and a thumbs up from Basic.

At the bar was Natasha, waiting to serve me.

'Hello, Tempest. Are you well?' she asked as she took the empty glasses

'Yes, thank you, Natasha. Are we friends again?'

'Same drinks, yes?' she enquired, dealing with business first. She was dressed much the same as always with one of those miracle bras that made her ample breasts defy gravity and a top that showed off a surprising amount of them. Her hair was getting longer, her natural, lustrous brunette locks falling over one shoulder to hang lower than her boobs. She positioned two glasses to begin pouring drinks, then glanced back up at me. She had made me wait a few seconds before answering my question. 'That, I think, depends on whether you still think you deserve a second chance and what you might do with it if there was one.'

From below the bar, Mr Wriggly had grabbed a bugle and was calling reveille to his two small round friends.

I was flapping my lips and failing to speak as usual. Mr

Wriggly was getting cross with me. If he had a foot, he would kick me in the two friends sitting just below him. It was an idle threat, but I put my brain into gear and formed a response anyway.

'Whether I deserve a second chance or not, is not for me to decide, but I will say that I feel we will both miss out if we do not pursue a second date.'

'A second date?'

'I'm counting lunch in Rochester as the first date. We were alone, it was nice, we kissed. It felt like a date to me.'

'Are you trying to get to date three, Tempest?' she asked, a single eyebrow raised.

My cheeks felt warm. 'That's not really how I do things, Natasha. I'm not looking for a date because I want a particular outcome. I would like to talk to you about what I do want if I can entice you into coming out for dinner with me.'

'Well, I don't know, Tempest. It might have to be something special if you want to *entice* me.' She was teasing me. She finished pouring my beverages.

'And take one for yourself,' I said as I handed over thirty pounds. 'When are you free?'

'How about Wednesday evening?'

'I'm always free, lady. If Wednesday works for you, then I will make dinner reservations and will pick you up.'

'Well, you have my number.'

'No, I don't actually. That was the problem. You wrote it on a note, and I don't know what I did with it, but I never saw it again. I'm not even sure I took it out of the restaurant with me after you handed it over.'

'Oh,' she said, her face colouring slightly. 'I thought that was just some excuse you came up with for not calling me.'

'No, I'm genuinely stupid. I lost your number and had

no way of getting it. I don't even know your last name and the Landlord, bless him, is very protective of you. I near enough begged him for your number, and he wouldn't give it up.'

'Bless him.'

That's not what I had said.

From behind me came a fake coughing noise. The chaps wanted their drinks and were being dicks about waiting while I sorted out my life.

'You go,' Natasha said. 'You're drinking, so this is not the time to talk properly. I will look forward to Wednesday. First though, give me your phone.'

I handed it over and watched as she created a new contact called Natasha Stow. She saved it and now I really didn't have an excuse. I didn't feel that I needed one though. I was back on track with Natasha, a woman I had been interested in for a long time.

I left her with a final smile and went back to the chaps, trying very hard to not look like the winner I knew I was.

I had snagged a bag of pork scratchings for the dogs to share. Their Friday night treat. I would usually split it three ways and eat a third myself, but in contrast to their trim waistlines after a week of getting far more exercise than usual in Cornwall, my waistline had expanded, and I was topping it off with several beers now. I was going to start a whole new regime tomorrow. I had already stocked my fridge and cupboard with the food I needed to be eating. So, while I gave myself the concession of a Friday night drinking with the boys, I didn't want to add to that with deep-fried pig skin.

The dachshunds were climbing my legs to get to them anyway, so I upended the bag and watched them do a damned good impression of a Hungry Hippos game as they made the crispy treats disappear.

The chaps wanted to hear about my time in Cornwall. They had seen the news reports and the reporter I had met there was still covering it, her face being beamed around the world no doubt as the treasure was to be slowly excavated and catalogued.

I launched into a long-winded tale of my Cornish adventure and the beer flowed.

Something Jagjit and Hilary were talking about had caught Big Ben's attention. He and I had been talking about his pregnancy dilemma, then he wasn't listening because he was paying attention to them instead.

'What's going on?' I asked.

'I was telling Jagjit that he needs to establish dominance straight away when they move in together,' said Hilary. 'I didn't and have always been the one taking orders instead of giving them.' He looked miserable.

'Is that how you see it?' I wanted to know. 'Anthea rules over you? Shouldn't it be mutual with both of you as equals?' I had never been married but just as I couldn't imagine being subservient to a woman, I would equally have no wish to dominate her either. That didn't sound like any kind of partnership to me.

'That's how it is. I let Anthea make some decisions, gave her the accounts to manage, that sort of thing and she just kind of took over. Before I realised it, I was operating to her schedule, doing what she told me. Fifteen years in I don't see how I can change that.'

Big Ben was shaking his head. 'Mate, are you sure you don't suck balls for a living? Women like to be dominated. Not in a manner that makes them feel diminished, but so they feel that you are their support, their strong arm to rely on, their big, manly man. Plus, in the bedroom, they all love to be dominated. Ever meet a lady that doesn't love to be spanked?'

'I've never tried,' admitted Hilary.

'There you go, mate. You could change the dynamic of your relationship with a little playful spanking. Pin that lady against the wall, give her a seeing to she won't forget, and she will want you to take the reins.'

'You have met my wife, right?' he asked.

Big Ben took a long swig of his drink and set it back on the table. 'All ladies are basically the same, buddy.' He claimed knowingly. 'Give it a try. What harm can it do?'

Hilary grabbed his glass while he thought about his answer. He opened his mouth to take a swig but stopped with the glass halfway to his lips. 'I don't know,' he concluded.

The group fell silent for a moment and when the conversation picked back up the topic had moved on to rugby and who was going to win this weekend.

Later, at home, I settled the dogs onto their side of the bed and slid under the duvet on my side. As I laid down to sleep, I thought about Natasha.

New Client, New Case

Saturday was one of the days when I habitually did not get up early to frequent the gym. I allowed myself the weekly concession of a night in the pub drinking on a Friday. I had done this even when I was in the Army, and even though I never had so much to drink that I felt groggy the next morning or had a hangover, it still seemed prudent to avoid thrashing my body with a gruelling workout when it was less than well hydrated. Going to the pub also meant that I was getting to bed later than I normally would, so I gave myself a lie in on a Saturday.

Today was like that, but I had added in the extra indulgence of getting a cup of tea and bringing it back to bed. The clock next to me claimed it was 0815hrs. I would get up soon as I had tasks to get on with. I had been away all week so had turfed my dirty laundry into the washing machine yesterday and into the tumble dryer last night as I went to bed. By lunchtime today I would have it all ironed and put away, would have cleaned the car and sorted out the house so that all was back to normal. It was going to take more work than I had expected though.

I had raced back from Cornwall last night in response to a message from Jane that suggested Amanda and Big Ben were in trouble. I couldn't raise anyone on their phones because, unbeknownst to me at the time, they were all being held captive by a crazy voodoo family. I had been able to hastily mobilize the police, mount a rescue and thankfully they were all fine, although somewhat the worse for wear. But the real shock had come once I was back in my house, had traipsed upstairs and turned on the bedroom light.

In my bed, was the client Amanda had stashed in my place to keep her safe. Amanda had forgotten to tell me she was here and forgotten to tell the client that I might come home.

She had screamed when the light woke her up and there was a man she did not know at the foot of the bed. I had screamed out of pure fright because she was screaming, and my poor sleep-deprived brain couldn't process the information fast enough.

Once I got my bladder back under control and managed to introduce myself, and once she understood that I was not there to do anything to her, I called Amanda, and we cleared the mess up. It was the middle of the night, and I really wanted to sleep in my own bed, but decorum dictated that I was on the couch downstairs until a more sociable time of the day. That had proven to be just after 0600hrs in Kimberly's opinion. She explained that she hadn't been able to get back to sleep and had called a cab to collect her.

I had thanked her and wished her luck, then fallen into the still warm sheets where sleep had taken me in seconds. I had been tired most of the day despite staying in bed until almost noon.

The bedding she had been sleeping in had gone into the wash and the spare bedding was what I was sleeping in now. I would rearrange it all, make the house look as I wanted it to look and then I would feel ready to run my business out of it and have my staff working here. It was not even close to an ideal solution, so among the tasks for today was contact Tony Jarvis and see how the rebuild of my office was going. I expected to be out of it for weeks, if not months and now I was back, I needed to look for somewhere more appropriate, albeit temporary, to work from.

I drained the last of my tea, swung my legs meaningfully over the side of the bed, argued with myself for ten seconds about the merits of getting another hour of sleep then reluctantly embraced the day. I had plugged my phone in downstairs to recharge overnight so didn't hear it ringing while I was upstairs getting a shower and brushing my teeth.

When I arrived in my kitchen, I saw the screen was lit and that I had four missed calls from the same number.

I pressed the kettle into service again and hit dial to call the person back.

I heard it pick up, 'Hello?' a man's voice at the other end. I judged his age as thirties probably. An adult definitely and without the wobble that might suggest an older person.

'Good morning. This is Tempest Michaels of the Blue Moon Investigation Agency. I have several missed calls from this number. How may I help you please?'

'Mr Michaels I am given to understand from your website that you investigate strange occurrences, things that cannot be explained. Paranormal phenomenon and such. Is that correct?'

'Indeed, Sir. My firm specialises in solving cases others

have dismissed or have filed as paranormal. What is the nature of your enquiry please?' I had just returned home from a week away, so I had no live cases open and needed paid work. Amanda had just neatly wrapped up a case for Kimberly (my unexpected house guest yesterday) but had almost done it pro bono despite employing others to help out. I suspected the books would record a negative for it. Other cases had paid well recently, and I would most likely have taken the case on if Amanda hadn't, so I had nothing negative to say about her actions.

Before I had to prompt him, the man told me why he was calling. 'I believe my stepmother used witchcraft to kill my father.'

Right. Witchcraft. Why not? I hadn't tackled witchcraft yet.

'I need to ask you some questions, take some notes if I may. Can you tell me your name please?'

'Of course, sorry. It's Michael Cotton.'

'Thank you, Michael. What can you tell me about the circumstances of your father's death please?'

He hesitated. I heard him breathe in as if he were about to start speaking but then stop.

I realised my potential error. 'Sorry, Michael, was it recent?'

'It was three weeks ago. It still feels recent. Sorry, I'm having a little trouble talking about it. It was very violent you see. The coroner's verdict was accidental death. She claimed my father was hit by lightning and there was a lightning storm on the day that he died. But the lightning hit him in the chest. I have been researching lightning strike victims and have learned that it never hits you in the chest. To be more accurate, it tends to hit you everywhere at once. My father was hit by a lightning bolt that exploded his rib cage and burnt his heart to a crisp. That just doesn't happen. There's another extraordinary element, though.'

'Go on.'

'He was inside his house.'

'Understood,' I replied taking notes feverishly. 'Where does the witchcraft connection come in, please?'

'I live in the same village as my father and his wife. Mum divorced him years ago. Not that I blame her, he was a cheating arse that deserved all he got, but I loved him nonetheless and I saw him every week. I got on okay with his new wife but the two of them seemed to be growing apart and then I noticed odd little things in the house. Dreamcatchers, that sort of thing. Odd symbols are written in chalk on the walls outside. I asked dad about it, but he hadn't noticed them, and he didn't know what they were or where they had come from.'

'Then he died suddenly, and she didn't seem surprised or bothered and then two weeks after his death an enormous cheque came through the post from a life insurance policy she had taken out. I don't think he even knew about it. '

'I went to the police, but they were content with the verdict and had no interest in reopening the case. I believe my father was murdered and I want you to help me prove it.'

It certainly sounded like a case to me. 'We need to meet Mr Cotton. Should I just call you Mick or Michael?'

'Mick would be better. I can meet as soon as you are available, Tempest.'

'Next question then. Where are you?'

'East Malling, not far from the research centre if you know where that is.' Indeed, I did. It would take me twenty minutes to get there, and I needed to walk the dogs and feed them and feed myself. Ironing would have to wait.

'I can be with you for 1030hrs if that is convenient. I just need your address.' Mick was only too happy with the speed of my response. I took his address and promised to see him shortly.

'Okay, dogs,' I called out. 'Time for a walk.' I got the usual response from them which was to be utterly ignored. They had been in the garden when we got downstairs, so their morning toilet needs had been taken care of. They had no need to go anywhere so far as they were concerned. They accepted defeat though and got up as I slid collars over their heads and clipped on their leads. It was a pleasant morning, and the exercise would do all three of us good.

There was dappled shade coming from the blue sky today as I walked through the vineyard. It was cool out, maybe no warmer than six or seven centigrade, which I believed to be cold for early November. There had been frost on the cars this morning. No doubt there had been frost on the hedgerows and fields also, sending the little creatures that lived there to hide in their warm burrows. The dogs were inspecting one such burrow now, each trying to nudge the other out of the way, their tails swishing back and forth with the exciting smell they had found. I ushered them onwards, enjoying the tranquillity of the countryside. In the distance, about halfway up the hill in front of me, I watched as the high roof of a truck could be seen between the trees. Any noise from it failed to reach my ears.

Back at the house, I took the dogs' collars from their heads and watched them scamper into the house. They were back to their routine of sleeping as many hours as they could. I had set some oats out to soak in yoghurt and milk while I was walking. I had meant to do it last night but had forgotten so overnight oats were now thirty-minute oats, but they were soft enough and once paired with nuts, fruit and seeds made a gloriously healthy breakfast. This was a good thing because I had weighed myself this morning and I had gained fourteen pounds. I had been slightly horrified but knew why it had happened. The answer was that I had been lazy for the last few weeks. I had been making excuses.

You might think several broken ribs are a perfectly good reason to avoid the gym and I would agree. What I should have done to balance the equation though was cut back on my calorie intake. If anything, I had increased it, and the scales were showing me the result. Now it was time to beat myself back into shape and that would include a hard session at the gym this afternoon.

Right now, though, I wanted to meet Mick Cotton and get my teeth into a new case. With my spoon delivering breakfast to my hungry mouth, I swiped my phone, brought up Amanda's number and dialled it.

She answered on the third ring. Typically, I had just put a spoonful of oats into my mouth. 'Hi, Tempest, what's up?'

'I have a case. We have a case. Probably,' I managed after a second of clearing my mouth with a swig of tea. 'I'm heading over to see the client now. I don't need you to do anything. Take as long as you need before coming back. I just wanted to let you know so you are involved.' I doubted Amanda would take any time off, she did not strike me as the sort, but she had been through the mill on the voodoo case, and I wanted her to feel she could have time if she needed it.

'Thank you, Tempest. I have a day of spa treatments and pampering planned. I need to get the icky feeling to go away. I expect I will see you first thing Monday though.'

'Very good. Well, that was all I called for.'

'Tempest?'

'Yes.' My heart beat in my chest. Having learned last night that Amanda and Brett were no longer an item, or were at least enduring a pause in their relationship, I was questioning whether there was any point in hoping I might have a shot. I still felt that she exists behind an invisible employee barrier where I could not send Mr Wriggly. Maybe it would be okay if it were she that removed the barrier. Was she about to ask if I was still interested in her?

'What sort of case is it?' she asked, sending a pin to burst my bubble and onwards into my heart.

'Err, witchcraft apparently. I shall know more once I meet the client. I doubt I will get much more than preliminary research done this weekend, but I can give you a clearer report on Monday.'

Amanda wished me good luck and disconnected. I went upstairs to change out of my walking boots and cargo trousers and into an outfit more appropriate for a client meeting. The dogs were gently snoring on the sofa when I checked on them. They would most likely not move until I returned in a few hours. I bid them goodbye, went out to my car, slid behind the wheel and headed for East Malling.

Dead Dad

I got stuck behind a tractor for about two miles on the winding road that leads out to East Malling and had to gun the engine a bit to make sure I arrived precisely on time and not late. My satnav took me directly to his door which he opened as I was getting out of my car.

Michael Cotton was relatively plain in every aspect of his appearance. Not that he was ugly, but he wore drab clothes, and he stood with his shoulders drooping which made him look smaller than he was. His hair was cut in an unfashionable style that ended just below his ears and made his head look like a spiky mushroom. His eyes didn't sparkle, which might have been from sadness, but I suspected it was more from a lack of life in his life. He was about my age but looked older.

'Tempest,' he said my name as he stepped forward to take my offered hand. I didn't attempt to give his hand a manly squeeze like I normally would. It was the right move as he simply grasped my hand lightly then let his fingers fall away again having barely touched them. 'Thank you for being punctual. I looked you up. You are ex-Army. My dad was too, and he was always a stickler for being on time.'

I had no response to his statement. I could hardly argue as I was very time conscious, but it made me feel odd that people were not only able to find out details about me but then did so and were content to reveal that they had.

I followed him into the house where he led me through to a lounge area that overlooked his garden through large patio doors – the type that fold to one side to open the entire room on days when it's warm enough to do so. The garden contoured downwards to a river at the bottom but not steeply and it was nicely maintained with clipped hedges and borders.

'Would you like a tea?' he asked, indicating for me to sit while he was still standing.

'Yes, thank you. White please, no sugar.' Mick left the room. Presently, I heard a kettle getting agitated and cups rattling on saucers. He returned a few minutes later with a tray that held a teapot and all the accompanying crockery.

He began talking while he poured, 'My father and his wife, Mabel, were married for twelve years at the time of his death. She was the woman he was having an affair with when mum left him. She was nice enough to me, but I was a teenager when the divorce occurred, and I always believe that she was only nice to me because she had to be. I think she would have displayed her ugly side if she thought she could get away with it.'

'I have no evidence that their relationship was breaking down. Certainly, dad never said that it was, but I felt a certain tension between them this year that hadn't been there before. Then the odd little trinkets started turning up and the symbols on the house. Now that you are here, I feel like I might have jumped to a conclusion. It's the lightning thing, you see. That is the bit that really doesn't fit. I made a copy of all the research I have done. I wanted to talk to some experts about it but have not been able to so far. Maybe you will have more luck.'

'Okay, Mick, tell me what it is that you want to get out of this.' It was an important question that I needed him to be able to frame for himself.

'I think… I think I just want to hear definitively if my dad did die of a lightning strike or not. I believe that he didn't. If you are able to speak with experts on the matter, Fulminologists I think they are called, and they conclude that lightning killed him, then I will stop. However, I think they will scoff at the idea, in which case something else killed him and I think my stepmother has been up to something. I have seen her meeting with four other women. I followed her a few times. Three of them are ordinary middle-aged housewives, but the last one is an ugly old crone.' I wondered if he had used those particular words because he was accusing her of being a witch.

'And if I'm able to show that a lightning strike was unlikely to be the cause of death?'

'Then I want you to find out how he was killed and if my stepmother was involved, I want her boiled in vinegar!' his voice rose to an angry crescendo with the last few words. Mick had been stewing over this for some time. 'Sorry,' he said, taking a sip of tea. 'What I mean is, I would like her to be brought to justice.'

I nodded my understanding then launched into my speech about the limitations of my powers. I could investigate and create a case, but I couldn't arrest or prosecute. I then opened the topic of fees at which point Mick laughed.

I tilted my head at him to encourage an explanation.

'Mabel got so much money from the insurance payout

that she gave me ten thousand and said that dad would have wanted me to have it. I think it was intended to keep me sweet and shut me up, so the irony that made me laugh is that I intend to use it to pay you to prove she's guilty.'

I wondered if proving murder would then make the claim void and all the money would need to go back but did not think that now was the time to voice it.

Mick got up and crossed the room where he opened a cabinet and retrieved a cardboard box folder. 'This is everything I have gathered so far,' he said as he handed it over. 'I have most of it electronically as well, so I will email it all to you as well.'

It would keep Jane busy when she returned to work next week. I thanked him for his time and for his business and made my way back to the door. We shook hands again and I promised him regular updates.

My watch told me it was 1153hrs, so I would get home for lunch, do some housework and get to the gym. I felt invigorated. I had a new case. I had a purpose for the days ahead. And I was going to get my body back into shape starting this afternoon.

CrossFit

I had given myself enough time for my lunch of tuna and courgette cakes to settle before setting off to the gym. I was dressed and ready for a hard workout when I got there. Much like martial arts, I never stuck to one discipline. I would switch from training karate, to judo, to aikido and then maybe krav maga as I enjoyed them all and each gave a different perspective on how to defend and to turn an attacker's moves against them. I had the same thing with fitness training in that I believe there was no singular right answer and that the only wrong answer was to do none at all. Some days I would pound away lifting heavy weights, other time I would pound away at the pavement running. I still swam occasionally although I found it to be one of the most boring forms of fitness training and sometimes I did CrossFit where one combined lifting weights and body-weight movements with explosive cardio exercises such as burpees and more endurance-based cardio such as running or swimming or biking.

I had a workout in my head that was going to kick my

backside, and it started with me dropping my bag and going back outside to run a mile. I kept the pace up, pushing myself as I completed the first element, then, already sweating despite the cool air, I went back inside and started throwing out rounds of overhead squats, pull ups, burpees, hanging sit-ups and squat cleans. I did three rounds of twenty of each and just as I thought I might die, I went for another one-mile run. By the time I got back to the gym for the second time I was soaked to the bone with sweat, but I had a second round of exercises planned. This time I performed three rounds of twenty deadlifts, twenty shoulder presses, forty press ups and twenty dips. Then guess what? I went for that run again. Convincing myself to push hard on the third mile loop was hard. My legs felt like jelly but after sixty-three minutes I touched the wall of the gym and stopped.

Then I promptly threw up.

I did make it to a handy rubbish bin though and avoided leaving an unsightly mess for the staff to tackle.

With legs that threatened to cramp, I performed ten minutes of warm-down stretches before collecting my bag, replacing my wet shorts and vest with a dry, cotton tracksuit and wobbling my way back to my car. I was going home for a soak in the bath.

Big Ben and I were out tonight, and I was driving. I volunteered to drive only because it meant I couldn't drink and would thus avoid unnecessary calories. I conceded that I might have one gin and slimline tonic though.

Remember, Remember

Big Ben didn't put up much of a fight when I said I wanted to get there early. Leeds Castle has enormous grounds. So big in fact, that I had once lost my car here for more than an hour and had to wait for most other people to leave before I could find it. That had been many years ago and I hadn't made the same mistake again. Also, the later you arrived the further away from the central area you would be parked. The further you would then have to walk to get to the festivities and the greater the search area for your car became when, in the dark, you couldn't find it.

I pulled up outside his house just as the clock was ticking over to 1900hrs. What can I say? Punctuality is a skill.

'How's the body?' I asked as Big Ben slid into my car. Big Ben had suffered some rough treatment at the hands of a family engaged in voodoo practices just a little more than twenty-four hours ago. I thought he was lucky to have no broken bones and only three stitches.

Rather than talk about the extent of his injuries, he

replied flippantly with, 'Lean, tanned, muscular and hand-some. Damned handsome.'

'Of course,' I responded. Big Ben and I had met in Iraq in 2003. There was warfighting to do, so although the conflict itself was quite brief, we got into a few scrapes and had gotten into a few since. I knew that he wouldn't open up about how he was feeling, but I wanted to give him the chance anyway.

'Is anyone else going tonight?' he asked, meaning other people from my circle that he might know.

None of the chaps at the pub were coming and I hadn't thought to discuss it with anyone else.

'No. I don't think so. I didn't discuss it with anyone,' I said.

'Why are we going again?' he asked.

'Because you said it was a great place to pick up girls and, as you all too frequently point out, I'm hopelessly single.'

'Well, it's a great place to pick up girls, if you are me. Anywhere that I am is instantly a great place to pick up girls.'

I swivelled my head to look at him in the darkened space of the car's interior. 'You are such a dick,' I assured him. This was typical Big Ben. He wanted to go somewhere and was certain to pick up a girl there. I was just his chauffeur and would most likely come home alone as he got a lift to a random lady's house.

He laughed. 'Don't worry, mate. There are bound to be some cast offs for you to pick from.'

'Utter, utter dick,' I concluded.

Most of the journey thereafter was conducted in silence. Big Ben appeared to be fretting, possibly about the two ladies that claimed to be having his babies. I thought about asking him about it, but before I could he hit me with a snippet of information I hadn't expected to hear.

'Amanda broke up with her boyfriend, did you know?'

'No. I thought she was really into him. What happened?'

'I did, apparently. When her place was full of spiders and she kind of freaked out I took her back to mine place and… Brett, is that his name?'

'Yes.'

'Well. Brett saw us together and assumed she was cheating on him. I don't know any more than that. Patience told me about it the other night.'

I wasn't sure how I felt about that. I felt sorry for Amanda, I knew she was rather enamoured with the stupidly handsome and rich Brett Barker. I wanted to say that I didn't like him but trying to be mature about it for a moment, I had to admit that I didn't know him. He and I had met as adversaries. Neither one of us had won, unless you were counting Amanda as the prize in which case I was definitely the loser.

I decided to just not think about it.

I was right about the parking, but we were not early enough to avoid being directed into a field. I followed the line of taillights into the dark and was waved into a space by one of the many attendants trying to manage the thousands of cars pouring into the castle grounds. Despite the hi-vis vest and torch, he was still having to avoid being run over by overzealous drivers trying to get their car parked and their hyped-up kids out.

Big Ben and I started down the hill to the castle. I turned around and took some photographs in the hope that I could find my way back by using what little navigation points I could find. Big Ben generously didn't bother to wait for me. I jogged to catch up.

As we entered the castle grounds proper, it was all lit magnificently with large floodlights that had been erected for the event. The castle itself was always lit at night. Light from inside making it look warm, more floodlights sunk into the ground outside highlighting the perfection that it was.

I spotted what I had been looking for. 'Gin tent,' I announced while pointing to our left, where a flag with the Fevertree logo could be seen waving in the sky.

Big Ben smacked his lips together envisaging the divine taste. 'Yes, please. Make mine a double,' he requested and produced a crisp twenty pounds note from a pocket.

'Top man,' I replied as I took it and began moving away from him. 'Where will you be?'

He took a second to look around, then pointed. I followed his line of sight and spotted two young ladies toting Guys on sack barrows. They were dressed in saucy steam-punk cosplay outfits. I knew why Big Ben had selected them: They both looked like Victoria's Secret models.

'I'll be over there,' he said, pointing at the two young women, 'scoring.'

'I bet burgers at the Oak that you'll strike out.' I figured it was fifty-fifty whether Big Ben could take one of these lovely ladies home tonight and that was assuming they were straight. They could easily be gay so I kind of fancied my odds. Honestly though, the burgers at the Oak are so good I was still a winner even if I was buying them.

'Challenge accepted.' I nodded then strode toward the gin tent, leaving Big Ben to do what he always does.

The gin tent was busy. Behind the counter were twenty or more well-presented bar staff. The chaps had stiff black shirts with the sleeves rolled up and charcoal aprons that contrasted just enough. Some of them had waxed mustaches that curled over at the ends. I don't know why, but I instantly felt assured, like a man with styled facial hair must be able to make a good gin and tonic. About twenty percent of the staff were female, dressed similarly but without the facial hair of course. They did all have long hair though and each of them had it pulled into a French plait.

I waited my turn patiently and whiled away my time inspecting the bottles of gin on display behind the raised bar. Making a choice would be difficult. Did I pick something new? Did I play it safe and go with something I knew? I searched along the rows until I spotted what I had hoped to see – a rare bottle of Chatham Dockyard gin. It was a local brew that one would not find outside of the County unless someone bought it and took it there. It had a wonderful after-hit of cardamom that I treasured.

Finally, I was next to be served. The two ladies in front of me had their drinks but were flapping around trying to find their purses. I gave them a moment, but it became clear they were without funds to pay for their beverages and were looking very embarrassed.

I stepped closer, 'Sorry, ladies. I couldn't help but overhear your plight. Would it be acceptable for me to pay for your drinks?' they eyed me uncertainly then looked at each other. 'I don't see any other way of getting to the bar,' I joked and thankfully it cracked the ice.

'That's very generous of you,' the one to my left said as I handed over the twenty pound note I already had in my hand. Her heritage was Jamaican maybe, my guess would be one of the islands in that chain anyway, but her accent was local, and she had most likely been born here. To my right the other lady had a trace of Japanese about her. They were both short, five feet five or six and both wore clothes that were appropriate to the November temperature. There were a lot of other women here tonight wearing huge heels to walk around a dark field and tiny skirts with skimpy jackets that revealed their assets. Their choice of course, but I liked that these ladies were sensibly dressed.

'You are very welcome,' I replied as I received my change and was able to place my order. I got my Chatham Dockyard gin with slimline tonic and a second for Big Ben but made his a double. I handed over more cash and got more change and turned to find the two ladies still stood behind me.

'Are you here with your wife?' the Jamaican lady asked.

Ah. This was what Big Ben was always telling me to look out for. An opening.

'I'm here with a buddy. I left him outside talking to some girls that were collecting for charity.'

Both girls exchanged a glance and rolled their eyes. 'You mean the titty-sluts in the steampunk outfits?'

'I think that would be an accurate description,' I replied neutrally. Mr Wriggly liked how they looked but I doubted it was the right time to voice his opinion.

'Shall we see if we can find him?' I asked as I moved away from the bar. 'He should be easy to spot. He's six foot seven.'

'Six feet seven?' How does he buy clothes?' The Asian lady asked, and I realised that I hadn't asked them their names or even introduced myself.

'I have never asked him that,' I replied rather than ignore her question. 'Ladies, it seems like a good time to do names. I'm Tempest Michaels.'

'Pleased to meet you, Tempest,' Asian lady said while putting out her hand. 'I'm Louise, and this is Angela. We work together. We are both single, but you probably could have guessed that since we are here with each other and not our boyfriends.'

At a different time, this would be welcome news. They were both pleasant to speak to, pleasant to look at and both had jobs and were single. Not that I really had a tick list, but it was always nicer chatting to a lady if I believed I might be interested. Now though I already had a date arranged with Natasha which was suddenly thrown into question because Amanda's relationship status had changed.

I turned back to scan the crowd and spotted Big Ben no more than twenty metres away. He was still talking to the two steampunk girls. They did not look very happy about it though.

'There he is. I said he would be easy to spot.'

Big Ben turned his attention away from the two honeys and instantly took in the two ladies accompanying me. He hit them with a smile that was probably designed to make them both go moist.

'Ladies, this is my good friend, Big Ben. Please be warned that he may try to chat you up. Ben this is Louise and Angela,' I said by way of introduction.

I handed Big Ben his cup of gin, tonic, ice and cucumber. Now all four of us had one and the two ladies were sipping theirs quite demurely.

'Good evening, ladies. A pleasure to meet you,' Big Ben started. 'How did Tempest entice you to join him?'

'He bought our drinks,' Louise explained.

'They were in front of me in the queue but their purses both seem to have been lifted. They had already been served their drinks, so I picked up the bill while they did the online bank, cancel your card thing.'

'You were very generous,' Angela acknowledged. 'I'm just glad I wasn't carrying much cash.'

'Me too,' said Louise. 'It will be a pain without any cards for a couple of days. Why do pickpockets have to target family events?'

'Because they know people bring cash and are often tipsy from the beer or gin tent and habitually do not pay attention.' I answered the rhetorical question.

Big Ben patted his pockets to reassure himself that his wallet was still there.

'Everything alright, Ben?' I asked.

Before he could answer, there was a loud whumpf noise as the fire was lit and it hungrily sucked in air from all around. Whatever accelerant they had applied to the dry timber was consumed in a half second as the flames lit the sky, light bouncing back down off the low clouds.

'Ooh,' said Louise.

I grabbed Big Ben's arm as the girls turned to watch the orange flames stretch for the sky.

'You okay?' I asked.

Big Ben hadn't answered my earlier question. 'Fine, mate,' he replied.

'So, what happened with the two steampunk girls? I took so long getting gin and helping the two ladies that I figured you would have shagged at least one of them by the time I returned, but there you were still talking to them. And they looked bored.'

'Yeah. It was weird. I felt like they were too focused on something else to notice me. I can't really explain it to you because that's what you get all the time.'

'You are such a pain in my butt,' I replied. 'Well, it's two-nil currently.'

'Talking to girls doesn't count, silly. How many times do I have to explain that? You want to brag, then bring me their knickers. Before we leave here tonight that is.'

I muttered several expletives under my breath. He had said it quite loud enough for them to hear and while neither one had turned, I saw that they had stopped moving and were now looking at each other as if wondering how to react. 'You could speak a little more quietly, you know. There will be no collecting of undergarments, thank you. I will have a pleasant evening and leave it at that.'

'That's your tactic? No wonder you never get any.'

'I got some last week in Cornwall, thank you very much. Twice, in fact.'

Big Ben appeared to consider that news for a moment. 'No, you didn't,' he concluded.

'Yes. I did.'

'Okay, I'll bite. What's her name? When are you seeing her again?' He was probing my story to see if it had holes in it.

'Roberta Masonberg and she's in jail now, so I will not be seeing her again.'

'Hold on. Did you get lucky because you were there by yourself? Was that your tactic? Increase your chances by leaving me behind?'

'I realise that I may begin sounding like a broken record through constantly repeating myself, however I feel I must once again point out that you are an absolute dick.'

He laughed hard now. He enjoyed being a dick. 'Seriously though, mate. Louise and Angela are attractive young ladies. You should pick one now so that I don't end up shagging the one you want.'

I was certain they had heard that as well. I shook my head and wandered back to them. 'Sorry ladies, my friend is a little gregarious.'

'He most certainly is.'

We all fell silent for a moment. It was becoming a painfully long moment when Louise asked if I was hungry.

'A little I guess.' I was lying, sort of. I was hungry, but I had no intention of eating what they had on offer here. Everything would be too calorific to fit in my new regime of fitness and health.

'Angela and I were planning to get some food after we went to the gin tent. Now we have no money, but we are starving. I was hoping I could give you something of value, my watch maybe as a deposit on a little cash so we can get ourselves a burger or something.'

I nodded. They were in a pickle. There were no cash dispensers here but even if there had been they had no cards to use. What was I to do? I could hardly have the ladies go hungry. 'I'll tell you what, ladies,' I said opening my wallet and peering inside. I had brought fifty pounds with me, which ought to have been more than sufficient but had spent almost forty on gin and tonics already. 'I can rustle up fourteen pounds and it's all yours. I think I can stretch that far.'

'Why?' Angela asked.

I looked at her.

'Yeah, why?' echoed Louise. 'For a moment I thought that you were just trying to get into our knickers. Your friend certainly seems to not care who he sleeps with as long as he sleeps with someone. But you haven't even tried a cheesy line.'

I could feel my cheeks colouring. I was thinking about the concept of being like Big Ben and taking one or both of these girls home. Of having lovely Louise naked in my bed. Mr Wriggly began to stir.

'Not really my style, I guess,' I managed to stammer out. 'You are both very lovely, but I guess the honest answer is that while the idea of a brief encounter has some enticing connotations, I'm not really looking for Miss Right Now.'

Louise and Angela considered that for a moment.

'Okay,' Angela said. 'Then I guess the burgers are on you.'

They both looped their arms through mine so now I was walking along with a pretty woman on each arm and feeling like an utter stud.

'And then you can decide which one of us you want to shag,' said Louise.

Bedtime

The dogs had spent the evening next door with Mrs Comerforth. They hated fireworks. They always barked and fretted even with me holding them and the television turned up. Their hearing was different to mine, so maybe my efforts were futile. Mrs Comerforth had triple glazing and had once commented that she never heard the fireworks at all. I had dropped the dogs off with her for them to enjoy an evening on her sofa watching television and probably eating biscuits. I collected them when I got home as she was still up. I thanked her as always and promised to visit the next day to tackle some rose bushes that had become over-grown and a gutter that was blocked.

When the fireworks ended, I had looked for Big Ben. I found him holding hands with a lady that was taller than me and was drop-dead gorgeous. Angela had made a comment that I hadn't heard. I doubted it was compli-mentary.

Big Ben was also surrounded by police. Not that they were bothering him. It transpired that while we were watching the fireworks and the girls were eating their burgers, Big Ben had been foiling a pickpocket gang's plans. There was a huge haul of wallets and purses spilling out of the bottom half of a hollowed-out Guy. The steampunk girls had made a run for it but had been caught before they got very far. Across the field, they were being loaded into the back of a police van along with four children, all of whom were crying.

'Ooh, that's my purse'. Louise squealed, pointing at the pile of purses on the ground by a police officer's feet.

'Sorry, you will have to wait for the evidence to be processed, Miss.'

Big Ben said some choice words, reaching down to pluck the one she was pointing to from the ground.

'Oi,' said the officer.

Big Ben ignored him and flipped the purse open. Then found her driver's license. 'Looks like a match to me.' He chucked the purse to Louise.

'That's evidence,' the officer hissed, but he did nothing to retrieve it.

Next to me, Angela was pointing to hers with equal excitement. Big Ben locked eyes with the much shorter police officer. The officer looked away and Big Ben handed Angela her purse as well.

'Thank you,' she said, opening it and checking the contents.

'Plenty of evidence left, kid,' said Big Ben in the general direction of the officer. 'Now. I'm going to take Elle here for some refreshments.'

'I thought I was taking you,' she pointed out.

'Oh yeah. I'm going to go with Elle for some refreshment at her place. Don't wait up.' He waved goodnight to me and was gone. A night of passion undoubtedly in store.

I turned to Angela and Louise. 'I guess this just about concludes the evening.'

'Have you made a decision yet?' Louise asked.

I hadn't realised they were being serious. They were both charming and attractive with great figures. How was a chap supposed to pick?

So, I said that I hadn't and that had been the wrong answer. Since I wasn't interested enough in either one of them to pick one over the other, I was getting neither. I was fine with that, at least, that's what I kept telling myself anyway. Big Ben would have said something entirely different which would have resulted in them both going with him simultaneously no doubt.

Nevertheless, I had driven home alone, and I was not all that upset. At home, I had made a cup of tea and taken it and the doggies up to bed with the box file I had been given by Mick Cotton.

I fell asleep before I finished my tea, waking later to find it stone cold on the bedside table and the box folder's contents almost entirely unread. I switched the light off, pushed the box folder onto the floor and let sleep take me.

Running, Research and Roast Dinner

I opened my eyes and glanced at the clock by my bed. It was 0653hrs which meant it was time to get up and attack the day. I'm sure that many, if not most people have a lie in on a Sunday morning. Maybe roll around a bit with their partner if they have one and wander around the house in their pyjamas for a while, drinking coffee and eating toast while reading the Sunday paper.

These were fantasy scenes from an alternate reality for me. I would happily change my life to have a woman in it, fast forward a few years to a point when we had grown used to each other and settled into co-habitual bliss. I didn't have that though, so I might as well get my lazy backside out of bed and get on with something more productive than fantasising.

Bull was tucked into the duvet looking very comfortable. His brother was under there somewhere. I could hear him gently snoring. Neither dog was inclined to get up though. I laced up my running shoes, peered out my bedroom window into the gloom and discerned that it was, in fact, raining. A steady drizzle by the look of it.

From the bottom of a cupboard, where I had a large, plastic box stuffed with odd bits of clothing I rarely wore, I found an old rainproof top. It was quite creased, but no one would see me and the rain would take the creases out.

I performed some stretches in front of the mirror by my front door, then opened it to discover that I had grossly underestimated the intensity of the downpour now occurring outside.

Tough luck, fatty. Get on with it.

With the gym instructor's voice echoing in my ear, I set off on my planned route. I didn't bother with music, I was going to use the next forty-five minutes or more to consider the witchcraft case.

My hair was soaked before I reached the end of my road. What did I know so far about the case? The instant answer was very little. I had looked through some of the paperwork Mick had put together before I fell asleep last night though. His research on lightning striking people was comprehensive if nothing else. Lightning strikes are rare, but when they do occur what the person actually suffers is called flashover where the lightning passes not through the body, but around the outside, travelling over the skin via sweat or rainwater to discharge into the ground. However, lightning can pass directly through a human body. When it does, it leaves an entry and exit wound to mark where the lightning both entered and left the victim. In his pack were printed pictures of people with Lichtenberg scarring – elaborate spider's web patterns where blood vessels have ruptured by the passing current. The effect was oddly pretty but probably very painful.

My breathing was becoming laboured as I slogged along

a dirt path through the woods going up Bluebell Hill. There was a hint of daylight to brighten the area, without which I would have no light at all under the canopy of trees where the steady rain fell in fat blobs. I acknowledged that the rainproof top was pointless. It had fought valiantly for a few minutes but was now just a sodden mess, stuck to my skin and weighing me down.

I was focusing on the lightning strike evidence because it was currently all I had, but also because I felt that it might prove to be the most important element of the investigation. Mick had said that he found evidence of other lightning strike victims where the lightning had entered the chest rather than anywhere else but had also said that it was highly irregular. I needed to talk to a Fulminologist then, show them some pictures and get their opinion. Mick said yesterday that if the scientists concluded that his father could have been killed by lightning then he would pay my fee and be done with it. I wanted to take a closer look at the stepmother though. I told myself that she could be completely innocent. I doubted it though.

I reached the halfway point of my run. There is a viewing point near the top of Bluebell Hill that walkers or hikers go to because it gives great views over the Kent countryside. Today, all I could see was grey clouds and murky, smudged outlines where the heavy rain obscured visibility. Somewhere behind it all, the sun was slowly coming up. I had the return leg to complete. It was mostly downhill, which you might think is easier than going uphill, but it isn't. It's quicker, but that's not the same thing. One can attack an uphill stretch, going downhill one had to constantly watch one's footing lest it goes out from under you. I have heard it said that if one runs downhill faster than you can fall then you will not fall. I'm not sure the persons saying that have it right though and was in no mood to try it out this morning.

By the time I got home, I was just as wet as if I had been swimming. I stripped out of my wet things on the stone tile of my porch, threw them in the washing machine and dripped my way upstairs to find the dachshunds just getting up.

I took them back downstairs and shooed them into the garden. Dachshunds do not like rain. They do not like it to the point that they will happily poop in my house rather than go outside when it's raining. Had I not stayed at the back door yelling instructions at them, they probably would have done exactly that. They were not quick about it though, they thought that if they just kept trying to get back inside that I would give in and let them, so by the time they were suitably empty, I was cold. The November air had a distinct nip to it, and I was naked.

As I closed the patio door I heard a rumble of thunder in the distance. The dogs barked at it. They were quite brontophobic. I glanced around but I saw no further flashes.

An hour later, I was clean and dry and warm and sitting at the computer terminal in my office with Dozer on my lap. His brother was asleep in a dog bed next to the desk. Neither one liked the storm that was now raging outside so were keeping me close.

My computer had grown two extra screens while I had been away. Jane had been upgrading undoubtedly. I was having trouble getting used to them. I had never had more than one screen before and wasn't entirely sure how to make this set up work. I assumed that I could have several pages open all at once and use the mouse to drag and drop them on the screens to the left and right of the one in front of me but was having no luck doing it. They just kept pinging back. I would ask Jane about it when she came back to work.

I wondered then how long she would take off. It was Monday tomorrow though and I was not going to expect her. If she turned up, super. If she didn't then it would be just like it was a month ago before I had hired her and I would manage.

I leaned forward to lift my mug of tea from its coaster on the desk to an accompanying grumble from the dog sleeping on my lap. Ignoring him, I knuckled down to do some research. Searching for lightning research centres showed me very quickly that the United Kingdom had a big one in Cardiff in Wales, right across the other side of the country and hardly convenient. Later, I would see if I could find someone there to speak to. Other than that, I found databases of persons injured or killed by lightning in the UK and lots of pictures, but nothing that was helpful.

I switched my angle of attack and looked into the step-mother. Most people have a social media profile even if they don't know it. There are some nefarious apps one can obtain that will find the intended person where they pop up on other people's profiles. Mabel Cotton though had her own Facebook, Twitter, WhatsApp and other accounts. An hour of fiddling around between the various pages, and by using my iPad and phone to have multiple pages open when I still couldn't get the screen sharing thing to work, allowed me to build up a picture of her life.

Mabel was not hiding her insurance payout. In fact, she was bragging about it. She had received, very recently, a cheque for one and a quarter million pounds and had announced it to her friends via Twitter with the hashtag RichAsF! There was quite a bit of back and forth between her and three other ladies. I was having trouble pinning the information down and would need to go to Land Registry to prove it, but they all appeared to live in East Malling and met at the Golf Club there regularly. They were going today if the feed on Facebook was to be believed. I looked out the window at the rain pouring down. Another crack of thunder punctuated my thoughts on the matter. No one was playing golf around here today.

Mabel's three friends were Edna Hinckley, Dorothy Myers, and Barbara Tremont. They each had other friends of course, which made it hard to pick out any threads of conversation. There was no grand statement to say that Mabel had killed her husband, but I did follow one exchange from six days ago which ended abruptly when Mabel had quipped about the girls looking forward to getting their cheques. She may have meant it as a joke and horrified the other ladies, but I wondered if there might be more to it than that.

I picked up my phone and called Mick. The phone rang and rang and then went to voicemail. I hated leaving voicemail messages so I would call him back later instead. As I put the phone down though, it started ringing. He was calling me.

'Good morning, Mick. Thank you for calling me back.'

'That's quite alright, Tempest. How may I help you?'

'I wanted to know where your stepmother was when your father died.'

'Playing golf. Or, at least, at the golf club in East Malling. She was with three friends. Not that she needed an alibi because it was recorded as accidental death, but she had one if she needed it. I thought it suspicious that she would be at the golf club on a day when there was a storm and I asked her about it, but she said that one didn't cancel plans with friends because of a little inclement weather.'

I thought it was odd, suspicious might be the wrong word, but definitely odd. I thanked Mick for his time and disconnected. I needed more tea. Dozer complained as I plopped him into the bed next to his brother. I figured he could snuggle up with him and sleep, but both dogs saw that I was heading to the kitchen and followed me just in case it was second breakfast time.

It wasn't.

While the kettle boiled, I called my parent's landline. I had the phone on speaker, so my hands were free to clean my mug, dry it and fetch a fresh tea bag from the cupboard. I had left my parents in Cornwall on Thursday night. They had last seen me leaving the pub late at night after an adventurous couple of days that had seen mum get kidnapped and tied up and my father and I fight some dead pirates while discovering the whereabouts of over half a billion in gold, silver, and jewels that had supposedly sunk several centuries ago. I had plugged in my lifeless phone that night as I was climbing into bed to find worrying messages from my friends back here. They were all missing, so I had thrown everything into the car, grabbed the dogs and raced across the country that night to find them. All I sent mum and dad was a text which they didn't see until the next morning. They actually said that they hadn't noticed I wasn't in the fold-out bed in our hotel room until mum read the text on her phone.

I hadn't called them since and they hadn't called me, so I did not even know if they were home or still in Cornwall. I got my answer when the house phone picked up.

'Hello?' Mum said after reciting her phone number.

'Good morning, mother.'

'Oh, Tempest. How are you?'

'More or less recovered from the week I took off to

recover.' I answered realising as I did so, how true the statement was. My planned restful week in Cornwall had been
nothing of the sort. 'I just called to check in really. After I
raced back here from Cornwall, I haven't spoken to you,
and I wanted to see if you were back.'

'Yes, we got back yesterday afternoon. We wanted to
stay on in Cawsand, but we couldn't remain at the Sea
Pilgrim pub because they closed it. The police that is.
Impounded might be a better word. Anyway, we were not in
a rush, so we drove along the coast for a bit and found a
nice B&B that we had stayed in before you were born. Do
you know what?'

'What, mother?'

'It was the same couple running it almost forty years
later. They are getting on a bit now though. Are you calling
to see if there's a roast dinner?'

'Not at all. I have plenty of food here. I really was just
checking to see if you got back okay.'

'Yes, yes. We are back safe and sound. When will we see
you?'

'Next weekend? I have work to do. I need to find a
proper office space to work from. It's not practical to work
from my house and I have a case that demands my
attention.'

'Next Sunday?' she asked.

'That works for me. I will be over for 1400hrs.'

'You mean two o'clock.'

'No, I don't.' I heard her sigh, then a quick goodbye and
she was gone. If there were any ill-effects from her brief
spell in captivity last week and the distinct likelihood that
her captors were going to murder her, then it hadn't
surfaced yet.

As I stirred my tea, a fantastic flash of lightning lit the

air, splitting the clouds in two it seemed. Before my heart beat again, the thunder hit, and the two small dogs began barking their discomfort once more. The sound was loud now, the storm right on top of us. I made a decision.

I knew that Mabel and the other ladies were going to be at the golf club today, but they would be in the clubhouse, not out on the fairways and greens, so I could listen to their conversation or pose as a new member and strike up a conversation with them.

I searched the East Malling golf club and confirmed that they took day members in. All I would need to pay for entry to the club was green fees for the day. I choked when I saw the price though. It was almost two hundred pounds just for a day membership. Nicely exclusive then. No need to worry about the local oiks turning up.

I called Big Ben. 'I need to borrow your golf clubs.'

'No problem. What for? You can't play. I tried to get you to play before, but you always said you were rubbish.'

'At golf? I am rubbish. I need to spy on some people at a golf club, and they will be part of my disguise.'

'Makes sense,' he conceded.

'I'll be over shortly.' I disconnected. I needed to clean myself up and change my clothing if I was going to an expensive, exclusive golf club. I was content that I could fit in but right now I was wearing slobby clothing that I had thrown on to do housework and research in.

East Malling Golf Club

The storm was unusually ferocious and prolonged. In the relatively flat open countryside of the south-east of England, we didn't get intense storms. No hurricanes or tornadoes to worry about. A lightning storm with gale force winds was as hairy as it got, but while a tree might occasionally fall it was rare for there to be any loss of life. This storm was being persistent though. Usually, the storms we got were brief, this one was into its fourth hour and was still going.

I knew where the golf club was. I had never been there but had driven by the entrance gateway many times. I followed the signs to the clubhouse and parked as close to the entrance as I could. Then I dashed to the door through the puddles before the sky soaked me for the second time today. Big Ben's golf clubs were on my passenger seat I realised when I got inside. I wasn't going back for them though. There was an umbrella in the bag, but the wind was blowing so hard I worried it would just turn inside out and break.

A bell chimed above my head as I went in, and I saw that I had unwittingly run into the shop. There was no shop assistance visibly in attendance, so I poked around wondering if there would be a way through from the shop to the main clubhouse. There was, of course, hidden in a corner. Had I looked up at any point I might have noticed the large sign pointing the way through to toilets, changing rooms and clubhouse.

I walked along a corridor lined with oak panelling to arrive in the front entrance that I had somehow missed in my dash from the car. It was double height with a vaulted ceiling and a marble staircase leading up to the level I was on.

I could hear faint chatter coming from around the corner. Following it led me into a bar and restaurant area that reminded me of the Ritz: It was palatial. Huge chandeliers hung from the ceilings. The expensive room was decorated like the inside of a palace might be if an important guest were coming. A pianist was tinkling away in the far corner and the room had a large terrace that gave a lofty view down onto the eighteenth fairway and green.

Naturally, there was no one outside on the terrace today and the glass doors to access it were shut against the harsh weather. The room was busy though. Small groups of men or women or men and women, families and all manner of ages, although I estimated the demographic to be middle-aged and upwards in general. One had to be successful in life to be able to afford to be a member here, so it did not surprise me that there were fewer young people around.

I knew what the four ladies looked like from their social media profiles. Another example of technology intruding into our lives uninvited. I spotted them as I made my way to the bar. Fortuitously, they were eating lunch at a table close to the bar so I sat as near to them as I could and ordered a diet coke.

It was hard to overhear their conversation amid the babble of background noise and the tinkling of the piano. I picked out the odd word though and I was able to watch their body language using the mirror behind the bar.

Mabel was sitting nearest me and thus had her back to me. Hers was the one face I couldn't see. She was clearly enjoying herself though. An upended bottle of champagne sat in an ice bucket by her left elbow. It seemed like she had either had the whole thing herself, or it was not the first bottle. The other ladies had glasses in front of them in various stages of emptiness, but Barbara looked like she hadn't touched hers. She looked nervous or worried or maybe she was just sick, but if so why come out to lunch at all.

I sipped at my coke and wished the other patrons would choose to be quiet so that I could hear what the ladies were saying.

I continued to watch, trying hard to disguise my attention. If they or anyone else was aware of me observing them, I couldn't tell, but I was left alone by everyone including the barman. Time ticked by in an uninteresting way and the ladies finished their meals. Well, I should qualify that. The plates were cleared but Barbara had barely touched her food and the glass of champagne that she hadn't drunk was swept up by Mabel. Mabel was telling her off for something, wagging her finger and making a big point about it.

'Are you a member here, sir?' a voice asked from behind me. I turned my head to find a giant bushy moustache attached to a face etched with thin red lines. The moustache was grey turning to white and the gentleman sporting it looked to be seventy or more. He was wearing a tweed suit that was mostly green but had intersecting lines through it in hues of dull yellow, brown and red. The trousers ended at the knee where they tucked into long socks that were tan in colour and finally they disappeared into a pair of wellington boots.

'I think you know that I'm not,' I replied to his rhetorical question. 'I was curious about the place. I recently moved here and wanted to see it for myself,' I lied smoothly. 'I had planned to play a round today, but the weather ...' I indicated to the windows.

'I'm afraid we have very strict protocols about non-members always being accompanied in the clubhouse by full members, sir.' He was being very polite. 'I really am sorry, but must ask you to leave, sir. The club will be only too pleased to receive your application for membership whenever you are ready, sir.'

I was about to reply when I noticed a change at the table of ladies. Barbara had received a phone call. There's nothing unusual in that, but the other ladies had all stopped talking. Even the inebriated Mabel, and they were listening intently to what Barbara was saying into her phone.

Barbara had her eyes closed and her head down. She ended the call and did nothing for several seconds. Then she lifted her head, opened her eyes and said, 'It's done.' It was loud enough for me to hear.

'Sir.' The gentleman at my shoulder reminded me of his presence and desire that I should leave.

I nodded my head and moved to follow him. He was leading the way out of the bar. At the table, the ladies, including Barbara, all looked jubilant. Her expression was that of a woman that had just received a great bit of news, that she had been expecting or hoping for, but hadn't dared to believe would ever come. To her left and right, were Mabel and Edna, both of whom were patting her on the arm or shoulder in congratulations. As I followed the tweed dressed gent out of the bar, I saw them all get up.

I went through a brief charade of obtaining the club captain's personal email so I could contact him about membership and arranging a trial round for free but soon made my excuses and went outside to see if the ladies were indeed leaving.

Sat in my car with the heater on and the wipers going, my patience was rewarded a few minutes later as all four of them emerged from the main clubhouse entrance. They tottered across to a large blue Range Rover, an older model with a private plate to hide its age. Dorothy climbed behind the steering wheel.

Death by Misadventure

I followed the Range Rover two miles back through East Malling. Quite where East Malling ended and West Malling began, I did not know, but we must have been getting close to the next village when the car indicated and turned up a driveway and towards a large, detached house that had two police cars outside it.

Now I wasn't sure what to do. I had a bad feeling about what was going on. Sitting in my car on the opposite side of the road weighing up my options, the arrival of a vehicle marked as County Coroner confirmed my assumption to be most likely true.

The house, I was certain I would later prove, belonged to Barbara and inside it was her dead husband, his heart exploded from his chest by a bolt of lightning from the storm today. What I wanted to do was go into the house and confirm it. I had no authority to do so though. No jurisdiction.

Calling Amanda might have worked a week ago, but she was out of the police now. She still knew people and might be able to call in the odd favour. Right now, though, I needed to get used to working without the benefit of having someone on the inside.

Would it hurt to try? Probably not. With that thought echoing in my head, I drove my car off the grass verge I had stopped on. Only I didn't. I put the car into gear and listened as the back wheels spun on the wet grass. I opened my door and looked back at the wheel behind me. If I continued, I would just dig a muddy hole and make it even harder to get out.

I swore but then saw the opportunity this presented: I had a legitimate reason to knock on a door. The only house I could see was the one with the coroner's van and the police cars outside of it.

I jogged down the gravel drive to knock on the door, hoping that I could convince them to let me in out of the wet whereupon I might overhear something.

The front door wasn't even shut! It was open a crack, so I gently, quietly pushed it open and stepped inside. This was as good as I could have hoped for. Voices were coming from deeper in the house along with the sound of camera shutters going as photographs were taken.

I edged forward. There was no one in this part of the house. I concocted a fast lie about knocking for help but finding the front door open and coming to look for help when no one answered. I doubted it would fool anyone, but I didn't really need it to. They wouldn't arrest me, I was fairly sure.

I crossed a hallway and came to a hub of sorts from which lots of rooms came off like spokes. To my right was where all the conversation and noise was coming. I moved quietly in that direction. As I got nearer, I started to make out what people were saying.

Before I got there though, a young female police officer came out of a different door bearing a tray full of steaming mugs.

I froze.

'Oh,' she said. 'Aren't you Tempest Michaels? I saw you on the news this weekend.'

I nodded. 'Guilty as charged. Can I help you with your beverages?'

'What? Oh, no. Ah, just follow me,' she said and went straight into the room where all the noise was coming from with me hot on her heels. 'I need to go back to take care of the widow and deal with all of that.' She put the tray down on a table and was gone. I guess she thought I was supposed to be here.

I had stuck my neck out this far; I might as well keep going, so I selected a mug from the tray and gave it a sip. Not bad. I was worried it might have sugar in it, but it was unsweetened. No one paid me any attention, so I sipped my tea and watched.

A photographer was snapping pictures as the coroner gave instructions. Two police officers, one of whom I recognised as Brad Hardacre, were standing around doing nothing much at all but were probably also waiting for instruction. All the work was being done by the person bent over examining the body.

I hadn't met a coroner before. At least, if I had I did not remember the occasion, but in my head, they did not look like the lady I could now see. She was bent over with her back to me, which is to say her peachy and perfectly rounded bottom was pointing in my direction. Mr Wriggly was filling my head with thoughts on the subject.

She was dictating into a recording device, probably for writing up her report later, her words mostly mumbo-jumbo to me as it was all complex medical terms. I listened though, staying out of the way.

'… wound to thorax consistent with lightning strike. No evidence of other injuries.'

She stood up at that point and gave me my first look at the victim as she moved around. I sputtered my tea as I had been taking a sip. The man's chest had been opened out like the lid on a can of beans. Several ribs were poking out, his clothing was soaked with blood and had been cut away to reveal the wound for examination. He was very, very dead.

Of course, having made a noise as I spat tea down my chin, all faces turned to me.

'Who are you?' asked the coroner lady. I was getting my first proper look at her too. She was my age or maybe a little older, perhaps even forty, but she was stunning. She could have been a swimwear model if she wanted with the figure I could see even with the layers of clothing.

'He's Tempest Michaels. A ghost hunter,' said Brad.

'That's not even nearly true, Brad, thank you. Apart from the name bit. You got that right.' I put the tea mug down and crossed the room to offer my hand. The coroner lady had on green plastic gloves though and they were covered in blood. She just looked blankly at me. I took my hand away. 'So, this all looks quite grisly. How do you think the murder is being perpetrated?'

'Murder?' the coroner lady tilted her head as if trying to work out what I was saying. 'How can it be murder? The victim was hit by lightning. PC Hardacre does this man have any right to be here?' she asked, turning her attention away from me just when it was getting interesting.

'I doubt it,' Brad replied. He'd been leaning against a window frame until this point, now meaningfully he levered himself off it.

Undeterred, I asked another question. 'If not murder, then what will your verdict be?

Death by misadventure?'

'Accidental death, Mr Michaels.'

'You genuinely think a lightning strike caused that wound?' I was pushing her. I wasn't sure why other than I didn't believe it myself and wanted to hear her defend her assessment.

'Get him out of here, please,' she instructed the two police officers. They moved toward me, but I offered no resistance. I had already seen more than I hoped to and learned a lot in the process.

I turned and left the room with the two officers following me. They were going to escort me from the property and make sure that I went away.

At the door, Brad had something to say, 'We are never going to be friends, man. But I heard about what you did for Amanda and Patience. I like those girls, so thank you.' He offered me his hand to shake.

I took it. He had a good grip. 'Now get out,' his partner said trying to look and sound tough. I grinned at him, nodded at Brad and went back out into the rain to find that it had largely stopped. I could still hear the constant drip of water filtering down through the trees, but the rain had all but completely left off now.

I heard the door shut behind me. They were content that I was leaving. I wasn't though. I doubled back and started looking around the outside of the house, making sure I kept away from the windows so no one inside would see me. I was looking for the runes Mick Cotton had described to me. I found the first one on the wall on the left side of the house. It was easy to see because it was three feet high – a witch's knot. I went back to the front of the building and had to scout around a bit to find the symbol there. The front façade looked to be free of any marking. In the end, I found it behind a plant pot close to the front door. It was the horned god. I would love to boast that studying all of this nonsense as part of my on-the-job training had given me the ability to identify these symbols by sight. Alas, I was doing it using an app on my phone. On the next wall on the other side of the building, I found a triple moon. I was willing to bet that there would be another symbol on the back of the house but I was certain I would be spotted if I tried to find it, so after a quick peek around the corner to see if it was obvious and easy to spot, I accepted that I would need to return another time if I really wanted to find out what it was.

The house was marked with wiccan symbols. There might be more inside, and I expected that I would find other artifacts if I were to have free reign to inspect the house.

My car was still stuck but that wasn't going to hold me up for very long. On the way back down the long driveway, I stopped under a few pine trees to collect pinecones and fallen bits of branch. These I shoved under the leading edge of each back tyre so that they bit in when I eased the car forward, allowing me to get moving. Once the wheels were turning, I was free.

The car dropped back down onto the road, and I took it home.

Groomsman Duties

Jagjit had texted me earlier to ask when I wanted to talk through the Best Man stuff. He wanted a stag party but had very specific ideas about what that should be like. He trusted that I would not ignore his wishes and organise an event with prostitutes or strippers and leave him tied naked to a lamppost.

He was due at 1800hrs but was late as usual. At 1812hrs he knocked on my door then called out as he let himself in. The dogs, who were barking before they made it off the sofa, saw who it was and fussed about his feet as he joined me in the kitchen.

'I brought beer with me,' he announced, holding a four pack of Cobra lager aloft in each hand.

'Thanks, man, but I'm off the sauce for the next few weeks.'

'Really? You were knocking them back on Friday night.'

I nodded. 'I was, but that was my last hurrah if you like. I'm on the fitness trail again.' I patted my love handles. 'I'm getting a bit tubby.'

'Yeah, you're really not. So, diet and exercise then?'

'I think of it more as training and nutrition. I just have to get my head in the right place. A few days in and the cravings will go. Then the benefits will start to show, and I will get addicted to fitness again.'

'If you say so.' Jagjit didn't run unless something was chasing him. He was content to work up a sweat on his X Box but the thought of going to the gym never entered his mind. He set the beers down, pulled one from the pack nearest him and took a long draft from it. 'All the more for me then.'

I looked longingly at the drinks but knew no good could come from it. I needed to avoid it for a while in order to lose the excess bodyfat I had gained.

'Down to business?' I asked.

He took a seat at my breakfast bar, and we started discussing the plan for the wedding, what he wanted for a stag do and who I should invite.

'Have you planned a honeymoon?' I asked when the question occurred to me.

He took another slug of beer and crushed the can before selecting another. 'We are going to Tignes. It's all booked.'

'As a surprise?'

'No, I didn't think I could organise something so important without involving her. Anyway, it was her idea.'

'Have you ever skied before? I don't remember you ever talking about it.'

'Yeah, man! I'm like Triple X only browner!'

I doubted that. I just hoped there wasn't a gulf of ability between them that meant she left him on the baby slopes every day.

'When do you go?'

'Right after the ceremony. There's a Eurostar service that goes from St Pancras directly there overnight, so we leave on the Sunday evening.'

'Sounds good. It has been too long since I hit the slopes. I should look into booking myself a week away.'

'Does Natasha ski?' he asked.

I frowned a little at the question. 'I don't know, but since we haven't been on a date yet, I will leave off planning our holiday together for a while yet.'

'Good point,' he conceded.

We talked some more after moving through to my lounge to watch TV. His mention of Triple X inciting a successful search for the film. I drank water while Jagjit worked his way through six of the beers and Vin Diesel did his thing.

By 2100hrs I had endured quite enough of watching Jagjit drink beer and I was getting tired. He had work in the morning too, so he wished me luck for my week and went home. We would most likely not see each other until next Friday night when I would have the even harder task of drinking water at the pub.

I had ironing to do, so I tackled the boring task while watching Jason Statham, then went upstairs to run a bath.

The day was over.

House Guest

Laying in the bath hours later, I was still wondering what I needed to do to move the case forward. I had gone to the gym again, this time for a weights session, which combined with the very healthy approach I was taking to my food since returning from Cornwall was making me feel not only physically better but, in many ways, mentally relieved that I was now tackling an issue I had been ignoring. Now I was soaking my body and getting it ready for the aches it was going to feel tomorrow when I would pound it again just as hard.

The case though was far less controllable than my fitness and nutrition regime. Barbara's husband had died in the exact same manner as Mabel's. There was no way it was a coincidence. This was murder, and someone had gone to a lot of trouble to disguise it as something that could be written off as a freak accident.

Who did I go to with this though? I wanted the coroner to reconsider her verdict. Who had been the coroner on the first case? That was a key question I needed an answer to. I would research it in the morning. I was secretly hoping that James/Jane would turn up for work as expected and in so doing give me the chance to hand the research over to him/her. He/She was better at it after all and it would mean I could pursue other lines of enquiry, maybe take on another case or find us a new office.

My doorbell rang downstairs, causing a cacophony of barking from the dogs as they ran from the sofa they had undoubtedly been sleeping on, to the front door where I heard their paws skid to a stop. They barked some more.

I had neither my phone nor a watch with me so I couldn't be certain of the time. My best guess was somewhere close to 2200hrs, a time at which I would not expect to have people ringing my doorbell.

I ignored it, believing that whoever was outside would get bored and wander off and the dogs would take themselves back to bed.

The doorbell bingbonged again though, eliciting another round of barking from the dogs. Still, I ignored it. It was late for it to be an opportunistic salesperson, or perhaps a well-meaning soul collecting for charity, but I couldn't imagine who else it might be. Regardless, I was in a nice, warm bath and felt no desire to rush downstairs, dripping with water to open the door to the cool late-Autumn air.

Several seconds ticked by. They had probably given up I decided. Then changed my mind when I heard the front door handle turning.

Someone was trying to get in!

I leaped from the bath and ran, snagging a towel as I went. The bathroom was right by the top of the stairs and the front door just beyond them. My wet feet quickly dried as the moisture was stolen by the carpet pile. Downstairs, the dogs were going absolutely nuts now to repel the intruder and I could feel adrenalin hitting my bloodstream. It was spiking my pulse rate.

I hit the bottom step… and stopped.

Hilary's woeful face was peering through a crack in the door. He was trying to calm the dogs and keeping the door almost closed so they could not escape. They had still not worked out that it was someone they knew and were in kill mode. Admittedly, an angry miniature dachshund is not that terrifying, nor is it likely to do much damage, but he was probably wise to keep the barrier in place.

'Hilary? What's up? What brings you here at this time on a Sunday?' I asked as I opened the door to welcome him in. Whatever had driven him to disturb my Sunday evening peace was insignificant, I could find out about it later. He had thought it important enough to come here so it was my task to welcome him inside.

As I opened the door, he saw that I was holding a towel around my waist with one hand while steam billowed off my skin. The dogs saw who it was and hopped over the doorsill to sniff him and I caught sight of the suitcase and duffel bag at his feet.

Oh dear.

'Anthea kicked me out,' he wailed.

I motioned for him to get inside. The cold air was biting at my wet skin, but he clearly needed to come in and be with a friend.

'I'm sorry. I didn't know where else to go.'

'Just come in, mate. Let's get you in the warm, shall we.' My mind was spinning. What did I say to a chap whose wife had booted him to the kerb? I got him in and closed the door. 'I think a stiff drink is called for.'

I fiddled with the towel so it would stay around my

waist and went through to the kitchen. I had a bottle of eighteen-year-old Scottish single malt for such occasions. I opened the cupboard it was in, swore under my breath because the level had dropped since I last looked at it, which probably meant my father had found it last time they dog sat, then poured a decent measure into two crystal glasses.

Hilary trudged into the kitchen after me, took the offered glass and upended it into his mouth.

'That's good stuff,' he said, taking a seat at the breakfast bar.

Err, yeah. It was. I poured him another and advised him to sip it.

'Do you need a place to stay for a while?' I was putting two and two together. He didn't answer for a second but nodded his head once quickly to confirm what I figured he had knocked on my door for.

I was getting cold. 'Listen, ah... I need to get some clothes on. I won't be a minute. I'll put your bags upstairs in the guest bedroom when I go up. If you want to talk, we can. If you don't, then stay here as long as you need.'

I gave his shoulder a comradely punch as I went out the door and left him staring into the bottom of his whisky glass.

I almost got to the door before he started speaking.

'I gave her a spanking like Big Ben said. I think I knew it would end badly but I did it anyway. I told her it was time for me to be the man and for her to learn her place.'

Christ! I could imagine Anthea reacting to that by going straight for the nuclear option.

'She just looked at me for a moment. I actually thought she was impressed like Big Ben said she would be. Then she kicked me in the nuts and dragged me out of the house by my feet. She threw my clothes out of the bedroom window. It was raining. I had to ask her for a bag.'

I was struggling to find something to say in response to his news. I couldn't remember what Big Ben had said, although I did remember the conversation from Friday night. I doubt he had intended for Hilary to have followed his instructions. He was most likely trying to be amusing. Or annoying. Big Ben did annoying very well.

'Hold that thought, buddy. I'll be two minutes.' I ran up the stairs two at a time, threw on sports trousers and a zip-through hoody and ran back down. By the time I arrived in the kitchen, Hilary had finished the second glass of whisky and left his stool. He was sitting cross-legged on the stone floor next to the oven with Dozer on his lap and Bull climbing on his right knee.

'I always wanted a dog. Anthea said they were too much trouble, and the children would just be upset when it got old and died.'

There was a little truth to that. I didn't want to consider how I would feel when my two little dogs got old. It was late on a Sunday evening, and I had planned to go to bed after my bath. The bath, of course, had been curtailed and I had a friend that needed a shoulder, so I clearly wasn't going to bed either.

I coaxed him off the floor and through to the lounge. He had downed two good-sized belts of whisky in the last five minutes, so I offered him coffee next. I couldn't see that getting smashed would do him any good.

He wasn't exactly chatty. Mostly he stared at his mug of coffee and looked lost. I asked him more about what had happened and learned that he had attempted to establish his dominance on Saturday evening. The resulting eviction had left him wandering the streets for the last twenty-four hours. His bed last night had been the bench in the bus shelter next to the park in the middle of the village. It was cold enough, now that we were into November, that he must have suffered and had probably got no sleep.

He needed a shower and a meal and some sleep, all of which I was able to provide. After an hour of talking back and forth, I was able to coach him into the concept of going to work in the morning, steadying his ship and letting the dust settle. He would speak with Anthea tomorrow and apologise. I was sure a truce could be negotiated and doubted their marriage was over – something he appeared to be very afraid of.

Finally, I got him off the sofa and upstairs. His things were in the guest room waiting for him although he didn't have a toothbrush, just some clothes which needed laundering before he could wear them as he had collected them off the wet grass outside his house.

As I shoved him in the direction of the bathroom, I went back downstairs to my utility room to put his clothes in the washing machine. As I came back up, I could hear the shower running. I was satisfied that he was no danger to himself. The sun would come up in the morning and bring new hope with it.

A New Start

I slept fitfully, the result of a dream waking me at 0112hrs. I had been back at the castle wall with Deadface and had once again let him go. In the dream I had watched him fall, watched his body break open as it hit the ground below. It was not the first time in my life that I had awoken terrified and knew from experience that I was best served to get up and get some water. Take a moment, if you will. I went back to bed and sleep came more peacefully but it was still fitful as if I was waking myself before I dropped into too deep a dream state where the terror might return.

The net result was that when I forced myself to get up at 0500hrs to get to the gym I was tired, not rested as I should have been. The fatigue was soon forgotten though as I began sweating, putting myself through another gruelling CrossFit workout. This time choosing the bike and rower instead of running. It was every bit as hard as the previous workout, my constant mantra throughout telling me that I would see the result of my hard work soon enough.

Sat at my breakfast bar later, dressed for the day and

eating a vegetable omelette, I heard a key in the lock of my front door. I glanced up at the clock: 0849hrs. The Jane shaped shadow outside turned out to be Jane, although it wasn't Jane at all because it was James for once. The killer dachshunds skidded to a noisy barking halt at his feet. They had identified the intruder and concluded that they could let him live.

'Hi, James,' I called out as he came in. 'I wasn't sure whether to expect you or not.'

'Hi, Tempest.' James was dressed in skinny bleached jeans, a pair of new-looking white Nike trainers and a white turtleneck sweater over which he had a down-filled, bright red jacket. Even though he had come as a boy today he was still wearing makeup. He looked very gay, but that was probably his intention. 'I gave some thought to staying off work today but decided I would most likely get back to feeling normal if I got back to my normal routine.'

I nodded. 'That makes sense.'

'Now that you are back, we can get back to usual routine. It would be nice if we were back at the office. Not that your place isn't nice,' he added quickly. 'But it doesn't feel like a proper place of work.'

'I know what you mean.' The dogs had checked James for food and since he had none, they had lost interest in him and were heading back to the sofa in my lounge. 'I have some research for you. I want to see if I can solve the office thing this week. I'm going out shortly.'

'Okay. Want coffee before you go?' he asked as he flicked the kettle on.

I wasn't going to say anything about it, but I was suddenly uncomfortable with him in my house. He was very familiar with it. I had thought that we might just use my house until the office was rebuilt but I knew now that I needed to rent somewhere new as soon as possible.

'Is Amanda coming in?' James asked as he opened my kitchen cupboard and helped himself to coffee.

'Yes, she is,' said Amanda. She was just coming through the front door. She also had a key. No sooner had I thought that I needed to get back all my keys, than Mr Wriggly voiced his opinion. He thought Amanda should keep hers. Just in case she ever felt the need to visit him in the middle of the night.

'Good morning, Amanda. How was your weekend?'

'It was very pleasant, thank you.' I really wanted to ask her about Brett and whether they had patched things up, but I kept my mouth shut.

'Yes, please,' she replied to James's unspoken question. He was holding up a coffee mug.

'So, what does the caseload look like? What do I get to do today?' she asked.

I spent the next ten minutes telling her and James about the witchcraft case. I showed them the pictures of the lightning victims and explained about the exploding chests. Both James and Amanda had made yuck noises at my description.

'What's next then?' Amanda asked.

'Well, I have a list of things for James to research. Not least of which is the coroner herself.'

'The one you described as super-hot,' Amanda clarified, a definite judgy tone to her voice.

'Did I?' Had I? I might have done. She certainly was quite attractive. I thought back to what I had been telling them, but the exact words I had used were eluding me.

'Yes. Anyway, if you have nothing immediate for me to do, I will start trawling emails and look for a new case.'

'Perfect. I'm off to see if I can resolve our office situation.' Heading to the door, I decided an extra layer beneath my coat was in order, it looked cool out, so I ran up the stairs to fetch a jumper.

As I turned toward my bedroom someone spoke. 'Morning, Tempest,' came a voice right next to my ear.

'Aaaaargh!' I replied, damned near wetting myself in the process.

With my head down and my mind on other things, it came as a shock when I bumped into Hilary on the landing. I had completely forgotten he was staying with me.

James and Amanda appeared at the bottom of the stairs. Both had leaped to rescue me from whatever foul fiend had caused me to squeal like a frightened girl only to find me sitting on the top stair holding my chest while my heart calmed.

'Everything okay?' Amanda asked.

'Hello,' replied Hilary, peering around the top banister so they could see him.

'Hi, Hilary,' James said slowly, undoubtedly trying to work out why he was in my house.

Amanda looked shocked. Then I remembered that she had never met Hilary and might now be questioning if I was bisexual. 'Amanda, this is Hilary. He needed a place to stay last night so he crashed here. I forgot.'

'You forgot?' Hilary repeated, somewhat affronted. I noted that he was having trouble keeping his eyes off Amanda.

'Yes, I forgot. I have been up a while and getting on with my usual routine. Last night is long behind me.'

'Charming,' he said. He wasn't actually taking offence, just making a point, I guess.

A thought occurred to me, 'Aren't you going to be late to work?' I asked.

'I already called in sick. One of the other department managers can cover for me for once. I don't remember the last time I had a random day off. I feel like I deserve one.' I had no opinion on the matter. 'Is there any coffee?' he asked looking down the stairs at the two faces still peering up.

Ten minutes later, he was downstairs with a hot mug of coffee cooling in his grip and a crumb-laden plate that had once held some toast. He was dressed in some old pyjamas I had found for him and a zip-through hoody. They were all far too big for his skinny frame but it hardly mattered.

He seemed far brighter than last night. The sun had indeed risen again.

'What is your plan for the day?' I enquired. I was hoping it included making peace with his wife so he could go home.

'Not sure,' he replied, then he looked like he was thinking about his options. 'Do you need me out of here?' he asked, indicating around to show that he meant my house, 'Or am I okay to stay a few days if I need to?'

I said the stupid thing that everyone does in such circumstances, 'Stay as long as you need, buddy.' As I watched his body slump gratefully with the news that he could live with me, I wondered what I had just let myself in for.

'Look, I have some business I need to attend to, so I'm going out. You will find a spare key in the utility room next to the front door. It will be easy to find. It has a label on it that says spare house key. Come and go as you please.' I wanted to give him a pep talk about fixing his marriage, but it didn't feel like the time. Maybe tonight.

I bid everyone good day and went out the door.

The New Office

I parked my car in its usual spot behind the office in Rochester High Street. In front of me was the ruined building that had once housed my office. Scaffolding clung to all sides of it now and a plastic canopy had been erected to protect the exposed interior from the weather. In one of the parking spaces was a large skip, half filled with debris that had been cleared from the building as they took it back to the parts that were still solid and could be built upon.

I looked in the skip. It was mostly roofing tile and burnt wooden trusses from the roof. The building didn't look as bad as it had in my memory. I went through the cut in the wall that led from the car park to the High Street. The Travel Agency owned and run by the chap that rented me my office, Tony Jarvis was almost untouched by the fire. The roof space was exposed where the fire had spread from my office but otherwise, he had probably just suffered smoke damage. The main office might only require some paint. He would not be able to reopen until it had passed safety inspection following the building works to fix the roof though. Maybe Tony would see this as a chance to update the shop – it was badly in need of modernising. That was his decision to make.

I turned and headed down the High Street toward Chatham. There was a line of real estate firms further down the High Street and that was where I was heading. I felt confident that one of them would be able to offer me a suitable office from the available property they had on their books.

I only got twenty yards though before I stopped. I had just walked by the solution to my problem. I was now staring at the gleaming glass frontage of the business formerly owned by Dr. Lyndon Parrish. There was a big sign in the left-hand window telling the world that the business was no longer operating. I didn't know he'd quit already. Maybe he'd moved on. Maybe his near-death experience with the Klowns had put him off pursuing a life as a paranormal investigator. Or maybe he realised that he was full of crap.

Either way, his business premises were purpose-built for what I wanted and were available. There was a contact number for the real estate agent on the notice. I stood in the street and called it. It was getting close to ten o'clock on a Monday morning, so the real estate business would be open.

My call was answered almost instantly. 'Good morning. Capital City letting and sales. How may I direct your call?'

I disliked the question. What did it mean, anyway? How did I answer? I ignored the question in the end and asked one of my own. 'I'm interested in the commercial property at 167 Rochester High Street. Can you connect me with someone that can talk to me about that?'

The lady was silent for a moment but then said, 'One

moment please.' Hold music replaced her voice: Mars by Holst, part of his Planet Suite.

It went on for nearly a minute before I was connected to the next person. In the cool air, my hand was getting cold holding the phone to my ear and I switched hands, but not ears because holding the phone to my right ear just felt wrong.

The chap now on the call assured me that the property was still available and gave me the monthly rental figure. I whistled quietly in my head when he said the number. It was more than I had expected, and a heck of a lot more than I had been paying for the office above the travel agent, but it was a proper office and came with a waiting area and separate offices for Amanda and me to work in. I was hesitating, but I knew I was going to take it.

I asked where the real estate firm's offices were. They were right in front of me, one of the firms I had been heading to when I spotted the vacant office.

I thanked him and told him to clear the next hour and to be ready for some hard negotiating. As I walked along the High Street, I found myself feeling elated for the first time in a while. Not that I was ever feeling down. I would never indulge myself with the idea that I could feel sorry for myself. I was privileged, and I knew it. But despite recent successes, I found that right now I felt like a winner. I smiled inwardly at how easy I was to please.

I got back to my house just after noon. Still feeling good and with a set of keys in my hand. I jingled them triumphantly at James, knowing that the action would force him the ask a question.

'That was quick?'

'It sure was. Remember True Paranormal Solutions?' I asked him, certain that he would. The dogs were buzzing around my feet wanting to be let out. I strode to the door and watched as they shot across the garden. Next door's cat was on the fence – this was a level one offence and was treated with the most stringent response. The cat just looked at them as they barked from the ground at the bottom of the fence. They were going nuts. The cat licked a paw.

'The rival place almost next door to the old office?'

'That's the one. It closed, and I just rented it.'

'Really?' James's face was beaming with excitement at the prospect.

'Really. I did some dealing, and we can move in as soon as we want.' The dealing I had done in the end was to haggle with the guy because I knew he worked on commission and could close the sale now if he was willing to be reasonable. I was playing sales chess with him, nothing more, because having backed him into a position he was uncomfortable with, I then told him I wanted the keys today and needed the paperwork done while I waited. He looked horrified, which was when I played my trump card and offered to pay close to the asking rent for the expedited service. I don't know whether I did really well or if he was inexperienced, but I got what I wanted, and he got a result, so I walked away believing it was fair deal.

'I think we should move in tomorrow, so I need to get a sign writer around to change the sign on the front of the building. Where's Amanda?'

'Amanda went to check something out. A potential client. Right, sign writers. You want to call them yourself?' James asked as the printer churned and spat out a sheet of A4 paper. I picked it up. Efficient as always, James had given me all the signwriters in the area.

'I'll call them shortly. You want a cup of tea?' I asked as

I headed towards the kitchen. Then I remembered something.

'Sure thing,' His voice drifted through from the other room.

I turned the kettle on then went back through to the office rather than shout through. 'Where's Hilary? Did he go out?'

'Yeah, said he needed to go for a walk about an hour ago,' James replied without turning away from the computer screen. It was probably for the best that he didn't mope about in my house. Having decided that he was not going to work, he needed to find something else to do with his day. The kettle button clicked off to announce the water was hot. I left the office.

'How did the research go?' I called back from the kitchen loud enough for him to hear me.

'I found your coroner lady. You were right about her being super-hot.' I was still sure I hadn't used the term super-hot. 'She was also the coroner on the first victim, the client's father.'

Was she now?

I scooped up the two mugs of tea and walked back through to my office/dining room.

Just coming off the printer was a photograph of the coroner. Victoria Mallory. James had taken the photograph from the coroner's department website. It listed her qualifications but gave away no personal information. I walked it to the wall and pinned it to a cork board I had there. Then I moved to a whiteboard and wrote her name, then the names of the two victims and linked her name to each of them.

I needed to gather a lot more information, but I also wanted to quiz Dr. Victoria Mallory. I wondered if she would agree to meet me. As with many other things, there seemed no harm in trying. I had a couple of schemes brewing, a couple of ideas to get inside the group of wives at the centre of this and find out more than they might willingly tell me. At this stage, I was unknown to the ladies, which might give me an edge.

The thing that was troubling me more than anything though was the incredibly violent nature of the death. Mick had said that his stepmother Mabel had an alibi for the time of his father's death. I also knew that Barbara had an alibi for the time of her husband's death. I was with her when it happened. So, if it wasn't lightning causing the freak deaths, and the ladies were nowhere near them when it happened, then how the heck were they pulling it off?

Witchcraft.

The answer presented itself for instant dismissal. I was stumped though. Try as I might, I couldn't come up with a way to make a man's heart explode out of his chest.

So, what did I need to do next?

'James, what else did you find out this morning? Did you get anywhere with lightning strike research or find a local expert I could talk to?'

'No local expert yet. The Universities around here just don't do meteorology. I wondered whether I might have more luck trying the radio or local tv stations to see if their weather presenter might have worthwhile qualifications. I haven't got that far yet though. What I did find was a similar heart exploding out of the chest incident from a couple of years ago.'

'Show me, please?' James pulled up a clip from a news report. It was more than two years old, and one had to read between the lines to understand what had happened. The brief report said that David Melrose had been killed when a freak lightning bolt entered his chest and caused immediate death. It did not actually say that it exploded his heart, but the suggestion was there.

'There are two more,' James said, 'Only weeks apart.'

He pulled these up as well and the printer started whirring as it began printing them. The news reports were inconclusive, but they were a lead of sorts. The three deaths spanned a period of just over a month in total. Each victim was a middle-aged man, and each left a widow. The deaths were all in Tipton. I didn't know where that was and had to look it up. It was just outside Birmingham.

'I wonder if there are any more?' I asked more of myself than James.

'I'll keep looking,' James answered anyway.

I nodded. 'James, I'm going out. Lock up when you leave. I'll take the dachshunds with me.'

'Okay, boss,' he replied.

Stake Out

I had the home address for each of the ladies and had driven to two of them before I found one that looked like it was worth staking out. At the first two, which belonged to Mabel and Edna, there was no sign of activity. I had been able to determine that Edna's husband worked in the city in a banking job of some kind. He probably earned good money, but despite that their house was the most modest of the ones I had seen so far, certainly it was far smaller and less grand than Barbara's place, which she didn't have to share any more on account of her husband being dead and it was much less opulent than the palace Mabel occupied. Mabel's husband hadn't been dead long enough for her to have moved to somewhere new already, at least that was what I was telling myself, so the house I had seen earlier was the house they had together.

Both Mabel and Edna looked to have gone out already. They both lived on the same side of East Malling and not far from one another. Barbara's house was all the way over the other side of the village, which through the winding roads was quite a distance. Dorothy's address though was right in the middle, so I went there next.

As I drove slowly by her driveway, looking to see if it looked like she was home, I spotted a car on the drive. I hadn't been able to identify what car she drove yet, but the bright white Mercedes SLK had her name written all over it. I circled around and found a place to park. I had the dogs with me, so I was going to walk them and accidentally lose one onto her property, so I had to chase it.

This was an easy effect to achieve. All I needed to do was suggest that there was a cat while letting go of a lead. The dog would do the rest. Once I had chased the dog down the drive, I could have a quick look around to ascertain if anyone was there. If the lady came out because she had seen me, I could retrieve the dog, apologise and make a show of having to chase the naughty creature.

I hooked the leads onto their collars and plopped first one then the other dog onto the ground outside the car. I had parked less than fifty metres from her house but had gone no more than ten metres when, ahead of me, her car appeared at the end of her drive, indicating to turn left toward West Malling.

I froze for a second, then scooped both dogs and threw them back into the car with an apology. I would walk them properly soon. This was exactly what I wanted though. She was going out, and I knew two of the other ladies to already be out. I was hedging a bet that they were meeting. I would only find out if I could get my arse moving and catch up to her before she took one of the many turnings available to her and was gone.

Thankfully, with so many routes to guess from, she headed straight for West Malling, and I was able to catch up to her. There was a silver BMW between us, so I was not too conspicuous I hoped, sitting two cars back in my bright red Porsche.

To prove that some days you just get lucky, I followed her all the way to West Malling where she swung into the main car park that serviced the small town. I didn't want to follow her in, but my luck held, and a parking space came available in the High Street as a car's reverse lights came on just ahead of me.

I had lost sight of Dorothy of course and would need to carefully catch up to her in the car park. When I got out of my car though I spotted, on the other side of the road, parked right in front of the Spangled Star public house, the Range Rover from yesterday.

Bull barked at me. He wanted to get out of the car and was telling me off. He was standing on the driver's seat and trying to work out if he could get through the gap between my leg and the door. Maybe he had business to attend to.

I placed both dogs by my feet on the bit of road between the cars. I wanted to have another go at eavesdropping on the ladies, but I had elected to bring the dogs with me and needed to make sure they were comfortable first. I crossed the road and walked them in front of the pub window hoping to see the four ladies inside.

I got a shock as they were at the table in the window and all looked at the man looking in at them. There was a fifth person with them.

I cut my eyes away and continued down the street. The fifth person was another woman, or at least I believed that to be the case. She was wearing a black shawl with a hood, her face hidden from view, so I was judging gender by the shape of the shoulders and back alone.

Walking down West Malling High Street, I was reminded how much I liked the place. There were so many wonderful shops to poke around in and not a franchise in sight with the exception of a coffee chain. I should bring Natasha here! I could collect her in my car. It was a nice drive that was unlikely to run into traffic anywhere and would give us a chance to chat. Thinking about Natasha made me feel excited. She had kissed me a while back and it had been very nice. I could imagine being quite smitten by her if we ever got that far.

The lead in my right hand jerked to a halt. I hadn't been paying attention and Bull was now hunched over in the street going about his business. It was less than ideal, but I don't think dogs consider such things. When they need to go, they go.

I checked my pocket to reassure myself that I had a baggy and waited for him to finish. I got a frown from a woman walking by. She was probably concerned that I might not pick up after my dog. I was an ardent fan of berating people for failing to do exactly that thing. Who wants to step in poop? I wasn't a fan of picking it up, who would be? But it went hand in hand with having a dog.

Task complete, I walked to the end of the road and then back up to the pub. There was a nice park in West Malling where I would take the dogs for a proper run around after I had spied on the ladies. Until then, the quick walk would have to do, and I would get them a packet of crisps from the bar as a reward for putting up with being messed about.

The pub had a back way into it via the car park. Rather than walk in through the front door and within feet of the group I intended to spy on, I came in through the other door instead. Weaving my way through the lunchtime crowd, I could see a space at the bar. I needed to be close enough to hear what the ladies were saying. It was the third time in a few days that I had been in close proximity to them. I worried they might have noticed me at the Golf Club yesterday and would now wonder why they were seeing me again.

It was a genuine concern, but I could do nothing about it now so dismissed the notion and went to the bar. I would keep my back to them and listen for their chatter. If I could, I would try to get a look at the fifth person. With my back to them the whole time I was sure they would not even notice me.

'Ooh look, Mabel. Dachshunds,' cried Dorothy, pointing at Bull and Dozer.

Of course. My plan to be inconspicuous had backfired. I had taken two small, cute dogs into an environment with women. The dogs immediately started wagging their tails. They were well-attuned to the cooing of women. It meant fussing and treats.

They were straining to get me over to the table of women, I was trying to get to the bar where I was clinging to the hope that the ladies would go back to their conversation and let me eavesdrop.

Dorothy was off her chair now though, as was Edna and both were happily ignoring me as they knelt to pet my sausage-shaped idiots. Both dogs had inverted themselves for tummy tickles and had their heads back and their eyes closed as the ladies obliged. Both dogs had a faraway expression on their face as they were transported to a happy place.

Dammit.

'Oh, aren't they lovely?' Cooed Dorothy.

'Can I pick him up?' Edna asked of me, it was the first time any of the ladies had looked directly at me. There was no sense in her eyes that she had seen me before. She had Dozer at her feet and wanted a proper cuddle.

'Of course,' I almost slipped up and said her name in my reply, catching myself only as the word formed on my lips. I reached down to unclip both dogs and watched as they were scooped into the air. 'I'll be at the bar, ladies.' I turned around. Maybe this would work out after all.

Edna and Dorothy went back to their seats, and I listened. Now, bear in mind that Barbara's husband was killed yesterday in the most horrible manner. One might expect her to be upset, inconsolable, tearful... pick an adjective you like but none of them would apply. With her three friends, it was business as usual. Barbara began berating Edna and Dorothy for being distracted by the dogs. They had important topics to discuss it seemed.

Watching in the mirror, I saw the mystery woman raise an arm. From the sleeve of the shawl poked a bony hand, withered and old. The motion caused the other women to fall silent. The hooded face turned toward me, and I saw the person inside for the first time.

It was a witch.

I couldn't find another word with which to describe her. Were a child to draw a witch this would be the result. Hook nose with a wart on it, on her chin and under her nose there were a few thick and very visible strands of hair that anyone else would have plucked or shaved. A giant brown mole on her left cheek had yet more hair growing from it, and when she spoke, I saw blackened and misshapen teeth. Her hair, what little of it I could see, was black, shot through with grey and unkempt inside the shawl. Her eyebrows were bushy and wild.

She locked eyes with me. It was quite deliberate, and she pointed a bony finger at me, pinning me to the spot.

'Spy,' she announced, her voice like fingernails on a chalkboard. 'He's spying on us.'

Whoever she was, how she had identified me, did not matter. I was not going to be able to eavesdrop on their conversation and they would be looking for me now which would compromise my investigation. I could worry about that later. Right now, I needed to leave and to do that I needed to get my dogs back.

'I think I'll take these, thank you,' I said, scooping the dogs from the laps of Dorothy and Edna. They both looked a little shocked, but then all the ladies did except for the witch. She was just watching me, her eyes accusing.

It was a little unnerving. She somehow knew who I was or at least knew my purpose in the bar. Had she just guessed? Did my actions somehow betray me? I was back at the door of the pub and walking away when I had a thought. I was busted anyway, so why not do something to advance my investigation?

I walked back to the table, pulled out my phone and took a photograph of the surprised witch's face. With a quick nod of thanks, I made good my escape. As I went, I emailed the picture to James with a request that he try to find her. It was a tough task I suspected but he surprised me all the time with what he could achieve on his computer.

I hadn't managed to get the dogs their promised packet of crisps and was now going to bundle them back into the car yet again. I paused before I got to it though, there was another course of action open to me.

Surveillance

I kept a few items of basic surveillance equipment in the boot of my car in a bag. One of the items was a small, battery-powered camera that linked to my laptop. It was very likely that all the ladies, except for Dorothy, had parked in the town's main car park behind the pub. I just needed to mount the camera in a place where it would pick up the cars as they left. I could see what car the witch was in, very probably get a shot of her number plate and through that James would be able to find out who she was. If she had a car and could drive, of course.

I hit the button on my key fob to open the boot and fished out the bag with one hand. It had a shoulder strap which I hooked over my head to fish around in it as I crossed the road. If the dogs were confused about where we were going or what we were doing, there was no sign of it. Both were trundling along happily by my feet, their tails wagging as they went.

Not far from my car, I found a convenient road sign that faced the car park exit. The camera had a magnet on the back so attaching it I barely broke my stride. I doubted anyone would see it, it was not much bigger than a fifty pence piece, but there was a risk it would get stolen, and it wouldn't do well with rain if the weather changed.

I gambled that the ladies were not going anywhere for a while having only just arrived, so I packed the dogs into the car and took them to the nearby park. I could leave the car at the park and walk back, find myself a shady corner to stand in and have myself a little stakeout until they left. I was also a little worried that they might know my car. The witch seemed to know me, so it didn't feel like much of a leap. If they did, then I wanted them to believe I had left.

Of course, I didn't really think she was a witch. She was just an ugly old lady, but my natural conclusion was that she was at the centre of the deaths. Possibly even the one causing them since the wives each seemed to have iron-clad alibis. How she was doing it remained a key question.

At the park, I wandered slowly back in the direction of the town centre, letting the dogs scamper back and forth. As they entertained themselves, I phoned Frank DeCaux, owner and manager of the Mystery Men bookshop in Rochester.

'Mystery men. For all your supernatural literature needs.' It was Poison who answered the phone. Ivy Wong, AKA Poison is Frank's very attractive assistant. She's his only member of staff, she's nineteen years old, and she has a thing for me that I was refusing to take advantage of.

'Hello, Ivy. It's Tempest. Is Frank there, please?'

'Hello, Tempest,' she purred down the line at me, her voice instantly demure and suggestive. 'He's right behind me. Somewhere you should be.' Her flirty words went straight to my groin. Mr Wriggly had been very grumpy with my decision to not pursue nocturnal activities with

Poison. If he could have sworn at me, he would be doing so right now.

'Tempest?' Frank's voice came onto the line.

'Hi, Frank. I have a picture to send you. I think this one is really a stretch, but I'm wondering if you can identify a person. Hold on.' I took the phone from my ear and switched it to speaker. 'Photo is on its way to you now.'

I waited for him to receive it and looked around to make sure I still had both dogs. They were just off to my left. I was on a path, and they were in the field it bisected. They were watching three crows. The large black birds were too far away for the dogs to have any hope of catching but close enough to make their dopey brains think they should try.

I made no attempt to stop them as they both took off. Stealthy as a one-man band going for a run, both dogs announced their attack by barking all the way across the field. The crows waited until the dogs were getting just a little too close, then took off. They flew fifty yards and touched down again, which was close enough that the dogs kept on running. As they neared the crows they took off again and the cycle repeated. They were getting good exercise and probably enjoying themselves.

'That's a witch,' Frank said.

I turned my attention back to the conversation with him. 'I'm sure that's what she wants us to think.'

'It's the heterochromia iridium that gives it away. Not that it cannot occur in ordinary people but in witches, it's very common. Combine that with the Wiccan symbol hanging from her neck and the three rings on her fingers, I'm certain that you have found yourself a genuine witch.'

I had to search my memory to dredge up the snippet of information that told me the term heterochromia iridium meant the person had different coloured eyes –

one blue, one green or whatever the combination was. I looked more closely at the photograph, and he was right; the left eye was brown in her case while the right was blue. Now that he had pointed it out, I was shocked I hadn't seen it before. 'Frank this will come as no surprise to you, but I do not understand the significance of the necklace or the rings.'

I heard him tut. 'The three rings represent their faith. Wiccans worship the Horned God of fertility and a Mother Goddess. The middle ring represents Wiccans on earth enveloped between the two gods. The odd things about their gods, of course, is that they have no names.'

'Why is that odd?'

'Because, Tempest, with the exception of the Christian faith, who are a bit arrogant in just calling their god, God, everyone else gives them names. The Romans, Egyptians, and Greeks all did. Even the Pagans had names for their deities.'

'Okay, so the pertinent news is that the lady in the photograph is a witch. My follow-on question is: Would she be able to make a man's heart explode from his chest?'

There was silence at the other end for a while. I was about to repeat myself when he finally started speaking. 'I, ah... I need to look something up.' Then he disconnected. Basically, he hung up on me. From anyone else, it would seem rude, but Frank's start point was odd. He went down the scale from that point depending on the day and the circumstances.

He would most likely call me back once he had something to tell me, or I would catch up with him later.

A few spots of rain began to fall, signalling the end of our walk. I called to the boys. They had given up their pursuit of the crows when the birds had finally grown bored of being chased and taken to a tree. Now they were snuffling at the base of a promising looking bush for rabbits.

For once they came when I called, bouncing off one another as they ran across the field to me. I clipped them back on their leads to escort them out of the back gate of the park. The town centre was no more than three hundred metres away, the time to get there insignificant.

No more than twenty-five minutes had elapsed since I left the town centre, and the ladies were still in their seats by the window. Opposite them was another pub, not unusual in an English village. If my knowledge was correct, there were no fewer than twelve pubs in West Malling and there had probably been far more than that a few decades ago. I slipped in through a side door, bought a diet coke plus a packet of crisp to feed the dogs and settled down to watch.

I may have mentioned this before, but stakeouts are boring. Really boring. I was sitting in a pub on a cool day in late Autumn and should have been happy to just idly sip a drink and relax. However, the mere fact that I was watching the window across the street made the time drag. It was not that I had a desperate need to be somewhere else, just that I was waiting for them to leave and had no idea how long the wait might be.

A long twenty minutes went by and suddenly they all started moving. The witch had her back to the window, not that I would have been able to see much had she been facing outwards. Light playing off the glass, passing cars and vans and the thirty metres between us all degraded what I could see. If only I had been able to place a one-way radio under their table, I could have recorded the entire conversation.

The ladies vanished from sight, heading further into the pub and probably out the back door to reach the car park.

Less than a minute later the white Mercedes SLK came into view as it left the car park. Then Dorothy came out the front of the pub and got into the Range Rover. The next car to leave contained Barbara. I watched for the witch.

Nothing.

Several cars left over the next five minutes, but each had a person at the wheel that was most definitely not an old crone.

I tapped my chin a few times, drummed by fingers, swore quietly and made a decision. I crossed the road, went in the front door of the pub and out the back. There was no other way out of the car park except via the entrance/exit I had been watching. Not for an old woman anyway. A fitter person could easily scale the six-foot wall that surrounded the car park, so she must have gone out on foot or by car in the time I was going through the pub. Regardless of the circumstances, she had given me the slip.

Then I remembered the camera.

Daytime Drinking

By the time I got home, I was very much ready for a cup of tea. I wanted a biscuit to go with it but denied myself the unnecessary calories and ate a banana instead. It was, probably, the same number of calories but the way my body would process and use them was vastly different.

I flicked the kettle on, took the dogs' collars off and put them into the basket on the shelf next to the front door along with their leads and the remaining baggies I had in my pocket. While my tea was brewing, I went through to the office to fetch the list of signwriters James had produced for me. I was itching to check the video footage from the carpark to see if I had, in fact, caught the witch on camera leaving the pub, but it could wait until I had made tea and sat down.

Checking the list of signwriters, I couldn't see that any of the firms on the list were better or superior to any other, so I started at the top and called the first number. They could absolutely do what I wanted, but not for another three weeks. I had no desire to operate out of an office that bore the name of a different business. I worked my way down the list, finally getting someone who could come tomorrow on the eighth call. They could come in the morning, remove the old signs, measure up and be back with new signs the following day or possibly the day after depending on what I wanted.

I was sceptical about their lead time for completing the work but did not voice my thoughts. I needed to provide them with a design, but if I did not have one, they could, for an additional charge, help me to produce one.

With that task done, I drank my tea and thought about what else I needed to do. Frank still hadn't called me back, but he would, so I was going to give him space and if I hadn't heard anything by tomorrow, I would visit him in his shop. I was looking forward to being back in Rochester High Street. I would have to break the news to Tony at the travel shop. He would be disappointed to lose the rent probably, but I would point out that he could charge more than he charged me and once the office was rebuilt, he could yield a greater income from it. I was paid up for the quarter anyway and would not ask for a refund.

I had been going over and over in my head how I was going to learn more about the four women. Now that the witch, or whatever she was, had identified me to them, there was no chance that I could spy on them or eavesdrop on them or even be anywhere near them unless I was in a very good disguise or invisible. But a thought occurred to me. Two of them were widowed and two of them were most likely disgruntled with their husbands. I wanted to know more about them, such as what Dorothy and Edna's relationships with their husbands was like. Were they unhappy? Did they have massive life insurance policies? Were they performing diabolical Wiccan ceremonies that cause men's hearts to fly out of their chests?

I couldn't get close to them, but I knew a man who could.

'Ben, I have a challenge for you,' I announced when he answered his phone.

'Yeah? Am I going to like this?' he asked, his voice guarded.

'Probably, yes. I need you to seduce some women, get them to lower their defences and obtain some information without them realising they have given it up.'

'Sounds easy. How many women?'

'Four.'

'Deadline?'

'How quickly can you get it done?' I asked.

'Well, I need their addresses, or where I can most likely find them. Photographs would help so that I can identify them easily. I had no plan for tonight, other than to go into town and pick up some women.' *Some women.* 'So, I can start right now if you like. Should have it all tied up before bedtime.'

I honestly couldn't tell whether he was joking or serious. I told him I was at home and had the information he needed here.

Something thumped against the front door. As I turned towards it, the dogs whooshed by either side of my ankles, barking as they went.

There was a figure on the other side of my door, but through the frosted glass, whoever it was appeared to be leaning on the door, their face was smooshed into the glass.

Curious, I opened the door. Hilary toppled in to land at my feet. The dogs stopped barking, surprised by the sudden human at their level. They climbed on his face.

'Hey, Tempesht. I found a...' he paused, partly because Bull had just licked his teeth and partly because he seemed to have lost the thread of what he was saying.

He was drunk.

'I found a pub. They had beer,' he announced with utter glee.

I looked down at the figure on the floor of my house. I didn't do drunk. I liked a few drinks, but once the alcohol started to impact my reaction time, which of course was almost immediate, I stopped. I never got to the point where I was a liability to others. Never had. Doubted I ever would. Nevertheless, I now had a drunk laying at my feet.

'Come on, buddy. Let's get you up.' I grabbed an arm, hauled him onto his very unsteady feet and walked him through to the lounge where I let him flop onto the sofa. 'Are you likely to be sick?' I asked. My concern felt legitimate.

'Goodness, no,' he replied as he sank into the cushions and made himself comfortable. 'I only had a few.' His arithmetic was questionable. 'There was a lovely barmaid. Well, I say lovely. She had a bit of stubble on her chin and the tattoos on her knuckles read LOVE and HAT. But other than that, she was lovely.'

'LOVE and HAT?'

'Yes, she lost the finger with the E on it in a fight when someone bit it off,' she sounded wonderful. 'We have a date at the weekend.'

I opened my mouth to ask whether that was a good idea, but the question died on my lips when I saw that he was now asleep. He began snoring. From the information about the barmaid, I surmised that he had walked to the pub in the next village. I had been in there once or twice, more from curiosity than anything else. The barmaid was something of a local legend, the legend itself being that if you got drunk enough you would wake up with her. It seemed she had a habit of preying on drunk young men and would carry them across the road to her house unconscious if necessary.

Hilary was lucky to have escaped if there was any truth to the rumour. I was standing in front of him, watching him sleep. I felt creepy, so I left him there to sleep it off. As I was leaving the room, Bull and Dozer were climbing onto his lap from either side. They would join him with their snores.

The Hag of Bluebell Hill

It was 1612hrs. I called Amanda. I hadn't checked on her all day. She was operating as an independent investigator, picking her own cases and bringing in fees for her services. I really liked how autonomous she was, but I felt I should check in with her every day and make sure she had all she needed, offer her my support, that sort of thing. She most likely had no use for me, but I wanted to touch base, nevertheless.

Her phone rang in my ear, but I could also hear it coming from somewhere else. As I looked up confused, she came through my front door holding it in her hand.

She said, 'Hi, Tempest,' as she closed the door behind her. I could see that it was raining lightly outside again. There were spots on her clothing where she had dashed from the car to the door and her hair, which was usually full of volume, looked a little deflated from all the moisture around. That said, she was still the most beautiful woman on the planet and we were alone in my house together.

Except we were not because Hilary was still asleep on my couch.

The dogs appeared, fussing around her feet until she petted them and cooed at them. Each rolled over to show her a belly to scratch.

'Hi, Amanda. I just called to see how you were getting on. James said you had a case but did not elaborate.'

'Have you ever heard of the Bluebell Hill hag?'

'Yes. An old crone that jumps out at cars or sometimes appears inside the cars. Scares the life out of the driver or other occupants and then disappears. Sometimes appears as a young woman but is mostly an old lady.'

'That's the one.'

'Someone asked us to investigate that old legend?'

'A gentleman by the name of Martin Boynes. I went to his house when I left here this morning and then went with him to the… hold on I need to back the story up a bit. Do you fancy a cup of tea?' she asked. She was taking her jacket off. It was warm in the house, and she had warmed up already. I tried not to watch as the action of taking it off made her boobs wobble about. Instead, I turned to the kettle and refilled it, then took two fresh cups from the cupboard.

As the kettle began making noise, she restarted her story. 'So, Mr Boynes got a speeding fine through the post. His wife recognised what it was, apparently, it's not his first. Anyway, she opened the envelope and saw, clear as anything, a young woman in a dress sitting in the back of her husband's car. She went nuts, as you might imagine, and accused him of having an affair.' Amanda produced a folder from her handbag, opened it, then handed me a photograph. It was the usual DVLA issue polaroid style photograph. It was not of great quality, but the woman, and more importantly her face, could be clearly seen.

'Did he hire us or did she?' I asked.

'He did. He wants us to prove to his wife that what she's seeing is a ghost. Gave me a fat advance too,' Amanda said, producing a wad of cash in a white envelope.

'I guess he's staring a costly divorce in the face otherwise. Did you explain to him that we spend all our time proving that ghosts don't exist?'

Amanda chuckled, 'I sure did. He didn't seem inclined to listen. He felt that if we could prove that ghosts don't exist, it should be easy to show that this one does. He had already done some research, so he knew that Bluebell Hill is recorded as one of the most haunted places in Britain.'

'Two seconds on google will show you that,' I added.

'Exactly, but he seemed to want to pay us to perform an investigation and come back to him with a pile of evidence that would suggest that he's not the first man to have found a strange woman in the back of his car on Bluebell Hill.'

I sipped my tea and remembered my manners, 'Would you like a biscuit?'

'No, thank you. I had better not.' I didn't press the matter, but I believed she could eat a biscuit if she wanted to. Her figure was perfect. Perhaps though that was because she avoided the biscuits.

'What is your early conclusion then?' I asked her. I was making conversation more than anything else. Just then the door handle turned again. I looked up and Amanda looked over her shoulder. The easily identifiable shape coming through the door was Big Ben.

'Hey, Tempest. Hiya, Hotstuff.' Big Ben pretty much refused to call Amanda by her name. He had latched onto the name I had given her when I first met her and did not know her name and now he wouldn't let it go. I had pointed out that she had learned it was a name I had given her and thus it was embarrassing to remind either one of us. However, he was an annoying tit, so he used it deliberately.

'Hello, Benjamin,' Amanda replied. 'I hear you have managed to get two different girls pregnant at the same time.'

His face fell, the smile that had been there a moment ago vanished in a heartbeat.

'Three,' he said.

'Three what?' I asked.

'It's three girls now. Some girl called Bianca phoned me this morning. I don't even remember her. Her period is nineteen days late and she wanted me to know.'

Big Ben looked genuinely panicked. I had seen him go into combat looking less worried than this.

'Well, that is a pickle.' I couldn't think of anything else to say.

'Where's the photographs and addresses?' he asked, his voice full of resignation.

'What are you up to, Ben?' Amanda wanted to know.

'Some top-level, top-drawer shagging.' Normally, Big Ben's reply would have been delivered with real gusto. Now though it was like he was accepting a chore.

Amanda rolled her eyes rather than comment and stepped to the side so that Big Ben could get to the pack I had placed on the kitchen breakfast bar for him.

'This isn't compulsory,' I pointed out. 'I have no reason to believe you will be able to get any information from them.'

Big Ben looked up from examining the pictures. His usual leering grin had returned. 'Who else could you possibly send on this mission. Besides, they will tell me anything once I have given each of them the greatest orgasm any of them will ever achieve.'

'Dear God,' Amanda muttered.

'It's there for you as well, Hotstuff. You only have to ask.' He ducked as she swatted at his head.

A noise came from my lounge and the conversation stopped as all three of us looked at each other. I called it a noise, but I should more accurately describe it as a large volume of gas being expelled from a drunk man's rectum via his anal sphincter. The fart had both volume and duration.

'Hilary is asleep on my couch,' I explained. 'His wife kicked him out and he crashed here last night, refused to go to work this morning and then thought a few beers was a good idea. I'm letting him sleep it off.'

Big Ben took a few steps back and to his right to peer through the doorway at him. 'That was some good farting,' He observed.

'Christ,' said Amanda, a comment that could have meant anything, but was probably tired resignation at men judging and scaling other men's farts.

Amanda and I joined Big Ben in the doorway. 'Amanda?' Big Ben started.

Amanda sighed, 'I doubt I want to hear the question you have for me, Benjamin, let alone want to provide an answer, but go on.'

'Do men often look that pathetic when they have had a few too many?'

'Yes. Always,' she replied instantly as if the answer were utterly obvious to anyone with a brain.

'I might never drink again,' he muttered to himself.

I was with him. Hilary looked a mess. He had one shoe

on and one off. His shirt was untucked to show his skinny belly, and he was half slouched, half dead-looking on the couch with a pool of drool forming on his collar.

'His wife kicked him out?' Big Ben asked.

'Yes, somehow he got it into his head that he should smack her on the arse and show her who is the boss in their house.'

Big Ben's cheeks coloured ever so slightly. 'Well, can't hang around. I have work to do,' he called out as he took the pack with the pictures and addresses and went back out my front door.

I was still in my lounge with Amanda and the sleeping Hilary. He shifted slightly on the couch causing us both to turn our eyes to him. So, we were just in time to see him idly scratch his balls in his sleep and then fart again.

'Let's go, shall we?' I asked as I turned toward the door and Amanda, but she was already gone.

'Where did we get to? Amanda asked. She was back in the kitchen. We stared at each other for a moment, trying to recollect where our conversation had left off before Big Ben had arrived.

Then I thought of something, 'Oh, I almost forgot to tell you; we have a new office.'

She had just taken a slurp of tea so raised her eyebrows for me to continue. I told her about the wonderful new building we were moving into the next day, what the increase in rent was, and what my plans were for it.

When I finished outlining my plans for the office, she agreed to help me set up tomorrow instead of doing case-work. We would meet there at 0900hrs and see what needed to be done. I had been inside briefly today, so I knew it needed a clean, but there was furniture inside that was now mine and all it really needed was a quick redecorate as I was not going to tolerate the large, framed pictures of Nessie and UFOs that adorned the walls currently.

'I remembered what we were talking about,' Amanda said.

'Hmmm?'

'Before Big Ben showed up. We were talking and then we couldn't remember where we got to. Well, we were talking about the Bluebell Hill hag and what I needed to do next. I need to do some research. That's my next step. I have a hunch about what the outcome of this case will be but don't want to jinx it yet.'

'Understood,' I replied. 'Got anything planned for the evening?' I was making conversation, being polite. It was the end of the day; the dachshunds had wandered into the kitchen to point out that it was very nearly their appointed dinner time and Amanda would be going home soon. It was for the best. At least that was what I was telling myself.

Last week, in Cornwall, I had met another lady and engaged in some naked fun with her. She had made me forget Amanda and I told myself at the time that the infatuation that had plagued me since the moment I met her several weeks ago, was in fact dissipating. Then on Friday, I had seen Amanda naked. It was not a sight I could erase, it was forever printed on my brain and was why I referred to her body as utterly perfect.

I had a date with Natasha in forty-eight hours though and every right to be excited about it. I could move on and be happy if I could just convince my stupid brain that the world's most perfect partner for me wasn't already standing in my kitchen.

I sighed internally.

'Nothing much,' she replied. 'I will visit the gym and get

some dinner in front of the television I think.' She was picking up her jacket and slipping her arms into it.

I showed her out and bid her a good night. As she pulled off my drive, I closed the door and went back to the kitchen where two black and tan sausage dogs were waiting impatiently for their evening meal.

Impressive

It was 1903hrs when Hilary woke up. He found me in my office where I was about to look at the video footage from West Malling. He looked bewildered and wanted to take himself to bed. I convinced him to eat a sandwich and drink some milk first though. He took both upstairs with him, which gave me the option of moving to the lounge instead.

I was having a fight with my conscience about the rum and coke that I wanted to drink. It was needless, pointless calories. I knew that, but I still wanted one even though alcohol would mess with my desire to lose weight faster than anything else I could consume.

Grumpily, I got a glass of water and sat on the sofa with my laptop and two dachshunds. The software with the cameras was easy to use, so seconds later I was scrolling through the footage looking for what I believed to be the right time. As I neared it, I slowed the playback and watched it at normal speed.

It was in colour and had quite good definition, not HD standard, but good enough to see faces in the cars. I saw

Dorothy leave and then Barbara. Then car after car until I appeared around the side of the pub, walked toward the camera and reached up for it. The screen went blank.

Had the witch hidden in the pub? Had she been in the ladies' toilet while I was looking for her? It was plausible. Disappointed, I closed the laptop and put it to one side

The rest of the evening ticked by quietly. I called and made a reservation at a Gastro Pub in the heart of West Malling. I was going to take Natasha for dinner, and I was going to make her feel cherished.

I thought some more about the case but couldn't develop a concept for how the women were causing the deaths. I wanted to be able to prove the guilt or otherwise of the ladies, although I was already certain they were guilty. However, to do that, I would need to first prove that there had been a murder. The coroner disagreed. A singular fact which made the case far more difficult.

I would need to arrange to bump into her somewhere. I needed to find a way to open her mind to the possibility that it was something other than lightning that had killed the two men.

Bedtime came around. The dogs were both asleep with their heads on my right thigh, one beside the other. I woke them, so they could pay a final visit to the garden then trudged upstairs thinking about the new office and what it would be like to work there. It was more prominent than the pokey, little thing I had inhabited previously, and it was much, much nicer.

Drifting off to sleep, I had one of those dreams that make you jump in your sleep. The witch had thrown a lightning bolt at me, I had jumped to escape it and woken myself. I looked at the clock as I settled back onto my pillow. It was 0015hrs.

Then my phone rang. I had forgotten to turn it off. Though tempted to ignore it, I suspected the caller would just call again after it had rung off. Reluctantly I rolled over to check the screen: It was Big Ben.

'Hey, buddy. What's up?' I asked blearily.

'I'm finished. Stop the clock,' he replied.

Groggily, I mentally scratched my head. 'Finished what?'

'Are you asleep already, slack arse? Real men are working, getting stuff done.'

'Yes, that's lovely, Ben. What are you talking about though?'

He tutted. 'You asked me to perform a task. I'm on my way home and letting you know that the task is complete.' There was some exasperation to his tone.

'I set you a … Hold on. Are you talking about the four ladies? Are you calling to tell me that you have shagged them all already?'

'Yeah. Took longer than I thought. That Barbara, she has got some energy. I tell you, when she said she wanted to…'

'NO!' I cut him off. The ladies in question were not unattractive, nor were they old, although they were all in the fifties, despite that, I did not need Big Ben filling my head with graphical images of his activities with them. 'How is it that you have shagged four middle-aged women in the space of six hours?'

'I'm not sure what you are asking. How did I manage to seduce and bed four women? Or how well did I stick it to them i.e. quality of shag? Because if you are asking the latter then the answer is that you will not need to worry about following any of them tomorrow because they will not be able to walk. If you are asking about how I seduced them all so quickly, then I would have to ask if you have ever met me?'

He was such a dick.

'Look, I'm kinda tired now. Four women in one evening does take it out of a guy. I'll come by the house tomorrow.'

'I'm moving to a new office tomorrow.' I told him about the place in Rochester High Street. He knew where it was.

'Okay, so I'll come by the new office around noon. I need some sleep first. I learned some stuff, but it can wait until then, right?'

'Yup.'

'Cool.' He disconnected.

Big Ben had shagged four women tonight while the closest I had got to some action was when I got an itch on my left nut and had to scratch it.

Disgruntled, I turned over and went back to sleep.

Moving Day

My morning ritual of getting up early to exercise went to plan, as yet again I made it to the gym. Just a few days into the routine I was already feeling better.

When I arrived home, Hilary was sitting looking miserable at the breakfast bar. His head was supported by his left hand while his right was cradling a cooling cup of coffee.

'Sore head?' I asked rhetorically.

His eyes managed to move upwards from the counter he had been staring brainlessly at, but the rest of his body remained motionless until he spoke. 'My life is ruined,' he announced.

I put my gym bag down, took milk from the fridge to make myself a power shake and sat down opposite him. 'This is the first time you have ever had a proper relationship drama, isn't it?'

He nodded solemnly. 'Anthea is…' he struggled for the right words. 'I have only ever slept with two women.' This was a somewhat startling revelation until I gave it a moment's thought. Hilary had been married for fifteen years and was in his mid-thirties so had married young. He was also not the sort of chap that inspired women to take their knickers off – kind of a polar opposite to Big Ben if you will. 'Anthea is everything to me. I don't know how to live without her.'

'Okay, mate, it's tough love time.'

He looked up at me, making eye contact for the first time because the tone of my voice was no longer soothing.

'I doubt that you and Anthea are done. You have been married a long time and have children together. You pissed her off, but you didn't commit a cardinal sin like getting caught in bed with her sister or anything, so it seems like a recoverable position. Whether this gets fixed or not may depend on whether you get off your arse and fix it. Get some gumption, decide what you want and find a way to get it. Go and win her back if that's what you want. When whining about it though, keep in mind that absolutely everyone else on the planet has had the pain of a failed relationship and each of them feels that their pain is worse than anyone else's. If you whine, no one will listen. So, sleep off your hangover and get your life back. Okay?'

He looked more miserable than ever. They were stern words, but I felt he needed a reality check.

'Serious talk over. Want some breakfast?' I asked as I got up and moved to the blender.

I let Hilary stew for a few minutes. Just before I felt the need to prompt a response from him, he thanked me for helping him and for not coddling him. He would be fine. I gave him more coffee, strong and black, and left him with bacon, eggs, and bread on the counter for him to turn into breakfast when he was ready.

Half an hour later, I was going out the door. I took the dogs to work with me. I would not have customers there today and I might get caught up in what I was doing and be late for lunch. Taking them with me made it easier. Somehow, I had packed all the computer gear, printers, whiteboard, and other paraphernalia into my car and James's Ford Fiesta. He had arrived at 0830hrs to help load it all up.

At 0900hrs we were just pulling into the parking spaces that were located at the back of the new office. It was all very new and exciting. Amanda's Mini Cooper was already parked in one of the spots. Her car door opened as I put my handbrake on.

'Hey, guys,' she said as she stood up. 'I got coffee.'

Marvellous.

There was a back door into the offices which was right in front of our cars. Like a kid at Christmas, and with the dogs buzzing around my feet, I found the right key and got the door open. It was a little stiff, but I could come back to fix that later. We all went inside, the dogs vanishing in the shadows until I found the light switches. The back door led into a corridor from which a utility room that had nothing in it and a small kitchen could be accessed. They were on the right as we made our way forward. The dogs had reached a door on the left and were looking between it and me expectantly. I turned the handle and pushed it open. On the other side was the main office, an open plan space with a reception desk and a seating area. To our right, at the back of the office, if one considered the High Street entrance to be the front, there were two offices. Neither big nor small, they were large enough to house a desk and an office chair plus two other chairs for visitors to sit on.

Dr. Parrish, the previous tenant, had left in a hurry. His Ph.D was still in a frame on the wall. He had left behind professional looking stationery and other office equipment. It was all still where it had been before he quit.

'Let's box it up,' I suggested. It wasn't ours and he might want it. We would put it all into a corner of the utility room and James would see if he could track the man down and give it back.

I had brought cleaning equipment from home so for the next two hours we polished and scrubbed and cleaned and brought the place up to an acceptable standard before we started moving our own equipment in. The two offices would be used by Amanda and me, James would be in the main room, but we would get him a better desk and set it up properly for him. One office was slightly larger than the other and looked likely to get more light through the window as the other was tucked in tight to the wall of the deeper building next to us and would thus often be in shadow. I did the decent thing and flipped a coin for it.

I lost.

Amanda laughed and ran into the better office with her box of bits before I could ask to go best of three. The dogs rushed in after her, curious about what it was that had excited her. They wandered out again when they realised there was no food to be had.

By 1100hrs I was getting peckish and wanted more coffee. We hadn't got around to setting up the percolator yet, so I suggested a spot of early lunch at the coffee house. Just then someone knocked on the front door. The dogs went berserk as always. They had no idea what they were barking at, but that never made a difference to them. The point it seemed, was to bark. The door was still locked, so I grabbed the keys and called out that I would be a moment while I tried to remember which one I needed.

The person outside was the sign writer. He had at least turned up. I pointed out the sign above the door and explained what I wanted. I had trawled the internet the previous evening and found an image I could use for our logo. It was a blue moon rising over a darkened forest. With the name of the firm displayed prominently underneath the moon, I was happy that it matched the nature of the business. He had ladders and an apprentice with him, so we left them taking down the old sign and crossed the road to the coffee shop.

The coffee shop, a daily refuge until my office burnt down, was a few yards further to walk now but we no longer had stairs to negotiate so it felt closer. Just as we were about to go in someone called my name.

I turned to see my father approaching. It was unusual to see him out without mother. Rochester High Street was walking distance from their house, so he had probably done just that.

'Hey, Dad. What's up?' I stayed behind and sent Amanda and James in ahead of me.

'You getting coffee?' he asked.

It seemed like a daft question, as I had one hand poised on the door handle of a coffee shop, but I let it go. 'Yes. Care to join us?'

'Absolutely. I need to talk to you about your mother's birthday. We can do that and drink coffee.'

The bell on the door chimed as we went inside. I wondered if the staff even heard it. It must ring several thousand times a day.

I joined Amanda and James at the counter. 'So, what about Mum's birthday? It's this Thursday, yes? Big party at your place.'

'That's right. Seven o'clock, don't be late.'

'As if.' Dad knew my thoughts on tardiness. Reminding me to be on time couldn't be what he wanted to see me for. I was waiting for him to get to the point though.

'Well, anyway, I thought I ought to… I wanted to talk to you about presents.' He was acting a little odd. Like he had an uncomfortable subject to reveal and was struggling to work out how. 'Can we, err… Can we go and sit? Can your friends bring the drinks across?'

I sent him to a table. Something was bothering him, I might as well find out what it was. I gave Amanda a twenty pounds note to pay for drinks and snacks. Ordered two coffees and asked her to get me a banana and an apple.

At the table, I said, 'Spit it out then.'

Dad was fiddling with a handkerchief. He laid it on the table. 'Well, I wanted to get your mum something special, but she never gives me any money, so I had been tussling with what to get her for some time. What do you think of these?'

Dad didn't look sheepish anymore. He looked like the cat that got the cream. He opened the handkerchief and sat back in his chair, his hands steepled under his chin. On the table was a brooch and a pair of earrings. Describing them like that though is like saying Buckingham Palace is a rather fancy house. Set into the centre of the brooch was a ruby the size of my left testicle. It was so big that to fully describe it one needed to use expletives.

The earrings matched, their rubies less daunting in size but massive, nevertheless. I gawped at the jewels, my mouth hanging open. I did not want to estimate their worth, it was somewhere between a lot and an obscenely large amount. I also knew where they had come from - a certain boat moored off Cawsand a week ago.

I looked back up at my father. He grinned and waggled his eyebrows. He had purloined himself a pocketful of the jewels when he went on the boat. I was starting to feel silly that I hadn't.

Just then Amanda and James started towards us. Dad folded the handkerchief and stuffed it back into his pocket.

'We got talking to one of the girls behind the counter,' Amanda said as she handed out the coffees. 'Hayley?' She was looking at me to see what reaction I had to the name.

'Yes,' I replied neutrally. I didn't know where she was going but she already knew Hayley. She and I had spent a night together about a month ago. Amanda had met her at my house wearing my shirt and very clearly nothing else having spent the night. What might have been something went south fast after she got confused about my assistant Jane and thought the two of us were an item making her the bit on the side.

'It seems that she was blissfully unaware that James and Jane are the same person.'

Oh.

'You should have seen her face, boss,' James said. 'It was a picture.'

'Anyway, I thought you would want to know,' said Amanda, locking eyes with me. 'It seemed to be important information to her.'

I looked across to the counter. Hayley was already looking my way and trying to catch my eye. She mouthed "Sorry" and mimed that she would call me.

Okay.

I shook my head to clear it. Suddenly Hayley was interested again. What next? I get home and find Poison naked and waiting for me in my bed? I told myself I shouldn't joke about such things, picked up my coffee and took a swig.

Amanda made small talk with my dad about the Bluebell Hill hag case and about her recent fun with voodoo. James played on his phone. I stared at the wall and vowed to pick one woman and see if I could manage a relationship. If it didn't work out and all the other women were gone again by then, well so be it.

'I might have something for you to look into actually, kid,' my dad said to bring me back to the room.

'Hmmm?' I grunted intelligently.

Dad ignored my demonstration of intellect and pressed on. 'There are some odd things happening at the yard.' He meant Chatham Royal Navy Dockyard where he worked an occasional shift as a tour guide on the ships they had there.

'Like what,' I asked.

'Odd noises coming from the rope room and no one there when we go to investigate. It's probably nothing. I shouldn't have brought it up. It's not as if they would pay for it to be investigated.' He shifted about in his chair, making himself comfortable, then had a thought. 'Why are you all in Rochester High Street? Your office burned down, didn't it?'

'I rented a new place. We are moving in today.'

'That was fast work.'

'Do you want to see it?'

'Sure thing.'

Amanda and James were chatting, and both had drinks and a piece of cake, so we left them where they were and took our coffees to go. Across the street, the sign writer guy was taking down the old sign, he and the other chap were on ladders to unscrew where it was attached.

I checked my watch as I went. It was 1137hrs, so Big Ben might turn up at any point. I showed dad around the new office and answered his questions about the increased cost of rent. He was just taking an interest; he had no genuine concern about my ability to manage my business and finances.

He did have some things he wanted to talk about

though. 'Now you know your mother is going to invite most of her friends from the church and that many of them will *accidentally* bring their daughters.'

I nodded. It was inevitable.

'Your mother is just going to keep on matchmaking until you find a woman of your own, you know.'

'It's not like I haven't tried, but I cannot just magic up a suitable lady, dad. I have a date this Wednesday, but whether there is a second date or a third etcetera, isn't something I can think about at this stage.'

'You want to bring her Thursday?' he asked.

'Not a damned chance,' I replied swiftly. Expose Natasha to my mother after one date? That was the sort of relationship test I would only subject a woman to if I was convinced she intended to marry me no matter what.

Dad chuckled, 'Probably a good idea. It does mean that mum will consider you to still be available and will thus be pimping you out to her friend's single daughters.'

'Not for the first time. Can I assume that Debbie will not be coming?'

'Uh, I think she might be. Her and her mother. Why?'

'Because she scares the life out of me.'

Dad chuckled at my discomfort.

'Is Rachel coming with Chris and the kids?' I hadn't seen my sister's husband for a long time.

'Apparently, so.'

Bull barked, the noise splitting the air and making me jump slightly. Dozer barked in reaction to his brother barking.

'Hey, it's the Michaels family.' Big Ben was coming through the door behind us as I was pointing out some of the office features to my dad. He was what the dogs saw fit to bark at.

I shook his hand. 'Hey, buddy.'

'Benjamin,' my dad extended his hand. 'I swear you get taller every time I see you,

'Mr Michaels, it's not my height that changes. I just keep getting more visually impressive.' Big Ben said as he took it. Looking around the office, he said, 'Nice place.'

'I have to be going,' my dad said. 'I'll see you Thursday.'

We shook hands again as he left. I was still shaking my head over the jewellery he had for my mother. She was going to be very happy with it; I was quite sure. There was a part of me that wondered what it was worth though. My sister or I would inherit the estate at some point in the future. Such things are inevitable. So, I was curious if any questions would be raised when we had it valued and discovered the ruby was worth half a million.

'Where're the others?' Big Ben asked. 'Jane and Amanda.'

'It's James today and they are both at the coffee shop. I expect they will be back soon. What did you learn last night?'

'To business then. I learned several things. Relearned, one might say as I had forgotten how enthusiastic older women can be.' Big Ben stopped talking as I had held up my hand. 'You have a question?'

'I just want to hear about things you learned that pertain to the case. Which of the ladies gave the best blow job is not going to help me.'

'Okay,' he replied, a little snippiness to his voice. 'The answer to that would be Dorothy, but since you don't want to hear about the interesting bits... Edna hates her husband. That became obvious quite quickly. He was out when I knocked on her door. She called him a cheating whatnot several times and was only too happy to get naked with me as she felt massively overdue some payback. I was able to ascertain that she has a massive life insurance policy on him and thinks that she will get to cash it in. She was suggesting that he had ill-health rather than openly talking about any intention to kill him. I got kind of the same from Dorothy, although she seemed disgruntled rather than filled with hatred. I couldn't find out from her if she had a life insurance thing going on, she didn't want to talk much at all and she couldn't for large portions of our time together because she had something in her mouth.'

I didn't need him to elaborate and was thankful when he didn't.

'Mabel said she was glad her worthless husband was dead. Those were her words. I asked her how he died, and she said it was a miracle – he had been hit by lightning inside their house when the bolt had come through the window. I asked her if she thought that was unusual to which she replied again that it was a miracle.'

To me, it just sounded really suspicious, but I had found a few recorded cases where lightning had done exactly that and struck a person inside their home. The cases I found though were never fatal. Too much of the lightning was dissipated as it hit the building.

'What about Barbara?' I asked.

'More of the same really. She bragged that her husband had died suddenly, and she was expecting a huge insurance cheque. She didn't go into how he had died though. I managed to ask the question directly, but her response was that he had died in an accident. She didn't elaborate, and I couldn't find a way to ask for more specific details.'

While he had been talking, I had found a scrap of paper and a pen and had jotted some notes.

Amanda and James came through the door. They

spotted Ben and exchanged greetings. He wasn't staying though; he had a golf match planned. As Big Ben went out the door, James went back to where he was setting up his computers. He had a pair of them on the reception desk with three monitors, to which he was now adding a fourth. He wanted one computer for regular work business such as invoicing and booking appointments for Amanda and me he explained. The other rig was for research. He had started talking geek speak when he was telling me what it would do, forcing me to stop him because it was just an odd language.

He had research to do already, both for Amanda and for me. I walked into Amanda's office. It already smelled of her wonderful perfume.

'What's your plan for the afternoon?' I asked her.

'Solve the Bluebell Hill hag case if I can.' She was putting things into her desk drawers, setting the office up to suit her. I imagine that in a few weeks it would all feel familiar, and we would both have personal effects in our drawers and on the walls. 'I was thinking about it last night,' she continued. 'I think that the only thing I can realistically do in this case is work out who the woman in the photograph is, find her and expose him as a lying philanderer.'

I shrugged. 'I'm confident it will not prove to be a ghost.'

'Yeah. My top theory is that she's a hooker. I might be wrong, and the man just has a girlfriend he doesn't want his wife to know about.'

'He must have been desperate to hire us. What outcome is he expecting?'

'I think he hopes that we will not be able to prove anything and that by muddying the waters he might be able to deflect his wife's accusation sufficiently to get away with it.'

'So, how are you going to tackle it?' I wanted to know.

'Inevitably I got to meet a lot of the local prostitutes in my last job, I know where to find them, so I will show a few of them the photograph and see if she's known. If not, I will get Patience to run the picture through the facial recognition database. Maybe she will show up there.'

'I forgot to ask: How is Patience?' She had been kidnapped and held captive last week. Nothing bad had happened but she had been tasered and drugged and stripped naked and threatened with death, so, all in all, it hadn't been a positive experience.

'She seems fine. They gave her a week off. HR insisted on it, and she has some holiday owed which she said she might take. Hey, do you want to come with me this afternoon? Or do you have leads to follow up on?'

'Come with you to see the hookers? I suppose I might learn something that could prove useful later.' I thought about it for a moment. I wasn't enthralled about meeting prostitutes. I didn't like that they existed. Not that I was being critical about their choices, more that I figured most of them didn't have a choice. I doubted it was the chosen career of many. I might learn something though. 'Yeah, okay. I want to take the dogs home first though and get some lunch. What time to do want to set off?'

'I'm in no rush, I guess. We can just go when you get back from lunch.'

I checked my watch: 1227hrs. 'Okay, I'm going for some lunch.' I turned my attention to James. 'James, can you stay a couple of extra hours and catch us up on email enquiries and such? We need to have cases lined up.'

'Sure thing, boss. Ah, Boss?'

'Yes?'

'You ask me to do extra hours all the time. Do you want me to just work full time instead?'

I hadn't given it any consideration. He was right though, he worked extra hours all the time. 'Nine till five?'

'Works for me.'

'Super. Oh, I forgot to ask. Did you get anywhere with the photograph I sent you?'

'The old lady? I'm afraid not. It's not a bad shot but she either doesn't have a driving licence or passport and has never been arrested, or the facial recognition software cannot find her for some other reason. Normally, I would expect to find her in under an hour, but she probably doesn't have a social media profile either.'

'Probably not.' I agreed.

I whistled for the dogs. Unlike at home, where they would just ignore me and pretend to be asleep on the sofa, here they had no bed so had been continuously sniffing around and poking at the boxes we had brought things to the office in. My whistle caught their attention, and they ran to the office entrance, assuming I was taking them somewhere. We were going out the back though, so I opened the door that led that way and called them again. They ran across the office, their tiny legs propelling them at a pace that always surprised me.

I waved to Amanda and James as the door closed behind me. This was all very new, but also quite pleasing.

Lunchtime Surprise

I called out to Hilary as I went through the front door with the dogs. I got no answer and there seemed to be no sign of him. He could have been upstairs sleeping soundly. I didn't bother to check as I was hoping his absence meant my harsh words earlier had driven him to seek out Anthea.

He might be with her now, talking things through. I pictured the two of them making up and chose to believe that must be why he wasn't here as I opened the back door for the dogs. They had enjoyed plenty of exercise this morning, I saw no need to take them for a walk. I sent them into the garden though, so they could empty their bladders and chase the birds away. I watched as they snuffled the bushes from my kitchen window while I mixed tuna, grated courgette, and eggs for my lunch. I formed the mix into patties and fried them in coconut oil. They would go well with a dressing-free salad.

The dogs barked to come in just as I was dishing the tuna patties onto my plate. I gave them each a treat from the dog biscuit jar in the kitchen and told them they were very good dogs. They didn't hang around to tell me whether they cared for my opinion on their behaviour. However, I was thinking that it might be nice to take them to the office more often. I could buy a new bed for them and have it behind my desk. Would they escape ever? That was the one concern. If they got out the front door, they were too inquisitive to hang around, they would wander off along Rochester High Street and then not know where they were.

My musings on the subject arrived at no conclusion, so I turned my thoughts to the case in hand. I needed to speak with Frank and find out who the mysterious old lady was. It was odd that he hadn't called me, but I hadn't called him either. I would make a point of going to his shop later. I also needed to speak with the coroner, I reminded myself for the umpteenth time. She could prove to be key if I could just get her to listen to the possibility that she had been mistaken about her verdict.

As I slid off the stool at my breakfast bar, someone knocked on my door. The dogs flew by me, they had been in the lounge, most likely dozing on the sofa, but there was an intruder to repel, and they would not be found lacking in their duties.

I wasn't expecting anyone, my natural tendency for caution fighting with my logical insistence that it was unlikely to be someone out to do me harm.

I shooed the dogs into the kitchen, calling out to the unseen person that I would not be a moment. With the terror hounds safely locked away, I returned to the door and opened it.

The coroner was outside.

Well, colour me surprised.

'Hello,' she said since I wasn't saying anything. 'Tempest, isn't it?'

The lady on my doorstep was every bit as attractive as I remembered her. She was definitely a couple of years older than me and probably was in her early forties, but she was still an absolute knock out. She was what I imagined Amanda might look with another decade or so under her belt.

I was just staring. Mr Wriggly growled that I should pull myself together. 'Yes. Yes, hello. Tempest Michaels,' I said as I put my hand out for her to shake. 'You have me at a loss.'

I elected to lie rather than reveal that I had looked her up.

'Victoria Mallory. May I come in?'

I was still acting startled. I did not know why she was here, but I needed to get a grip and be polite. I wanted to quiz her about the verdict in the lightning strike case and now I had the perfect chance.

I smiled warmly. 'Please.' I indicated inside and held the door for her.

'Did I hear dogs?' she asked.

'Yes. I'm afraid I will have to let them out.' I checked her feet. She had on a nice pair of heels and the exposed skin was sheathed in what was either pop socks or possibly tights. I wasn't going to ask her which, but the dogs would most likely claw it. 'I will have to field them, or they will claw your legs.'

I opened the door and snagged them both before they could get to her. Pinned under my arms they began growling. Both had their hackles raised and were straining to get to the new lady. I couldn't remember them ever taking an instant dislike to someone before.

'Are they alright?' she asked.

'Sorry about this,' I replied. I had intended to calmly introduce them to the lady. They would sniff and wag their tails and then, once they had established there was no food to be had, they would wander back to their beds. That's what they always do. Not today though. Bull was wriggling to be set free and curling his top lip back to reveal his teeth. 'What is wrong with you, dogs?' I asked them. No answer was forthcoming, but it was clear that they were not going to play nicely.

'I won't be a moment,' I advised the coroner as I turned. I took the dogs into the lounge and shut the door. Whatever business the coroner had for me would be conducted in the kitchen or the office.

I walked back through to find her checking her hair in the mirror by the front door. 'I'm glad you are here actually. I was planning to track you down.'

'Really?' she said. Her voice sounding very interested.

'I need to talk to you about Bernhard Myers. I have good reason to believe that he was not killed by lightning and was murdered by a twisted ring of women that are colluding with one another to bump off their husbands.'

She looked at me with a strange expression, then she laughed. 'Goodness, I thought you were serious for a moment then.'

'I'm serious. Your verdict is wrong. You were the coroner on another case a few weeks ago with a similarly unusual death were you not.'

'I don't think you should question my verdicts, Tempest. I don't think you should question me at all unless you intend to ask me why I came here this afternoon.'

Okay, I'll bite. 'Why are you here?'

'Because you are the sexiest man I have ever seen, and I have just got to have you.' Before my brain could even process what she had said she had closed the space between us and had her lips on mine. I opened my mouth to protest but suddenly had an extra tongue in it.

Mr Wriggly was downstairs doing stretches and limbering up like he was getting ready for some hard exercise. I tried to back up, but one pace brought me to the wall, and she pushed me against it. I needed to push her off me but bringing my hands up to shove her away only resulting in me grabbing two handfuls of breast.

'Yes, treat me rough,' she moaned as she bit my neck.

'Sorry, Victoria,' I said, finally getting my hands onto her shoulders. 'This is not...' What? I was struggling to finish the sentence.

She took a step back. Looked at me quizzically, then ripped her blouse open. She had on a sexy black lace bra that pushed her boobs together and up in an entirely pleasing manner. A sheepdog bra my father would call it because it rounds them up and gets them pointed in the right direction.

I shook my head to clear it. 'Victoria, I'm not interested in having sex with you.' There, I had managed to say it. I wasn't sure it was true, but I knew it was supposed to be.

'Oh, really.' She looked down at my trousers. 'Try telling him that. I think I'll just give him some oral encouragement and see how you feel about it after that.'

Suddenly she was on her knees in front of me and trying to undo my belt.

Then Amanda walked in. I guess she had got used to coming and going when my house had been the office because she didn't knock, she just turned the door handle and walked in.

'Oh, good lord!' she blushed, her eyes bugging right out of her head as she took in the view in front of her. Then she stepped back outside and slammed the door shut with her outside.

At least it had broken the spell, and Victoria was getting up from her knees again.

'This is disappointing, Tempest. Do I assume that she is your girlfriend?'

I wish! Mr Wriggly had some clear intentions for Amanda.

'Business partner,' I replied, 'But that makes no difference at all to this situation. I want to talk to you about the lightning cases, but I don't think taking our clothes off is a good idea.'

'I can't see why not, Tempest.' She was at least buttoning her top back together. 'I'm not wrong about the lightning victims. You should stop wasting your time looking into it. Oh, you're bleeding.'

I turned to look in the mirror mounted on the wall behind me. There was a trickle of blood on my neck where her passion had taken the form of some biting.

'Here,' she said as she dabbed at it with a tissue before I could take out my own handkerchief.

'I think I should go, Tempest. I'm not done with you though. I still intend to have you. If you don't have a girlfriend and you are not gay, I do not understand why you would refuse me.'

I was struggling to explain why not either. Mr Wriggly still had a full head of steam that seemed unlikely to dissipate in the next few minutes. A chap cannot listen to a half-dressed woman tell him she wants to play with his meat and two veg and not have an involuntary reaction. Can't be done.

She was standing far too close to me, her boobs all but touching my chest, but very much filling my field of vision.

'If I have to revisit the lightning victims' cases to achieve that then so be it. Here's my card.' She produced a card from a pocket, reached around and placed it in my left buttock pocket. Then she patted Mr wriggly, giving him a quick squeeze between thumb and forefinger before reaching for the door and leaving.

'Call me,' echoed back through the door as it closed.

Amanda wasn't outside that I could see. I would call her in a minute and try to explain what she had witnessed. I doubted she would let herself in any more.

Shaking my head and trying to think boring thoughts, rather than remember the sight of the top of Victoria's head and heaving chest as she had knelt in front of me, I walked through to the kitchen. I filled the kettle and turned it on. I needed to pee, the previous cup of tea now ready to leave my system but the liquids ejection system was not currently in a useable state. I didn't want a cup of tea, I was hoping instead that performing a mundane task would distract me.

My phone beeped: An incoming text. It was from Amanda apologising for interrupting me and telling me that she had found the girl already and my house was on the way to where she was going. She had dropped by to collect me.

How do I answer? This was now the second time Amanda had come to my house and found me with a woman. I couldn't help but wonder if such awkward circumstances had already ruined any chance for her and I. Then I grimaced at myself for still considering how I might one day find myself in her arms when I already had a date with Natasha tomorrow.

I checked out the window. Amanda's car was not outside. However, I was not surprised that she hadn't waited. Thankfully, Mr Wriggly had given up hope and gone back to sleep, grumbling at me as he did.

With my bladder finally empty and my belly replete, I considered what to do with my afternoon. Speak with the coroner was still on the list, but I needed to leave it a day before I called her. I had no other leads and had intended to go with Amanda to see the hookers. Amanda and I had spent far too little time together, almost none since she started working for me. Despite the embarrassment, the best course of action was to call her, find out where she was and join her. I would explain what she had seen and maybe save some face.

Otherwise, I would just have to explain it tomorrow. Muttering to myself, I dialled her number.

She answered as it began ringing, 'Hi, Tempest. All done?'

She was making fun of me. Perfect. 'Hello, Amanda. Yet again you catch me with my pants down.'

'I'm really sorry about that. I should have knocked. I just didn't think. I was going in and out of there for a week, so… muscle memory?'

'It's fine, Amanda. You didn't disturb anything. I was trying to fight her off.' No comment from the other end. It probably hadn't looked like I was trying to fight at all. 'I doubt that was the impression you got,' I conceded. 'The lady is the coroner in the lightning case. I met her at Bernhard Myer's house, and she tracked me down.'

'There's no need to explain, Tempest. We just work together. You're my boss for that matter. Lunchtime blowjobs are none of my business.'

'I get that. I do, but…' I realised the futility on trying to explain my innocence and the likelihood that Amanda genuinely didn't care what I got up to. 'Look, I'm calling to find out where you are, so I can join you. You and I should work together more than we have done.'

'Oh. Oh, okay. I'm in Maidstone, near the prison. There's a kind of prostitute pick-up point at the bottom of Wheeler Street. You know where that is?'

I did. I said I would meet her there in ten minutes. I got off the phone, checked my pockets, patted the dogs and went out the door. It had stopped raining, and the sun was trying to come out.

Hookers

Parking was easy in this part of Maidstone at this time of the day. There were rows of terrace houses, so it would be awful later, but it was almost devoid of cars at 1402hrs because the residents had taken them to work.

Driving here, I had considered whether Amanda meant that there would be prostitutes here right now or if she knew some that lived nearby. Were hookers in high demand just after lunch on a Tuesday? I had no frame of reference. There had been prostitutes readily available near many of the barracks I had been sent to during my time in the Army. I had never felt the need to frequent them though. I knew men that had, of course. Prostitution was legal in Germany and well-controlled so one could argue that some of the seediness was eliminated, but I was either too tight-fisted or too reserved to ever hand over money for an act that should be a bit more special than what I imagined one would get. Big Ben had likewise never visited the brothels, but in his case, he had no need and had always claimed that he felt affronted by the concept as they should be paying him.

I spotted Amanda as I got out of my car. She had most likely spotted me and had made herself visible. As I looked over, she waved to make sure I had seen her and went back inside a house about thirty metres down the street in the direction of the town centre.

I went to the house and found the front door still open. 'Hello?' I called out as I went in. It was a small terrace house, the type with just one window on each floor at the front of the house because that was all it was wide enough for.

'We're in the kitchen,' echoed back through the house. All the terrace houses I had ever been in were of a similar design. A short corridor from the front door led to the stairs. To the right was a living room just about big enough for a sofa and a TV, to the right of the stairs as one reached them was a dining room and beyond that a kitchen. Beyond the kitchen was a toilet that would have originally been accessed from outside the house - an outside loo. I wondered if there were any houses left anywhere that hadn't been converted to allow internal access to the bathroom.

The house itself was tidy enough, there was no mess visible, but its décor needed a refresh. I could hear voices ahead of me, one of which I could identify as Amanda's. As I reached the end of the corridor, rounded the stairs and entered the kitchen, I found her talking to a young woman in her early twenties. It was cool in the room because the window behind her was open, and she had a cigarette in her mouth. Most of the smoke was being drawn out of the window by a breeze but there was enough of it for me to smell it and know I would need to wash all my clothes as soon as I got home.

'Hello,' I said as I extended my hand. 'Tempest

Michaels.' I offered her my card, which was a natural action rather than because I wanted her to have my number.

She took my hand and despite her tiny frame and minuscule hand, she had a firm grip. I told myself not to think about what she practiced gripping. She took my card, inspected it briefly and produced one of her own as she told me her name was Stacy Jenkins.

'That's my real name.' she explained. 'The name on my card says Stacy Sukks because that's my stage name. I'm an adult actor as well.' She boasted. I had no reply that would sound acceptable to my ears. I looked at her card.

Stacy Sukks, Adult Actress, Female Companion, and Escort
Anything goes. Get it here every time!

Beneath the text was an email address and a mobile phone number so the holder could get hold of her easily when they wanted to get it, I assumed. I put it in my pocket only because I couldn't work out what else to do with it.

'It's mostly girl-girl stuff but I'm thinking of branching out into...'

'You were telling me about Tiffany,' Amanda interrupted before Stacey could say anything more.

'Oh, yeah. She should be back soon. She had a home delivery to take care of?'

'Home delivery?' I repeated dumbly, missing the point.

'Yes, that's when we go to someone's house for sex rather than them picking us up somewhere.' Stacy supplied.

Lovely.

'Anyway,' Amanda tried to steer Stacy back onto the topic of interest. 'You recognised the man in the photograph I showed you.'

'Yeah, that's Martin. He always says his name is Bob,

but Tiffany and I learned to check bloke's wallets for their driving license long ago. Much safer to know a bloke's real name. He's a regular.'

'And the girl in the picture?' Amanda prompted, holding the picture up so I could see it was the one taken by the speed camera.

'That's Tiffany.'

Amanda put the photograph away. 'It would seem that Martin likes to pick up young ladies for sex. I'm not sure what we are supposed to do with the case now. He wants us to prove that the lady in the photograph is a ghost. The only thing we can show is that it's not.' Amanda was clearly asking my opinion about what to do next.

I scratched my head, both physically and mentally. Did we expose him to his wife? It felt like the decent thing to do. Did I then return his money? No, we had been paid to conduct an investigation and had done so. It had cost us time, and we billed hours even when we did not arrive at a successful conclusion. So, the bill stood, but what about the result? It wasn't my job to balance the scales in their marriage or stand in judgment of other people's actions. I investigated and reported my findings. Often this resulted in a criminal prosecution for someone because they had committed a crime. Again, I passed no judgement.

'I think this is the same as any other case. Our investigation is concluded so your next task is to present the client with a written report detailing our findings.'

She nodded. 'I'll go back to the office and do that now.' Amanda turned back to Stacy and thanked her for her time. Stacy shrugged.

Back outside the house in the cool Autumn air, I paused waiting for Amanda to join me. Spending time with Amanda was… unsettling. Finding the right word was difficult. Even after distracting myself with Hayley and Roberta, and even with the impending date with the gorgeous Natasha, I was still undeniably bewitched by her. There was something about her, something intangible that to me meant that she would always be…'

'Were you waiting for me?' Amanda's voice suddenly by my ear made me start.

I turned to face her. 'Sort of,' I replied. I was looking at her beautiful, wonderful face again. I had just been thinking about her, my entire train of thought focused on how perfect I thought she was and now she was standing in front of me once more, waiting for me to speak. I tried to find something intelligent to say. I failed. 'I hadn't decided what to do next. You said you were heading back to the office?'

'It feels like the case is closed. This is how it works, isn't it? I select cases, I solve the cases and bill the hours, right?'

'That's what I do,' I replied.

She nodded, looking to the middle distance while she thought. I wondered what she was thinking. Then she looked at me again and an uncomfortable silence stretched out for a few seconds while we both waited for the other to speak.

Then, inevitably, we both tried to speak at the same time, stopped, tried again and finally, I held up my hands and asked her to go first.

'Will you be in the office tomorrow?'

'That's my current plan.' I considered that for a moment. 'Maybe we should make it a standard thing that we meet at the office each day before we go off to tackle our casework.'

'Okay. Sounds good. So… see you in the morning?'

'Yup.' I turned to go then turned back. 'You know, I really was trying to fight her off earlier. She caught me by surprise and then you walked in before I had a chance to do anything.'

Amanda grinned at me. What the heck did that mean? 'Tempest.' she looked down, smiling, then looked back up with a lopsided grin. 'You are a good-looking guy. Women are going to be drawn to you. It doesn't surprise me. Don't worry about it.'

I just stared at her, dumbfounded. I had no response. I was treading water, lost in a sea of relationship confusion. Before I could form a coherent response, she chucked me on the arm and headed down the street towards her car.

I watched her go, her perfect bottom swaying from side to side rhythmically as she went. I sighed and turned my eyes away. I shouldn't be looking at it anyway.

I needed to buy flowers. I had a date with an attractive woman that was, in contrast to Amanda, actually interested in me. I needed to focus on her and take my head out of the clouds.

I took a final look at the sky and as Amanda drove by me with a brief wave out her window, I started walking toward the town centre where I knew there was a good florist.

Buying Flowers

I had been in the flower shop many times before. The flowers I had bought there though were more often for my mother than they were for a lady I was romantically interested in. Today was different. Today I was buying flowers for an elegant, well-spoken, eligible lady I was taking out for dinner. I selected a simple spray of carnations as they looked healthy, and the florist had them in a variety of pink hues. They were paired with an abundance of green foliage and wrapped for delivery. I swiped my card to complete the transaction and left the flowers to be dropped off at Natasha's address in the morning.

Task complete, I left the shop confident that Natasha would feel suitably positive about her choice to join me for dinner. I decided to head home. Jagjit had asked me to be his best man, so I had a speech to consider. I also had the small problem of Hilary to deal with. His presence in my house was nothing more than a minor inconvenience at the moment, but that was because I believed it to be temporary.

I needed to get him back on his feet and back with his wife and kids.

Arriving home a few minutes later though, a sense of dread settled into the pit of my stomach.

Big Ben's car was parked on my drive.

I walked through my front door, stepping over the dachshunds as I closed it behind me. I expected to hear voices coming from the kitchen or the lounge, but the house was silent. I called out anyway, then poked my head through a couple of doors when no answer came back. The dogs were whizzing around my feet, standing on the toes of my shoes whenever I stopped moving long enough for them to do so. They wanted my attention, and I couldn't tell how long it had been since they were last outside, so I grabbed their leads, popped their collars over their heads and encouraged them back out the front door.

If Hilary and Big Ben were not here, then they were most likely in the pub. I started walking in that direction. It was cool out bordering on cold. The forlorn trees were now all but bereft of leaves, clutching pathetically at one here and one there as they fluttered in the breeze. Soon winter would be upon us and my small dogs would need to wear their specially made coats whenever I took them out. Today, for the short walk I had planned, there was no need for such protection.

I guessed right. I could see Big Ben's head through the window of the pub as I approached. Both he and Hilary were in our usual spot, a half empty glass of beer in front of each. They looked up as I entered.

'Chaps,' I said in greeting. Hilary looked better than he had this morning, not that it would have been hard to achieve an improvement.

'Hey, Tempest,' replied Big Ben. Hilary nodded his

greeting. 'Hair of the dog for the ailing man,' Big Ben explained.

I looked at the bar. I had no intention of drinking, I would get a water if the landlord appeared, but he was absent, probably somewhere in the back doing a vital task of some kind. I took a seat.

'How are you feeling?' I asked Hilary.

He took a sip of beer. 'Much better, thanks. Sorry about yesterday. And this morning. And for the whole thing really, I guess.'

'I felt bad about him following my daft advice,' Big Ben cut in. 'So, I came to make amends and get him back on the right path.'

'Jolly good. I'm sure Anthea will be only too pleased to have you back. Have you spoken with her already?'

'What? Oh, no I'm not moving back home. I'm going after a younger version with bigger boobs. That has always been Big Ben's advice on how to get over a breakup. I've heard him tell you and Jagjit and others exactly that several times.'

I narrowed my eyes at Big Ben. At least he had the decency to look embarrassed. 'I'm not sure that should apply in your case, mate,' I said.

'Nonsense,' Hilary scoffed. 'I need to get me some new boobies. I called this one,' He indicated Big Ben with his head, 'to give me some advice on picking up women. I know it's all he ever talks about but, to be honest, I have never actually listened before.'

This sounded like a terrible plan. Hilary needed to go home to his wife and children. He also needed to improve the terms of his relationship with his wife so that she didn't push him around so much, but that was just the kind of man that he was. Were he able to change, I suspected that he would have done so a long time ago.

He hadn't done talking though. 'I also think I should look at new career options. I have been doing the same job ever since I left school. It's boring.'

'What do you propose?' I asked, hoping we could talk about jobs and not women for a while and maybe circle back to the subject of not cheating on his wife shortly.

'I'm not sure. I thought I might try a few different things. See what I like.'

Okay. Well, at least he hadn't settled on a new career already. Now I just needed to convince him to avoid doing something rash with a free-thinking local lady and hope that he didn't feel the need to keep his date with the awful barmaid from the Watermill pub in the next village.

'It's all quite liberating being kicked out by one's wife. I have never felt so free, so filled with opportunity. What shall we do tonight?' Hilary enquired

'I have a couple of dates,' Big Ben replied.

Hilary looked at me, his eyebrows raised in question. I had heard of this phenomenon before. The newly single suddenly have a new lease of life and want to get out and party because they have not done so for so long. It takes them a while to realise they are no longer twenty-two and that they are genuinely happier at home reading a book and tending their geraniums.

'Sorry, old boy. I have cases to work on, a date of my own to plan and no desire to be out chasing girls.'

'Just me then,' he announced as he drained the last of his pint. 'Can I get a lift back into town?' he asked Big Ben.

'Sure.'

'And direction to where the easy girls hang out.'

'Yup.'

I felt the need to interject. 'Hilary, wouldn't you rather spend the evening at home with your wife and children? I'm sure Anthea misses you and is just too proud to say so. Maybe you should talk to her?' My stern advice this morning hadn't worked clearly. I was working my way down the list of available tactics and was starting to worry I would need to act myself at this rate.

Hilary was not to be budged though. Somehow, in all this, he had found some drive and determination. 'Not a chance. I'm armed with fortitude and a hearty bag of chat-up lines provided by my good friend Ben. I'm going into town to give a lady exactly what she deserves.'

Dear God.

'Ready?' he asked Big Ben. Hilary was already out of his chair, poised like a sprinter getting into starting blocks. Big Ben looked at me, his pint halfway to his lips. He shrugged, finished his drink and he too stood up.

'Don't wait up,' Hilary called as he went out the door of the pub. I could hear someone moving around in the depths of the pub now, most likely it was the Landlord on his way back to tend to his customers that were now leaving. There was no one else in the pub and I had no need of a drink, so I followed the chaps outside. They were heading back to my house. Rather than follow and listen to any more nonsense, I pointed myself toward the village green where the dogs could have a good run.

The sky was darkening. It was close to 1600hrs and a time of year when the evenings set in early. I had my house to myself for the evening, a fact I was thankful for, but I thought it likely Hilary's plan for the evening would end badly.

Conversation with the Client

Dinner was grilled chicken thighs, lentils from a tin, spinach and pine nuts. It was healthy, muscle-fuelling food and I was going to get in a workout before bed, so I felt justified in the large portion I gave myself. The dogs licked the plate clean before it went into the dishwasher along with my cutlery and the two dishes I had used to prepare the meal.

Finding Victoria's workplace was on my list of tasks for tonight. Without her willingness to concede that her verdict of accidental death might be wrong it would be very hard to get a court case started for murder. I intended to politely confront her at her place of work. She had cornered me, so maybe I could turn the tables on her. She seemed to want to have me near her, so I would try to use that to my advantage.

I wondered if I was clever enough to pull that off.

First though, I needed to call the client. I had promised Mick semi-regular updates and hadn't provided them. I stroked Bull's fur as the phone rang.

'Hello.' I recognised my client's voice.

'Mr Cotton, this is Tempest Michaels of the Blue Moon Investigation Agency.' The formal and full introduction was almost certainly not necessary, but it felt right to remain professional. "Hey, Mick, Whassssuppp?" wasn't really my style.

'Tempest. I was hoping to hear from you. Do you have news for me?'

It was a good question. 'I can report that I think your stepmother is guilty.' I heard his breathing pause. 'I have no proof of anything at this time,' I said quickly before he got too excited and stopped listening. 'I have tracked your step-mother and her friends and have colleagues investigating various elements of their lives.' This was completely true. Thanks to Big Ben, I could reliably tell my client how each of the ladies sounded when reaching orgasm. I figured that bit of detail could be withheld in my report though. 'I have met with the coroner that recorded the incorrect verdict of death and will be meeting with her again soon.' Hopefully with less erection involved next time. 'This is, I'm afraid, little more than a courtesy call. I have little to report at this time.'

'That's okay. It's just nice to hear that I'm not crazy and making it all up in my head. You really think my dad was murdered?'

I gave myself a few seconds to consider my answer. 'I really do.' I really did. 'I have to admit though that I have no idea how they have done it. Getting the result you want will not be an easy task.' I realised I sounded like I was pumping him for more money and had to back pedal quickly. 'I'm not after more money. I just want to be clear that to secure a conviction I will have to provide unequivocal proof, and I think that's going to be tough.'

'Why is that?' he asked.

'Because they will not open a murder investigation when the coroner has recorded accidental death unless my case is watertight. To create a watertight case, I may need to catch them doing the same thing again.' As I said the words I acknowledged to myself that they were probably true. I hadn't thought the problem all the way through until that moment. Now I wondered how I would do that.

I could hear Mick making hmming noises at the other end of the line. he was probably considering what I had told him. 'I guess all I can do is wish you good luck then.'

I thanked him, put the phone down and relaxed back into the comfort of the sofa. I had wandered through from the kitchen to the living room while I was talking to my client. The dogs had followed me and assumed their usual positions either side of me. I was deep in thought about the case, still trying to work out what I was facing.

I'm not sure how much time went by with me sitting like that, churning the case in my head, but when Bull sneezed to break my concentration, it was 1946hrs according to the clock. I sat up, causing the two dogs to jump down to the carpet. They were probably expecting a walk, so I obliged while I continued to think.

Ten minutes into our peaceful meander around the village, I forced myself to change the topic and think about something else. I was getting nowhere, and it was frustrating me. Instead, I considered the task of the Best Man's speech I needed to write. I had a few weeks but to get it right I needed to perform some research into the victim/groom.

Jagjit and I had been friends for a very long time, more than three decades in fact. However, I had been absent for a large chunk of it pursuing a military career and anecdotes from when we were seven would not fill a speech. He had brothers that I would have to speak with to recruit their help. Not that my intention for the speech was to embarrass him, I merely wanted to find the best material so that I could throw in one or two amusing stories.

As we neared the pub, both dogs tried to pull me towards it. I tugged them back to the correct path, arriving home less than two minutes later. Untethered, they scampered away for a drink of water as I took myself upstairs to get changed. I had successfully avoided the lure of the pub, so I was going to compliment my fortitude with a workout. This one I would perform at home in front of the TV using my own body weight as resistance – do enough press ups, burpees, and sit-ups and you will burn a truckload of calories. They would also ensure my goal of getting back to trim would remain on track.

Bedtime came soon enough. Hilary was still out or had perhaps come to his senses and gone home to his wife. I had no messages from him and dismissed the idea of messaging him to find out what he was up to. I felt it was right to let him work this out for himself. The noise of his return woke me though. The clock claimed the time to be 2257hrs – early to be home after a night on the town and unlikely that he had found the available woman he left the house in search of.

I laid my head back on my pillow and let sleep take me.

Early Morning Office Stuff

My new morning routine of rising early, beating myself half to death in the gym and eating a vegetable-filled breakfast, was long behind me by the time I arrived at the office. During the night I had received a text message from Frank which simply asked that I find him as he had information for me. He hadn't elaborated on what the subject matter would be during our meeting, but I assumed it was the witch. I hadn't seen Hilary before I left the house. He was sleeping off whatever booze he had imbibed, and I saw no reason to disturb him. I would check on him later.

There was a steady drizzle of rain again today. It made the pavements glisten and the guttering gurgle. I didn't mind it, but it meant the sky was so much darker than it otherwise would be, the result of which was that it felt like night still when I got to work, and I was yawning.

I got to the office at 0823hrs, beating James to work for once. He was one of those people that got to work early every day. He had only been with me for a few weeks though so perhaps his keenness would dissipate as the months went on. It was 0847hrs when he came through the door, a Hello Kitty umbrella in his hand to keep the rain off as it had increased to a downpour. The umbrella had pastel-pink piping around the edge and a small plastic kitten hanging from the tip of each spoke. The pink matched his eyeshadow and lipstick too closely to be a coincidence.

'Morning, boss,' he called as he walked through the office. I had heard the back door open in the quiet of the office, then lights coming on as he opened the door that led from the back into the main office, heralded his arrival. I was sitting in my office, at my desk doing some research. It was too early to visit Frank. I would go after 0900hrs when his shop would be open. I had been trying to find information on Victoria Mallory. It still felt odd that she had thrown herself at me, but I wanted to find out more about her to fashion an argument that might convince her to reopen the file on the two lightning deaths.

I needed a way into this case. I knew the ladies were guilty somehow but had nothing I could take to the police or even tell my client. It did not help that I still couldn't conceive how they had been murdered with lightning. How does a person achieve that? My other angle of approach was the witch. I kept referring to her as the witch even though I knew she was no such thing. Quite what I could do about the witch that would be of help I hadn't yet worked out. The Wiccan symbols, the insurance policies and the very presence of a haggard old lady were all tripping my Spidey-sense though. Something was amiss, the witch was involved. I just didn't know how.

'You want coffee?' James asked.

'I do. I'll go though.'

'Everything alright?'

'Yeah. I'm wrestling with the witch case and need to take a walk. I'll go to the coffee shop. We ought to resupply the office with beverages. Did you check the fridge? Does it work? It never occurred to me to open it yet.'

James was turning his computer on and taking off his jacket to hang up. 'Yeah, I checked it yesterday. Shall I get milk and teabags and stuff?'

'No, I'm going by a couple of shops, I'll do it. I'm going to pop in and see Frank as well, so I might be a while with the coffee. Are you okay to wait?'

'Sure.'

I checked my watch. It was 0858hrs. 'Amanda will be here any minute I expect. I'll get her coffee too. Let her know I'm at Frank's, please.'

'Of course.'

If I waited sixty seconds she would most likely walk through the door, but I had no reason to hang around. I would see her soon enough.

It was raining hard outside. I went out the front door of the office and shut it behind me. People were rushing by, trying to get to work in the rain without getting wet. I turned my face up to the sky. The rain didn't bother me. I had no desire to get soaked but I doubted that would come to pass. Instead, I would enjoy the rain because it was part of the natural order of the planet. Plus, my skin is water-proof, and I refused to run just to limit the amount of water that would hit my clothes.

So, I strolled to the coffee shop, a lady in a skirt, heels and nice rain mac coat arrived at the door just as I was reaching for the handle. I held the door open so that she could get inside first. In turn, she graciously insisted I join the queue ahead of her.

I had decided, in crossing the road, that I would get my coffee now and take it to Frank's, then get coffee for James and Amanda on the way back. I would stop for groceries before that.

At the counter, I ordered a skinny Americano to go and moved to the end to wait for it. I spotted Hayley moving around in the back, preparing food. Did I want to attract her attention? I hadn't thought the situation through, but it occurred to me now that little good could come from it. If Hayley had finally worked out that I hadn't been messing her around, then she might wish to pick up our relationship where it had left off. Mr Wriggly was suddenly paying attention.

Hayley had wanted to get naked, and play hide the sausage. That was where our relationship started and ended. It was most gratifying. I had enjoyed her company immensely. Mr Wriggly had enjoyed her willingness to have no clothes on. But what did I do now? I had moved on; I had a date tonight. Even if I didn't, I was too interested in Amanda to consider a second round with Hayley a good idea.

Before she could spot me, my coffee was ready, and I left the shop. I would be back soon to get drinks for Amanda and James and would have to find the words to make it clear to Hayley that she and I would not be picking up where we left off. As I went out the door, I reminded myself that I had no good reason to believe that she was still interested.

Time would tell.

I sipped my drink as I walked around the corner to Frank's bookshop. The Mystery Men was an odd little place that was invisible from the street unless one looked directly at the door on the ground floor that led upstairs to it, or one just happened to be looking up and spotted the sign sticking out from the wall ten feet above one's head. Frank sold books, graphic novels, comic books and memorabilia that all tied into the paranormal. Everything in the shop was of the same theme and much of it was non-fiction, a term I thought odd since the subject matter was pure fiction. Was it an oxymoron to claim to write non-fiction about supernatural creatures?

Pondering that question in my head led me to his door. I pushed it open and went up the stairs. As the shop's interior came into sight, I saw Poison serving a pair of mid-teenage boys. They were a little scruffy and scrawny looking, although I would never voice such an opinion. Being fair, they looked like most teenage boys and very typical of what one might expect to find in a comic book and graphic novel store.

Poison was playing to the audience, being engaging and harmlessly flirting with them as she bagged up their purchases. Poison looked up as I came into the shop. She smiled in my direction but stayed focused on taking their money and making sure they would be back next week to buy more.

I busied myself looking at the figurines on display inside a glass cabinet. Each of them had a price tag with at least a couple of zeros. I couldn't identify more than half of the figures, if I had it right though, the rarer the character, the more desirable it was and thus the higher the price tag it could demand.

'Hi, Tempest. Are you after Frank?' I turned to see that the two boys were on their way out of the door, it tinkled its little bell as they left. Poison was leaning on the counter, looking at me through her fringe in a way that went straight to my groin. Goodness, she was pretty. Too young for me I repeated in my head several times.

'Yes, please,' I replied. 'Is he here?'

'FRANK!' she yelled through to the back of the store behind the counter.

Silence followed her shout. Two seconds went by, then three and just when I was beginning to feel awkward, I heard someone moving in the depths of the store. Footsteps, audible because there was no other noise, preceded Frank's untidy, thin frame appearing in the doorframe behind Poison.

'Oh, hi, Tempest,' Frank said as he came into the shop. He was holding a small fish tank in which I could see a frog.

I was used to Frank being different. I applauded it, while at the same time I always found myself scratching my head while trying to follow his logic. 'What's with the frog?'

He rolled his eyes as he placed the aquarium on the countertop. 'It's not a frog, Tempest. It's a toad. A Salem toad to be precise. You do know what makes a Salem toad special, don't you, Tempest?'

'It has opposable thumbs?' I guessed.

Frank hung his head in defeat like a teacher with a particularly dumb student might. 'No, Tempest. A Salem toad reacts to the presence of witchcraft.'

'That would have been my second guess.'

Frank ignored me, 'It's just an early warning system, of course. The toad will warn the owner that a witch is nearby.'

'How does it do that?' I was trying not to smile as I imagined the small amphibian conducting witch trials.

'It farts.'

'It farts,' I repeated with derision or disbelief in my voice. Even I couldn't decide which it was. Frank didn't reply though. 'So, you have to carry the toad around and watch its butt for an excess of escaping gas and then you know that somewhere in your vicinity is a witch. Do I have that about right?'

'Yup,' Frank replied. He had been watching the toad but shifted to face me now, his face serious. 'The photograph you sent me, Tempest. That's a witch. There aren't many around anymore, not since the great purge of the Salem witch trials, but they are out there, and more dangerous than they ever were because their magic is more focused.'

'Can you expand on that?' I asked.

'Okay.' Frank held up his hands to make a pot shape. 'Imagine all the magic in the world is finite. It's shared unevenly between however many persons are born with the skill to practice it, or wield it, if you will. As the numbers of these people increase or decrease, the total amount of magic remains the same but becomes more or less concentrated depending on the number of available recipients. With far fewer witches around and very few sorcerers, each of them has become quite powerful. The power is still shared unevenly, of course, so the most powerful will be incredibly dangerous.'

'What about the lady I took the picture of then?'

'Given that she's killing men by making their hearts explode from their chests, I would say she was very powerful indeed. Wouldn't you?'

Normally I would respond to such goading by explaining to Frank what was really going on and how the crime was more likely to be being committed. In this case, though, I still hadn't come up with a way to make lightning, let alone how to then instruct it to hit a person while they were safe inside their house. It was perplexing.

'Why is that there's only a finite amount of magic?' I enquired. It was a detail that was bothering me like there was a hole in his story.

He raised his hands. 'Why is the sky blue? That's just how it is.'

'So, what can you tell me about the witch in question?'

'Not a lot, I'm afraid.' He paused for a moment while he put on a pair of white cotton gloves, then squatted below the countertop. I listened to the sound of a key in a lock and then what sounded like a padlock being moved and then a length of chain being dragged through a hasp. Eventually, he reappeared holding an ancient looking book, the cover of which looked a lot like crocodile skin. 'Never touch dragon skin with your bare hands,' he advised as he put the book down. 'This is more than two-hundred years old and would probably still eat through my skin if I wasn't protected.'

I opened my mouth to respond, but I couldn't form a sentence that felt like an adequate reply. Instead, I chose to ignore his delusion.

He carefully turned some pages, found what he was looking for and turned the book to face me. He pointed to a crude drawing, 'The art of controlling lightning has been largely forgotten by today's magical practitioners. Of course, most of today's practitioners are almost entirely harmless. The Wiccans are the best-known group but what they do is more of a religion than an arcane art. I have not heard of anyone performing dark spells of this magnitude. Not ever. I have reached out to some of the people that work in this field, they might be able to provide more information on what you are facing this time. Vermont Wensdale should be able to shed some light.'

Vermont Wensdale. Now there was a name that kept cropping up. He was as bonkers as Frank but far more dangerous. Where Frank might study, Vermont would seek to slay.

I scrutinised the drawing. It was of a crone in a cowl, like the wicked witch from Snow White. She had her arms aloft with lightning arcing above her. The effect was to make it look as if she was controlling the lightning and opposite her was a man, strong and tall, whose body was drawn as if the lightning was passing through his chest. Above and below the drawing was writing in very old English. It was barely readable, and I gave up after a few sentences.

'I can't read that,' I said, pointing to the passage. 'Can you give me the general gist?'

He rolled his eyes again and turned the book around so that it was the right way up for him to read. I watched as he traced along the lines of writing with a finger.

I leaned in close to see what he was reading. 'The spell requires three parts of the chosen to activate it, essence, presence, and seed. These help to form the link between the source and the earth, so the practitioner can guide it through their intended victim.' Frank and I both jumped as a huge peel of thunder echoed through the air to punctuate the macabre subject.

We looked at each other, our faces inches apart as we were staring at the book. Neither of us said anything, the timing of the thunder undeniably eerie.

Poison began laughing at us. She was holding her phone and sniggering, then turned it so we could see the face and pressed a button. The thunder sounded again: She had downloaded an App.

The little cow.

Frank shook his head and looked back down at the book. 'The spellcaster must bind the source, that's the light-ning, to the chosen using the three parts and has to be present when the spell is cast to guide the source to its target.'

'Sounds simple enough. What does it mean by essence, presence, and seed?'

'Oh, err, essence would be blood, presence has to be a physical part of the body like a piece of skin or maybe some hair.'

'What about seed?'

'This is old stuff. Seed means exactly that.'

'So, the witch needs to gather blood, hair, and semen? How does she get hold of the victim's semen?'

'Are you kidding?' asked Poison, her face incredulous. 'Boys give away their semen for free. I could get a dozen samples in half an hour just by going into the street and asking.'

I volunteer as tribute!

Ignoring Mr Wriggly's thoughts on the matter, she was probably right. How difficult would it be to get seed from a man? Pretty tough if you looked like the old lady I had seen with the four murderous wives of East Malling.

For the case in question, she could obtain it via the wives. I was going with the premise that the witch/old lady was pulling some kind of murderous scam. Were the wives in on it or not? Were they complicit? And, if so, did they believe they were killing their husbands with magic or did they know it was all nonsense?

'You are going to carry on looking into this case, aren't you?' Frank asked.

I shrugged my shoulders. Of course. 'I don't think there's a witch at the end of this, Frank. I will admit I don't know how the murders are being committed, but I doubt a witch is doing it.'

'She used lightning to explode their hearts, but you

don't think it's magic?' Frank was stood with his arms folded, looking at me sceptically.

'Nope. When I work out what is going on I will let you know.'

'Bye, Tempest,' Poison called as I started to move toward the door. She pressed the button on her phone again to cause another loud peal of thunder and grinned at me.

I waved a quick salute to her and Frank, then stopped in the doorway as I remembered something. 'Almost forgot. I moved into Lyndon Parrish's office yesterday.'

'Oh,' Frank said.

'I think we can assume he has quit the paranormal investigation business. Anyway, I have a stack of framed pictures that need a home if you promise not to just flog them on eBay.'

'You mean the big ones he had on the walls? Of Tunguska and the Patterson-Gimlin Bigfoot...'

'And all the other ones he had. You can have them all if they are going up in here.'

'Tempest you are a gentleman and a scholar,' he replied, a smile revealing how pleased he was with the freebies. They were good quality frames, and I could probably have sold them, but they went well with Frank's theme, and he had never once tried to charge me for his perpetually available advice.

'I'll bring them around later.' With that, I was gone. The door closed behind me as I descended the stairs.

Groceries with a Side of Violence

I stopped in a co-operative store on my way back to the office. We needed basic office supplies such as kitchen towel and toilet rolls, tea, coffee and sugar and I grabbed some biscuits and a quality box of tissues because it was not unusual for clients to begin blubbing while telling their tales of woe.

My brain was largely in neutral for the task, I was thinking about the lightning, but managed to select, pay for and pack my groceries on autopilot, only coming back to reality when I stepped back out of the shop and into the rain. I was supposed to be picking up coffee. I had left the office more than ninety minutes ago now. Chances were that Amanda and James had gone for their own rather than wait for me and since my hands were now full of bags it was going to be difficult to carry coffee if I got it.

I would go back to the office and head out again if necessary.

'There he is.'

I looked up to find the source of the voice. A fat bloke

was advancing toward me from in front of my office as I approached it. He was flanked by two other equally over-weight men. They were all forged from the same biological soup and had to be brothers.

I had labelled him as fat because he clearly had a beef with me, and I was instantly feeling a lack of generosity. My hands were full of bags. He looked like he wanted to get frisky and there were three of them.

'You want to tell me why I paid you money to have my wife throw me out of my house?' He had closed the distance to me and was yelling, spittle flying from his lips in his excitement. Adrenalin was coursing through his body, making him twitchy and potentially dangerous.

I forced myself to relax as his brothers joined him. They were stood three abreast, each of them looking at me, each of them taller and heavier than me. I kept the bags in my hands and looked slowly and calmly at each in turn.

I was going to have one go at diffusing the situation, after which I was going to get some exercise if necessary. 'Sir, you have me at a loss. You appear to believe I have been involved in some misfortune you have suffered.'

'He doesn't even know who I am!' The man said, throwing his arms in the air. 'I paid you to prove the woman in the back of my car was a ghost and you went and found a prostitute.'

Ah. Now I could join the dots. I had only seen his face in the dim light of the photograph Amanda showed me and I had been looking more closely at the woman in the picture. This was Amanda's client, Martin Boynes, the one that wanted us to prove ghosts existed.

'It's my understanding, sir, that the lady in the photo-graph is indeed a prostitute.'

'It's a ghost!' he screamed in my face. He reached for

my jacket, grabbing the front of it with both hands. I remained calm, but it was almost time to act. 'You have ruined me. I paid you to get me out of this.'

'Hit 'im, Martin! Go on!' goaded the brother to the right.

'I would advise against that,' I replied, my voice still calm though my adrenalin was beginning to make my pulse race.

'Why? There's one of you and three of us,' the same brother observed. His arithmetic was not as accurate as he thought though.

'Wrong.' His face wrinkled up in confusion. 'There's *only* three of you.' I'd reached the end of my patience and Martin was still screwing up my nice jacket. In one motion, I dropped the bags, their contents spilling at my feet, and reached up with both hands. My right hand went over his arms to grasp his left wrist. I turned it against itself by forcing my thumb into the join between his thumb and forefinger to break his grip then rolled the arm down and toward me. My left arm arced up with a high elbow that struck against his temple.

Controlling his left arm, I swung him to his right and into his brother there to form a barrier. The brother to his right could now not get to me. The brother to his left was now behind me and starting to react. I kicked my leg out behind me into the inside of his left knee. I needed space more than anything, I couldn't afford to let them get hold of me.

I changed direction to push hard against Martin. He was trying to pull away from me, so the sudden shift in momentum propelled him into his brother and sent them both sprawling. They were on the wet pavement, and I had space between me and the third brother. He had recovered his balance after the kick to his knee though and was coming for me.

I let him come. His weight would become my weapon. As he closed the gap, I let him grab for me, but I was falling back as he came, making his centre of balance move beyond his leading foot. Had he swung a punch I would have needed to parry it, but he didn't, he tried to grab hold of me, wanting to slow me up so his brothers could join him. It was a sensible tactic, the three of them moving together would quickly overpower me. He hadn't planned well though, just as he started to tip forward, I stepped tight into his body, spun as I grabbed his lapels and threw him over my hip.

Three men down. I was so magnificent.

They were getting up, still looking angry, but also now looking wet and a little confused about what had just happened.

'Chaps I see no particular benefit to any of us in trying a second round. Shall we move to the office instead?' I had no desire to sit down with them, but even less interest in finding myself engaged in a full-blown street brawl that would most likely lead to someone's arrest. People, most probably tourists, were already staring at us as they hurried by. Were it not raining, they might have formed a small crowd by now.

Martin did not feel inclined to agree to my proposal though. Thankfully, he didn't want to fight anymore either. His preferred option was to call me some names and threaten to set his lawyer on me. I was impressed by how many swear words he was able to string into a single sentence. He was done though, his adrenalin expended without the victory he had expected.

I held my ground, patiently, calmly waiting for them to

walk away. Only when they turned to go did I allow my hands to shake. My pulse was through the roof. I was also soaked right through to my skin and my shopping was all over the ground. The coffee jar had cracked open when it hit the street, the tissue products were damp and expanding from the water that had penetrated the packaging. I probably needed to buy it all again.

I trudged back to the office.

Amanda started speaking as I came through the door, 'Be careful if you go outside again. Mr Boynes is out there somewhere.' Amanda was bent over at the computer desk reading something with James. When I came in, she glanced up but hadn't taken in my bedraggled appearance. I waited for her to finish what she was reading and look up again. Finally, she did. 'Oh.'

I was standing in an expanding pool of water, and my clothes were skewwhiff. 'Mr Boynes and I met. He seems displeased with our service.'

'Yes. He was here a few minutes ago threatening legal action against us. When he left, I thought he had gone home or to work. Are you okay?'

'I'm a little damp. The groceries are mostly ruined also.'

'So they are,' said James who had come over to take the bags from me. Amanda had also crossed the room to help me. She was wearing a dress again. It was elegant office wear and paired with brown leather knee-high boots. She looked incredible yet again, forcing me to remind myself how good Natasha looked. I pictured Natasha wearing the same outfit. Then I caught a whiff of Amanda's perfume and almost sunk to my knees. She had the ability to completely distract me. I needed to be somewhere else.

'I need to go home and change my clothes.'

'What do you want to do about Mr Boynes?' Amanda asked.

It was a good question. 'I wasn't able to get any sense out of him. He said his wife had kicked him out.'

'She read the report in the email I sent him. I got the impression that he has given her cause to check his emails. I wrote the report and emailed it to him yesterday afternoon. It outlined our findings – mostly that the girl in the back of his car was a prostitute by the name of Tiffany Roberts and not a ghost. His wife intercepted the report, I guess she has access to his email somehow, and he arrived home to find his clothes on the front lawn.'

I considered what Amanda had just said. 'I don't think we need to do anything about Mr Boynes. He's guilty of trying to use us to cover his tracks. His attempt failed. We investigated and reported our findings. We even emailed them to his personal email address that he supplied us. That his wife doesn't trust him is not our problem. I doubt he will be back.'

'I hope not.'

'Okay. I'll bring fresh groceries back with me. I should be less than an hour.' I patted my pockets to make sure I had my keys and phone and went through the office and out the back to my car where I squelched a little as I settled into my seat.

It was turning into an odd day.

Black Eyes and Top Chat-Up Lines

The dogs rushed to the door as I opened it. The sound of the rain meant they couldn't hear me approaching the house so for once I was inside with the door shut before they got to me. I was dripping slightly, the dachshunds electing to keep their distance as a mark of how much they disliked getting wet.

The TV was on in the lounge. I could hear voices and music drifting through.

'Are you in, Hilary?' I called out, certain that he must be.

'Coming,' his reply came back a second before he appeared in the kitchen doorway in front of me. He had a black eye. A real corker of one and a fat lip to go with it.

'You okay?' I asked.

'You mean this?' he asked, wafting a hand in the direction of his face. 'I tried some of Big Ben's top chat up lines. Apparently, ladies do not like to be told that their breasts look heavy and asked if they would like me to hold them for a while.'

I felt my jaw drop a little.

'They also don't like to be told they remind me of my pinky toe because they are small and cute and am probably going to bang them on my coffee table later. But the one that tipped the balance was Big Ben's sure-fire icebreaker.'

'Oh, this I have got to hear.'

'So, you walk up to a lady, and you ask her if she wants to play the rape game.'

'The rape game!' Oh, my lord.

'Then, when she inevitably says no, you reply with "That's the spirit" and the ice is broken because you both laugh.'

Okay. Now my jaw was hanging slack. I had to wonder if even Big Ben could get away with such lines. On seeing the black eye, I had assumed that Hilary had simply got into a fight. Even the fights you win usually result in some injury, but now I judged the facial marks to have most likely have been the result of his amorous advances.

I asked him, 'That was a girl?' I pointed at his face.

'Three of them actually.' He looked quite despondent.

'I need to get out of these wet clothes and get back to work, mate. You should tell Big Ben that you got action last night with three girls at the same time and leave it at that.'

'That's funny.' He smiled at least. Then he left me alone as I started to pull off my clothes.

I stripped in the small entrance lobby of my house, the coolness of the air on my damp skin causing goosebumps to appear. The clothes went straight into the washing machine, but I left the door open as I would add more clothes to it from the basket upstairs and put on a full load.

I could have dried myself with a towel, restyled my hair and dressed in fresh clothing but I was already naked and cold, so I got in the shower and turned it up to hot.

Ten minutes after getting home, I was coming back downstairs with an armful of laundry to go in the washer, dressed in dry clothing and ready for whatever came next.

Following on from my research last night I had decided while lathering shampoo into my hair, that I would visit the coroner at her office and see if I could sweet-talk her into showing me the case files for the first victim. I would play the role of the amorous man and hopefully get what I needed before she got what she wanted.

Her office was in Pembury hospital, a large modern facility on the way to Tonbridge. I had done the research on her myself last night between other tasks, but I wanted to tie up with Amanda and James before I set off. I had planned to get together with them this morning, my plans spoiled by Mr Boynes and his brothers.

When I came downstairs, I found Hilary hanging around dressed to go out.

'Going out?' I asked.

'I thought I would come with you, if that's alright? I'm bored here, and I cannot go back to work looking like this.' He explained, wafting his hand at his eye again. 'Would you have something for me to do?'

I thought about it for a moment. I couldn't come up with a good reason to say no. If he didn't want to go to work maybe I could use him to help me find the witch or watch the ladies. They knew me now, so I couldn't easily stake them out and my car was too conspicuous. Not for the first time, I considered that I might need another car, one that blended in.

I grabbed my keys and phone. 'Sure. Let's go.'

Crop Circles

I had planned to stop for groceries on my way but a text from James to say he had dealt with the task from petty cash negated my need to do so. Hilary was largely silent on our ride to the office, so I filled in the void by telling him about the witchcraft case. He was horrified at the thought of a man's heart exploding from his chest. However, he was not convinced that there couldn't be a witch behind it all.

'You haven't met my mother-in-law,' was what he said when I asked why. 'That's where Anthea gets her fire. That woman always loathed me. Still does, I expect. Probably congratulated Anthea on throwing me out.'

I wanted to retort with more advice about getting her back, but I had gone over the same ground enough times already.

Amanda and James were in the office when we arrived. There was fresh coffee percolating into a pot which made the office smell divine and a bowl of fruit on the side next to it – handy for when I wanted a snack.

James looked up as we came in. 'You have a couple of calls. One from... Wow!' James had seen Hilary's black eye.

Amanda poked her head out of her office. 'What's going on?'

'Hilary got into an altercation last night. A three on one situation.' I failed to mention that it was ladies and that they slapped him around.

'Goodness,' she said as she came closer to inspect the damage.

Hilary also elected to keep quiet about the gender of his opponents, instead tilting his head toward the light to give Amanda a better look.

'That's a good one.'

'Isn't it?' he agreed.

'Well, I think it makes you look dangerous,' she concluded. She was being generous. Hilary didn't look dangerous at all, and he weighed less than I could bicep curl. Nevertheless, the comment had the intended result as Hilary puffed out his chest and looked proud for a moment.

'Have you found a new case?' I asked to move us on from Hilary's face.

'I think so. There are crop circles and other odd events happening out near Cliffe Woods.'

'Don't forget the missed calls,' interrupted James while waving a post-it note at me. He had written on it with a pink pen that had a fluffy unicorn mounted on the end. 'The first name is the same lady coroner you wanted me to track down the other day.'

'Is that the one that...'

I cut her off quickly before she could finish the question, 'Yes, Amanda. That one.' The one last seen by Amanda kneeling at my feet with her boobs hanging out.

I thanked James for the note then looked at it properly. The second name was my client, Mick Cotton.

'Did Mr Cotton say what he was calling for?' We had only spoken last night.

'Err, no,' James stuttered. 'No, he did say it was fairly urgent that you called though. It was only a few minutes ago that the call came in. He said he couldn't get you on your mobile number.'

That's odd. I took out my phone. It was off. I pressed the button to give it life, but no life was forthcoming. Had I damaged it tussling with Mr Boynes and not noticed? Had it somehow run out of battery power? I poked it brainlessly with my IT ignorant fingers for a few moments before accepting defeat and handing it to James who had seen my plight and was patiently waiting for me to hand it over.

I turned to Amanda, 'You were telling me about crop circles?'

'I will forward you the enquiry to read, but I already phoned the client. Clients I should say since there are three of them. Crop circles have been appearing randomly for a while in the cornfields.' Cliffe Woods was a remote village the other side of the river from our office in Rochester. It was probably less than ten miles away, but the journey there took in a plethora of tiny, winding back roads so it felt twice as long and would take most of an hour to drive. 'The crop circles are little more than a nuisance, I think. We first heard about them a couple of weeks ago, but they are now reporting that their dairy herds are all producing luminous milk and that strange craft have been spotted in the air.'

'Craft plural or singular?' I wanted to clarify. We had wandered over to her office, so she could show me the email, but something on the desk in my office had caught my eye.

'I should check that,' she replied. 'It was Kieran Fallon I spoke with. His number is the one on the email, but he has two other farmers he works with that have reported the same problem. They work as a cooperative, so they are all in trouble if they have to keep throwing their milk away. Mr Fallon said they were only a few weeks away from going bust if they cannot sell their produce.' Amanda had been explaining the case and not looking at me. Now that she finished speaking, she saw that she only had my partial attention and followed my gaze.

'Oh, yes. Frank dropped it off. He said, "Tempest forgot to take this with him and he's going to need it to survive his latest case." Then he left it on your desk and went back to his shop.'

On my desk was the damned toad in its tank.

'Did he explain what it is?' I asked her.

'Nope. I wasn't willing to ask either, he seems safe enough, but he sure has some odd ideas.'

'It's a Salem Toad. Apparently, it's quite rare, and it has a unique adaptation that manifests in the form of flatulence when it's brought into the vicinity of a witchcraft practitioner.'

Amanda laughed out loud, then stopped, 'You're serious, aren't you?'

I shrugged. 'Frank is. I think it's just a frog.'

I hung my head. I had a toad to look after. How much care did a toad require to survive? What did I feed it? 'Did he leave any care instructions?' I asked her.

'I don't think so,' she called through the office to James to check that Frank had left nothing with him. The answer came back negative.

'What are you going to name him?'

'What?' Now I was looking at Amanda. Her latest question had carried the girlish glee that I had heard before from other ladies when faced with a kitten or a puppy. She was bending down to inspect the amphibian, the move pushing her perfectly rounded bottom out towards me.

I moved to join her by the tank to avoid staring where I should not. 'Why would I name it?'

'You have a pet frog, sorry, a pet toad. You have to give him a name.'

I sighed. Girls and pet names. 'It's not a pet. As soon as I can return it…'

'Him.'

'What?'

'It's a boy. Frank said so.'

I screwed up my face, perplexed. 'How would he know?'

'I expect it has little boy toad bits under there.'

I looked at the toad. It looked back at me. 'Whatever, I'm not naming it.'

'I think it looks like a Kevin,' she announced. I stood up and made to walk away. 'Don't forget to take Kevin with you when you go,' she called after me.

I turned back to find her smiling at me with encouragement and amusement. I showed her my gritted teeth at which she laughed again, the sound like angels playing music.

'So, the crop circles is an interesting case. Have you already committed to it?' I forced a change in subject.

Graciously, she let me off the hook about Kevin the toad and came back to the real world of work. 'No, but I was about to call him back and arrange to visit them. If they can see me today, I will go this afternoon. Otherwise, it will be as soon as possible, so I can determine if there's a real case here.' It was exactly what I would do.

'Let me know how you get on. We need to build the

caseload. We seem to be moving from one to the next with very little overlap at the moment.'

'Yes, there are plenty of enquiries though.'

'Plenty of crazy ones,' James chipped in from his seat at the front reception desk behind us. James read all the incoming emails and had learned to sift the worthwhile cases from the idiots looking to hand over their money when there was no case to solve.

Amanda went back to her office to start planning her investigation and do some research. I watched her go, then turned to find James and Hilary looking at me expectantly.

They wanted me to give them things to do.

'I got your phone working,' announced James handing it over.

'What was wrong with it?'

'Nothing that I could see. I pressed the one button, and it started.' Exactly what I had been doing. I often worried that I was just too old for technology even though I was still in my thirties. Somehow, I always needed to find a teenager when I had an issue with my phone or laptop or whatever.

I thanked him, took it anyway, and showed him the picture of the witch. Hilary leaned in to see it as well.

'Is that your witch?' he asked.

'It's an ugly old lady. But yes, that's the witch. Think you can find her from a picture?' I asked James.

He screwed his face up a little. 'Well, if she has a criminal record or a social media profile or has appeared in a paper in the last few years then probably, yes. It will be a question of luck more than skill though I think. Can you send the image to me?'

'Um, yes.' I knew how to do that one, so I fiddled with the phone a bit and sent it to his work email address. 'Done.'

'Cool,' he said as he swung back behind the desk and clicked his mouse.

'What shall I do?' Hilary asked. 'I can make coffee. Anything is better than doing nothing and stewing.'

'You really want to help out here? Don't want to go back to work or home to your wife?'

He shook his head. 'I'm not ready for work and they owe me holiday anyway.'

'What about Anthea?'

'I'm not ready to beg for forgiveness. I don't think I should have to.' It was the first time that he had acknowledged the concept that he might.

'In that case, I do have a task for you. A secret mission you might say.'

His eyebrows rose to the top of his head.

Mick Cotton

I called my client when I had finished explaining to Hilary what I needed him to do. He had been enthralled with the task, which came as a surprise because it was not a task I could find much excitement over. I shook his hand, said a few motivational words and slapped his shoulder as he squared his jaw and left the safety of my office behind.

Mick Cotton had answered his phone immediately. It hadn't even had time to ring at my end. His reason for calling was simple: He had found a rune on the outside of his house and was quite rightly concerned about it. Obviously, I had abandoned my outline plan to track down the coroner and was heading there now.

The sky was dark. A storm was out there somewhere. I couldn't see the lightning but every now and then I thought I heard thunder above the throaty roar of my car's straight six engine. I had always loved nature's great displays of power; the spectacle of a lightning storm was something to behold if one had a good view of the landscape. Now though, it gave me a feeling of unease. What were the

Witches of East Malling up to? Was there another murder planned? They knew about me somehow, forcing me to keep my distance, but had they somehow found out that Michael Cotton had hired me and now planned to remove him? Who had inscribed the rune on his house?

The route to his house from Rochester took just over half an hour and meant I skipped lunch. I was hoping to come back via my house when I was finished at Mick's, so I could walk the dogs and get something to eat. I would find out soon enough if that plan would come to fruition.

It was just after one o'clock when I pulled up at his house. He had clearly been watching for me as the front door of his house opened before I could exit my car. I threw him a wave as I stood up.

He looked relieved to see me. He also didn't look entirely well. His skin was pale, his eyes bore bags beneath them as if he hadn't slept at all, but mostly he just looked like he was fighting off a particularly harsh cold.

I didn't comment, but gave him an opening to do so, 'Mick, how are you?' I asked as I approached him and shook his outstretched hand.

'Thank you for coming so quickly. Why do you have a frog?'

I sighed deeply. I couldn't possibly explain, even to myself, why I was carrying the toad around. I had tried to leave the office without it, but Amanda had grabbed it and chased me down. With her fantastic eyes locked onto mine, she could have told me to do anything, and I would have complied. Kevin the toad was going to be my co-pilot. Mr Cotton was still looking at me, waiting for me to answer though. All I could do was shrug.

I guess he wasn't really all that interested because he accepted my answer and moved on. 'Let me show you the symbol.' He wanted to get straight down to business. I followed him to the front of his house where he picked up a large flowerpot to reveal the rune hidden behind it. The symbol was eight inches high and made using a basic white stick of chalk but whoever had made it had clearly had to move the flowerpot to do so and had intended for it to remain unnoticed.

'How did you find it?' I asked.

'Accident,' he replied, then filled in the blanks before I prompted him for more information. 'I lost my keys, and I kept a spare one underneath the pot. Only thing was, it wasn't there. So, I have a Wiccan rune on my house just like the ones I found on my father's house before his death, and someone has my front door key.'

'So, how did you get in?' It felt like a valid question.

'I also keep a spare key for the back door hidden under a rock in the garden as an extra extra just in case. Thankfully, that was still there, and I could get into the house. Now though I'm thinking I need to change the locks.'

'Did you check for other runes?'

'I did. I didn't find any. You want to check again?'

I nodded then performed a left turn, put Kevin the toad on the doorstep and went to inspect the outside of the house. The symbol hidden behind the plant pot by the front door was a triple moon. I found the same symbol on Barbara's house when her husband was murdered.

We moved to the left side of the house as one looks at it from the road. Mick claimed to have already looked, but he had done so with tired eyes as I saw the witches knot symbol almost immediately. It was marked in chalk and no more than an inch in height, tucked into the eaves. The person making the mark would have needed to use a ladder.

I continued to the rear of the house, passing through a

gate to get there. His household waste and recycling bins were located near to the back door that led out from his kitchen. There I found the third symbol, a horned god behind the recycling bin. I took my phone from my pocket and dialled Frank's number. I had a question.

His voice came on the phone, 'Tempest. Did you get the toad?'

'Oh, you mean Kevin?'

'Kevin?'

'Yes, Amanda named him for me.'

'Jolly good. Just keep him close by and keep an ear for his gas. He will produce a high-pitched shrill sound from his anal sphincter when your witch is nearby.'

'Frank, I have a question. The houses of the victims all have Wiccan runes marked on them...'

'Are they on all four sides?' he interrupted, his voice was suddenly intense.

'Yes.'

'Is the horned god one of the symbols?'

'Yes.'

'They were marked for death. They are not Wiccan symbols either. They are ancient Pagan symbols, some of which have been adopted by the Wiccans. This is old world witchcraft, Tempest. Dangerous, deadly stuff.'

'Right. Well, I'm at the client's house now and he has symbols on his walls just like the victims did.'

'Tempest, I'm not feeling all that well,' Mick said from behind me.

Frank was still on the phone, his voice a desperate plea in my ear, 'Tempest you have to get out of there right now. Get your client and get him to safety. Bring him to me, I know people that can cast shielding spells until the witch can be trapped.'

I was looking at Mick. He looked ill. His skin had a glassy sheen to it, and he looked to be shallow breathing. Before I could say anything, his eyes rolled back, and he collapsed. I dropped my phone in my bid to catch him. It clattered behind me as I dove forward to stop his head hitting the stone slabs of the path.

Then the storm hit.

Death's Door

Once again, I was wet. It was just starting to rain, but the ground was already thoroughly damp from the earlier downpour. A huge peal of thunder had boomed overheard as Mick collapsed.

I may have saved him from striking his head on the hard ground, but he was unconscious now and unresponsive. I positioned his head on my legs and reached back for my phone hoping it was still functioning.

It was.

I dialled three nines. An ambulance was coming.

As the rain picked up its pace, I checked his pulse to find it weak and thready. He was significantly unwell. The ambulance would come from Pembury and could not get to me soon enough.

In the end, it took twelve minutes, my directions on where to find us thankfully sufficient to lead the paramedics directly around to the back of the house. I was instantly superfluous, but they didn't hang around trying to wake him or determine what was wrong with him. In less than a minute he was on a stretcher and heading to the ambulance parked in the street outside. Rain was pouring down on us.

I squelched around to the front of the house, snagged Kevin from the doorstep where I had left him and ran to my car. I spun it around and followed the Ambulance at speed back to Pembury where I then spent the next three hours doing nothing much at all. I was sitting in a waiting room in the accident and emergency department. Periodically, I would wander over to the desk and ask if there was any news. The answer was always the same: I would be updated in due course. I had elected to leave Kevin in the car believing that he may draw too many questions.

Questions like: Who's the idiot with the frog?

I had tried to dry out some of my clothes using the hot air blower in the gent's toilet, but apart from making my damp clothing warmer, I achieved very little. One of the ladies on reception was kind enough to have someone bring me a towel but mostly I was just wet and cold and used the towel to reduce the amount of dampness I transferred to the chair I was sitting on.

Having time to pass with nothing much to do allowed my mind to drift. It kept circling back to the minutes I spent hugging Mick to keep him warm and protect him from the rain. All the while I had been doing that, I had been waiting for a lightning bolt to strike us.

The storm was overhead, lightning flashing across the sky. Sitting on the cold, wet floor I felt exposed and had been glancing behind me continuously while my paranoia imagined the hook-nosed crone creeping up to send the lightning coursing through my chest.

This case was weirding me out more than others had.

Eventually, just when I was considering that I should just leave and return later, a doctor appeared. He was a tall man with a dark beard shot through with grey. The grey extended into his hair to give a salt and pepper effect at the sides.

'Mr Michaels?' he asked as he approached me.

'Yes.' He extended his right hand, so we shook while I waited for him to tell me something.

'You are a friend of the patient?' he asked. I replied that I was, even though I knew it was stretching the truth. Explaining that he was my client and I was hunting a witch for him would take too long, get confusing and potentially stop the man from telling me whatever it was he had to tell. 'I'm afraid Mr Cotton has been poisoned. Do you know where he might have come into contact with Anthrax?'

The startling question led to a police interview a few minutes later. I had no time for it and no option but to answer their questions either. Their concern, it seemed, was to do with terrorism and whether my client was, in fact, brewing Anthrax at home as a biological weapon and had accidentally poisoned himself. At that point, I came clean about who I was and the nature of my involvement with him. I had no doubt whatsoever that the Witches of East Malling were behind his ill-health, but I left that part out, secure in the knowledge that the police would not listen to me and were most likely duty-bound to conduct a full investigation into Mick's life now anyway.

They took my details, and I was finally allowed to leave. My client was seriously ill, but according to the consultant doctor I had spoken with, he would most likely pull through. They had placed him into a coma as part of his treatment.

Walking away from the hospital, I found myself convinced that he was the third victim in this case. I didn't know why yet, but I was getting angry. The ladies were killing their husbands and had turned their attention to another man. Where or when would they stop? Better yet, who would stop them if I didn't?

It was a good question. I was going to visit the police station in Maidstone where I was at least known. I doubted I would be able to get them to see reason, to consider that there might be a sinister coven of middle-aged women being led by a wicked old crone into murdering their husbands and lesser relatives. It sounded improbable, even to my ears. However, I had to try. If I could get them to start digging, then maybe I could prevent another death.

Mick Cotton would wake up and when he did, I intended to be able to report that his case was closed.

Maidstone Police Station

Though I was wet and cold, I went directly from Pembury hospital to the police station not far from my house. I had fire in my belly.

I regretted my decision soon enough.

I had a relationship of sorts with Chief Inspector Quinn. He was not the top man at the Maidstone station, but he acted as if he was and he was senior enough that he could make things happen if he wanted to. Our relationship was based on the fact that he really didn't like me, and I kept doing my best to give him reasons not to.

At the front desk was a young woman that knew who I was. I suspected we had met at some point, or she had been present on one of the many occasions when I had been arrested for being in the wrong place. Whatever the case, she addressed me by name before I had the chance to speak.

'Tempest Michaels, everything okay?'

'I'm here to report a murder.' I knew the statement would get their attention, the desk sergeant working behind her looked up immediately, then pushed back his chair and joined me at the front desk.

I didn't know his name, but he was another cop that I recognised so he probably knew who I was too. 'That's a very serious accusation,' he said. Was it derision I heard in his tone.

'Actually, it's two murders and one attempted murder,' I corrected myself.

'Goodness, well we had better give you our full attention then. Is it Casper being less than friendly this time?' Okay, so it was derision. The lady cop looked like she was ready to pay attention to me, she was probably friends with Amanda and Patience and thus had an alternate opinion about me from them. Her Sergeant clearly thought my paranormal investigation business was a sham, or that I was a con man or something. There were plenty that did still.

'Perhaps I might have a quick word with Chief Inspector Quinn?' He didn't move. 'Fetching him is your swiftest way to get rid of me,' I assured him.

He continued mocking me, 'I'll get right on it then.'

'Sergeant, I intend to make a statement regarding a double murder. If you don't get off your fat arse and pay attention to me, I will personally name you in the press when I solve the case and make it very clear that the police once again refused to act when a heinous crime was reported to them.' I had kept my tone calm and even but had allowed the volume to rise sufficiently that it carried back through to the rooms behind reception where a stack of officers would be working. The general din of noise coming from there stopped.

The desk sergeant's eyes widened at my threat. Less than a week ago I had made CI Quinn look ridiculous on TV when Amanda had solved the Voodoo case that he had been happily ignoring. The TV people had loved it, and I was quite confident that I could call the number on any one of the business cards I now held and have a news crew outside the station within the hour.

The desk sergeant knew it too, everyone had seen the clip of CI Quinn and I. Being fair to myself, it hadn't been my intention to make Quinny look so bad. He had done all the work for me by being pompous and refusing to see the warning signs.

The desk sergeant opened his mouth to retort. I had no idea what he was going to say, and I never found out because a fresh voice joined our little conversation.

'I'll take it from here, thank you.' CI Quinn had appeared in the aperture that led to the front desk from the room behind. He was in uniform as always. I was beginning to wonder if he slept in it. 'I will take your statement, Mr Michaels.'

Jolly good.

Wordlessly, he opened a door to allow me access to the station and led me through to an interview room. I walked by the open plan main office where dozens of cops were sitting at desks or performing tasks of some kind. I got a couple of nods, one from Brad Hardacre, the cop that had kicked me out of Barbara's house on Sunday, but most faces just stared.

Quinn started talking as we sat down, 'What seems to be the problem, Mr Michaels.'

'Ian,' I started. I had learned his first name from watching the TV playback of the interview last week. On the screen beneath his face, it had displayed Chief Inspector Ian Quinn. I was using it now because he refused to use mine. He stiffened visibly when I did as if it was a verbal assault. 'There's a man in Pembury hospital suffering from

Anthrax poisoning.' That got his attention. 'That man is my client. He hired me to investigate the death of his father, a man that was recorded as killed by lightning while standing inside his house. The accidental death that you will find on his autopsy is wrong. He was murdered. A second man was killed by the same method just three days ago at a house in East Malling. The two dead men were known to each other. Both wives had taken out large insurance policies. I believe the two wives are colluding with two other women and a fifth person who is performing the murders while the wives ensure they have airtight alibis.'

'Two men killed by lightning?'

'Yes.'

'Inside their homes.'

'Yes.'

'And their bodies were examined by an appointed coroner?'

'Yes.'

'And accidental death was recorded as the verdict?'

'Precisely.'

'And your client has Anthrax poisoning?'

I couldn't be bothered to keep saying yes, so I simply stared at him, waiting for a question that was worth answering.

'Tell me about the fifth person.'

I launched into a description, doing my best to not call her a witch. But I was bored now and could see it didn't matter what I said to him. He was too focused on trying to belittle me and probably had some grand plan for looking superior as he had me escorted from the station shortly. When I finished speaking, I noted that during the fifteen minutes we had been in the room he hadn't written down a single word.

'I hope you'll forgive me when I ask what it is you would like me to do about any of this.'

I sighed. It had become a week of sighing. 'Ian,' he stiffened again but didn't attempt to correct me, 'I'm going to record a statement. I want you to open a case and investigate it because I believe there are at least two more men in serious danger. If a further murder occurs and you have not acted, I will make it clear to the press that you were privy to pertinent information that could have prevented it.' It saddened me that I had to keep threatening people to get them to do their job.

'Then I encourage you to do so, Tempest.' His tone had changed to one of finality. 'You take the credit for cases I have solved, you wreck press interviews and belittle the efforts of my team.' This wasn't about his team, this was all about him and his power trip up the promotion ladder, but he wasn't done yet. 'The very existence of your investigation agency is an insult to the criminal prosecution system, and I intend to put you out of business.'

I stood up. I was wasting my time. 'My statement?' I asked.

He spat his answer at me, 'Get out.'

If I could record no statement, I could never claim that the police knew about the murders and ignored them. It would be clever if it wasn't so damned irresponsible.

The sea of faces in the station watched me as I went by once more heading back toward the door that led out into the reception area.

'Be careful out there,' advised the desk sergeant with a chortle.

A Date with Natasha

I got home from the station right on time for the dogs' dinner. They met me at the door, sniffed me suspiciously as I was wet again and backed away. It was standard practice for them to go outside whenever I got home, but they hated the rain, and it was still drizzling.

They both ran to the back door, saw the rain and changed their minds about wanting to go out. I shooed them out anyway and since I was already soaked and cold I went outside with them and stood on the patio to make sure they got on with their business and didn't just hide under a bush.

When I had let them back in and given them their bowls full of dog meat, I finally got out of my wet clothes. They went into the washing machine as a bath ran. I had been cold long enough that I wanted the warm water to penetrate deep into my core.

I had arranged to pick Natasha up for our date at 1900hrs. Our table was reserved for 2000hrs, so I had allowed time to arrive and park and get a drink and very definitely sit and chat for a while. I had spent very little time alone with Natasha, just one lunch, but I knew her to be charming to spend time with and able to converse on a diverse range of topics.

As I soaked in the bath, glad to finally be warm, I idly fantasised about having a relationship with Natasha. For a long time, I had wanted a woman in my life, someone I saw many times a week and that I would one day convince to move in with me. I had a picture of co-habitual bliss that was feeling just a little bit more pressing now that one of my good friends was getting married. Jagjit still lived with his parents. They had a big house, but he and Alice were already spending almost all their time at her flat and were looking at property together. He would be moving out of the village and in with her in the next couple of weeks, I was sure.

I came to a decision as I bobbed about in the warm water: I needed to sabotage my chances with Amanda. I had been ready to put my attraction to her behind me until Big Ben had revealed that she was suddenly single again. She was single though through a case of misunderstanding. If I intervened, would they repair their relationship? It would be better for me if she were dating someone else. I was sure of it. Just as I was sure she was not interested in me and that openly pursuing her would drive her from my firm and my life.

I dried my hands, picked up my phone and called Big Ben. When he answered we had a brief discussion where he repeatedly asked if I was sure about my request, but in the end agreed to find Brett and explain what he had seen. He closed with some advice on what to do with Natasha's chest in true Big Ben fashion.

The alarm on my phone pinged just as I put it back

down. I had set it just in case I fell asleep in the bath or lost track of time. I had a poor record with dating ladies; life just seemed to get in the way. Tonight, I was going to be on time.

Getting dressed, I had to open a window to see if it was still raining. I would collect Natasha from her door, not just pull up at the curb outside and the rain meant that I needed to carry an umbrella with me to ensure she stayed dry in her transition from her house to my car. I also needed to know if it was still raining as the dogs could do with a walk. It was though, the steady drizzle of an hour ago had picked up. I would leave them sleeping on the sofa. They would not thank me if I forced them to go out in the wet.

I gave each a pat on the head and a quick scratch behind their ears, promised them a biscuit upon my return and left them to snooze the evening away.

I acknowledged, walking to the car, that I had a faint fluttering of nerves regarding the date tonight. I thought this meant that I was genuinely interested in Natasha and thus hoping to not mess it up.

It was a short drive to her place in Rochester, the address in a new estate developed close to the river and the brand-new railway station. I had never been to the estate before. The area had been industrial warehouses until just a few years ago and hidden from sight behind the large brick-built elevated railway that ran over the river and skirted the town centre before continuing toward the coast. One had to drive under the rail track to access it, but the road had always been there for traffic entering and leaving the industrial estate.

My satnav delivered me to her door, a shiny new link-detached place. Probably two bedrooms and a bathroom upstairs and a kitchen/diner and living area downstairs. It looked spacious enough and to my knowledge, she lived alone. On the short driveway, in front of the garage was a car that I had seen many times before in the pub car park. I hadn't known it was hers until now.

Natasha was in her kitchen, a room that dominated the front downstairs aspect of the house. She saw my car and threw a quick wave to show she had seen me. I doubted that she expected me to get out of my car to escort her from her door and that was why I was going to do it. Not just this once, but forever more if I got the chance.

'Good evening, Natasha,' I said smiling as she opened her door and faced me. 'You look utterly lovely.' She also smelled wonderful. The scent, whatever it was, hit my nose in a way that gave Mr Wriggly a tap on the shoulder to wake him up. She was wearing a fitted cream dress that hugged her curves and a pair of navy-blue heels that matched her coat. In her left hand was a small clutch bag.

Hi, Tempest,' she said as she stepped under the umbrella I was holding for her. The umbrella wasn't big enough for both of us to easily be under without being arm in arm, so I moved to step out and hold it over her head. Smiling, she looked at me quizzically, 'Where do you think you are going?'

Then she reached her free arm up to loop it behind my head and pull me into a gentle kiss. It was lip action only but there were fireworks coming from downstairs as her ample chest crushed into mine.

She broke the kiss and leaned her head back, so she had enough distance to bring my face into focus. 'That's better. Now take me for dinner, I'm starving.'

Mr Wriggly had been willing to bet we were going straight back inside her house for a hearty evening of shagging, but I was okay with him being disappointed. I had been attracted to Natasha from the moment I first saw her behind the bar in my local pub. Until Amanda came along and confused the heck out of me, Natasha had been everything I wanted in a woman and tonight I was taking her out. I had to consider myself lucky.

In the car, we chatted about what sort of food we each liked and whether she had eaten out in West Malling much, or at this restaurant at all. I learned that like me she didn't eat out much. There were too many unguarded calories in restaurant food, so tasty though it always was, it was best avoided in practice.

I found a parking space right in front of the restaurant. Occupying a position in the High Street, it had no car park of its own. The rain had stopped but I took the umbrella with me in case it began again while we were inside.

Always think of the lady first.

We both skipped starters and ordered thick steaks with creamed spinach and asparagus. When the waiter asked how she wanted her steak prepared, I was pleased to hear that she liked it rare. I have my steak as raw as a chef is prepared to send it out. I always felt that cooking it ruins the flavour and have an unnecessary frustration with people that asked for it well-done.

'How did you come to pick dachshunds?' she asked, changing subjects as the waiter walked away.

I took a sip of my deep red wine, savoured the intense earthy notes and cleared my mouth before answering. 'A whim combined with a selection process. I wanted a dog, but I knew I didn't want one that required grooming and lots of care and I wanted one that was long-lived. I didn't want a big dog, and I certainly didn't want one that barked a lot. There are so many breeds to pick from, so I tried to be objective and scientific in my selection process, but I had fallen in love with dachshunds when I was a little boy and part of me couldn't escape the desire to have one. Looking back now, I cannot tell if my selection process singled them out as one of the viable options or if I tailored the selection process to select them. Regardless, the breed ticked most of my boxes, so I searched until I found a reputable breeder and suddenly I had a tiny dachshund puppy to look after.'

'Was he your first dog?'

'Yes. With Dad in the Navy, it probably wasn't practical to have a dog growing up and it was only me that wanted one. My parents like the dogs, but I don't think they have ever considered owning one themselves. Have you ever had a dog?'

'Me? No, I'm more of a cat person.'

Ooh! Big black mark right there.

Natasha talked about having cats growing up and that she had just lost her cat a few months ago when it finally gave up aged just shy of nineteen years old. She acknowledged that it had been a damned old cat but now she was thinking about getting a new one and couldn't decide if she should get a kitten or go to a rescue place.

Our steaks arrived, looking delicious and thick and meaty and wonderful. I can report that mine was all those things. I had to slow my pace to stop myself from devouring it. I ate alone so often I worried that my manners might slip.

We elected to share a dessert and chose the cheese board. It complimented the wine she was drinking. I had bought the bottle and allowed myself a small glass leaving her just over two glasses to drink.

Two hours of pleasant dinner conversation slipped by easily, neither of us having to look at our watches or wonder when it would be polite to escape. The bill came all too soon, the restaurant was closing soon, and we were one of only two couples still being served.

Natasha offered to pay half. This was always the potentially awkward part of the event, primed with pitfalls where I might inadvertently suggest she couldn't afford it or was somehow not supposed to pay because she was a woman. I smiled and asked if it was okay for me to pick up the cheque this time. I had arranged the date and felt privileged to be out with her. I thought about making a joke out of it where I suggest she could pay me back in other ways but dismissed the notion as I was likely to make a hash of it and come off as predatory rather than cheeky.

I thanked the waiter, left a tip and helped Natasha into her coat. Outside it was not raining, but the pavements still glistened with wet under the streetlights and thunder rumbled to let us know there was a storm out there still somewhere.

I held the car door for her and closed it before getting in myself.

'Thank you for a lovely evening, Natasha,' I said as I started the car. I was looking at her from my seat, her dark, sexy eyes locked on mine. 'I had a really nice time.'

She bit her lower lip as she decided how to reply. Then, she leaned over the transmission tunnel, her intention to kiss me obvious. I met her halfway, our lips parting as the kiss deepened and became quite intense. She broke it after a few seconds, one hand holding my face as she pressed her forehead against mine. Her eyes were closed.

She took her hand away and slumped back into her bucket seat. 'I like you, Tempest. Take me home.'

I wasn't sure what that demand meant. Whether there was hidden meaning in it, but I turned the key and did as I was told.

Marked for Death

The clock in my car displayed 2301hrs when I pulled up at my house. Natasha hadn't invited me in. I was telling myself that was the right thing to do. I was very interested in her and was happy to wait for the intimacy to occur naturally and at the right time. That said. I was horny as hell now.

I had parked in front of her house and opened the passenger's door to let her out. The bucket seats are so close to the ground that getting out can be a chore. I offered her my hand and was rewarded with a view of her stocking tops as she demurely swung her legs out. We kissed again, but I had deliberately left my engine running to show that I did not expect to be invited inside.

I walked her to her door, asked her to decide if she wanted another date and get back to me with a proposal for it. I explained that I would be very happy to see her again and would make myself available, work permitting, at any time that suited her.

All in all, the date could not have gone better.

Hilary's car was on my drive. To perform his secret

mission today he had first needed to fetch it from his house, a part of the task he was least happy about and had said he could only do it if Anthea was out. I was curious to hear how he had got on, but he had gone to bed already. The dogs had been asleep on the sofa but were at the door when I opened it having heard my car no doubt.

While the dogs scampered in the garden, I tidied the kitchen. In my haste to get out this evening, I had left tea mugs on the side which needed to be moved into the dishwasher, and I had to empty the waste bin under the sink plus a few other small jobs.

I could hear Bull and Dozer barking at something, so they were not at the back door trying to get back in and were probably glad that the rain had left off for a bit.

The storm was still out there, the black sky lit sporadically as lightning flashed behind the clouds.

I was about ready for bed but not desperate to get there so I was going to spend a little time sitting with the dogs, reading a book and sipping a rum and coke. I was off beer and hadn't had a drink since Friday night; one spirit with diet mixer didn't seem too extravagant.

Moving around the kitchen I detected an odd smell. Something pungent and a little unpleasant. I checked the bin, giving it a tentative sniff. It wasn't that. I looked around wondering if I had knocked something down the side of the oven or refrigerator.

James had been here while I was in Cornwall, maybe he had a little accident and hadn't cleaned it up properly and now whatever it was, was beginning to fester in a dark recess of my kitchen. A horrifying thought, however, when I pulled out the oven to see behind and under, there was little more than dust and one very dead-looking pea. The refrigerator revealed a similar picture.

I stood up and scratched my head. The smell persisted. I took to sniffing my way around the kitchen, a tactic that provided the answer soon enough.

I was smelling Kevin's farts. Lovely. The toad and his little tank were on the kitchen windowsill where I figured he would get light during the day and was constantly in my eyeline to reduce the likelihood that I would forget to feed him. He was going back to Frank tomorrow.

Bull barked his request to be let back in just as I dropped two ice cubes into the dark liquid. I left it fizzing as I went through the house to let them in.

The ground outside was still wet, small puddles showing on my patio and across the path that wound around the garden. The rain had been persistent for several days, saturating my lawn which was now covered in worm casts. In turn, this meant the dogs came into the house with muddy feet every time they went out and my attempts to keep the mud off my carpet by placing towels down hadn't been as successful as I had hoped.

This time I caught them both as they attempted to run between my legs, pinned them down and dried their feet. They expected a biscuit, so once I let them up, they each ran through to stare at the cupboard in the kitchen and wait for my arrival.

I selected two gravy bones, collected my glass from the side and began an intricate dance where my feet had to dodge small dogs that were bouncing around beneath me, constantly moving and trying to keep their eyes on the prize in my hand. In the end, and before I fell over, I gave up and threw the biscuits, one to my left and the other to my right.

I placed the drink on a coaster on the small table I kept by my sofa and went to sit down whereupon I realised the book I planned to read was on the windowsill in the kitchen next to Kevin the toad and his small tank.

I didn't bother to turn the light back on in the kitchen, there was enough light coming through from the lounge for me to see by. Kevin was over by the sink; the book was in front of it. As I picked it up though, the lightning flashed again and there, outside the window, was the witch.

My heart thudded in my chest.

The split second of light had thrown her into silhouette while simultaneously illuminating her face from the reflected light off the windowpane. She had been looking right at me, but the darkness returned instantly, and she was gone.

I was running through my house though. Too fast to turn, I slammed into the wall in my lobby, rebounded off and ran for the back door. Ripping it open, I scanned around for her as the two dogs zipped by on either side of my feet. They vanished into the dark and for the umpteenth time, I wished I had gotten around to installing a light in the garden.

Lightning provided a fresh snapshot of the trees, bushes and six-foot-high fence that surrounds my garden but there was no sign of her. Forty feet away, at the other end of my house was a gate that led around to the front. I ran to it, but it was still bolted and padlocked so the only way in or out was through the house or over the fence.

How did a woman that age scale a six-foot fence, I asked myself? My brain returned the obvious answer: She couldn't.

Unless she had a ladder!

I ran across the garden toward an area that the moon-light didn't penetrate. Fronds from bushes snagged my clothing. Bull barked his excitement and danced in front of me, the moonlight catching his eyes more than anything else. I dodged around him, continuing my search for the old lady in my garden. Touching the wall, I could see all the way along it to the corner.

There was no ladder propped against it.

I checked a few other spots where I thought she might be able to climb over without being easily visible but there was nothing to find. I cursed myself and pulled out my phone. She must still be hiding in the garden. Under a bush or behind the shed, watching me and waiting for her chance to escape.

I turned on the phone's torch function, flooding the ground in front of me with bright, white light. I glanced at the house. Had she slipped inside and gone out the front while I was running around the garden?

I was so dumb!

I sprinted back to check but there were no muddy or wet footprints in the house. I turned back to face the dark and called out. 'There's no way out of the garden. Please show yourself. You will not be harmed. I'm not armed.' If I caught her, I was going to call the police, but no reply came back and though I looked for it, no movement beyond the trees blowing in the breeze was there to be seen.

With the torch and the dogs, I continued to search around under bushes and in dark corners for a good ten minutes. I was certain there was nothing to find though. Had the lady been in my garden, the dogs would have found her in seconds.

Accepting that she was no longer there I returned to the house, but once back inside the warmth, a question occurred to me: What had she been doing in my garden?

I could continue to ponder how she had escaped but

what she had been doing felt more pressing. I suspected I already knew.

Thirty seconds later I had confirmed what I had guessed. Right outside my kitchen window, a few inches up from the ground was a chalk-drawn witch's knot. She had been inscribing runes on my house.

I was marked for death.

Angry Wife

My sleep had been plagued by dreams and for the first time since moving into the house, I had locked all the doors before I went to bed. I considered waking Hilary to alert him to the trespasser in my garden but left him to sleep instead as I was struggling to convince myself there was any actual danger even though I felt quite unnerved.

Despite the later bedtime than my usual, I was up at 0500hrs to continue my fitness regime. I was distracted though, going through the motions of lifting weights and hitting the treadmill rather than feeling fully engaged with it. I needed to talk to Hilary when I got home and would wake him if he was still asleep.

I came back through my front door at 0654hrs, the sweat from the gym making my clothes stick to my skin. It was cold out though, the air penetrating through the damp-ness of my sweatshirt to chill me even as I was sweating.

At the top of the stairs, two small, pointy, black and tan dog faces were staring down at me. I went most of the way up and scooped one under each arm. They ran for the back door, their little legs moving even before I plopped them on the carpet.

The toilet flushed upstairs immediately before Hilary himself swung into view.

'Hi, Tempest. How did the date go?' Hilary seemed much improved, his mood almost buoyant in comparison with recent days.

'It was very pleasant,' I replied as I flicked the kettle on to boil. I would eat and cool down properly before I went for a shower.

'I didn't hear you come in,' he said with a grin. 'Did you...' He made a motion reminiscent of humping a dead cat which was probably supposed to enquire whether Natasha and I engaged in coitus. I could never understand why people thought it better to substitute adult conversation words for actions instead as if they somehow made the topic more palatable.

'I got in at 2300hrs and you appear to be confusing me with Big Ben.' The kettle clicked off. 'Coffee?'

'Yes, please.'

I took two mugs from the cupboard next to me. I took a tea bag for mine. 'I need to tell you more about the witch. She was here last night.'

'Here? In the house?' His voiced shot up an octave.

'In the garden. Come on, I'll show you.' I took him into the garden where the first rune was chalked below the kitchen window then walked around the house while I told him about my search for her and confusion about how she could have escaped. As we went back in the front door, I asked him how he had gotten on yesterday.

'Exactly as you expected – I struck out. I'm fine to keep with the task though, give it another go today. It was much more interesting than my usual job.'

'You are returning to that next week though, right?' I couldn't have him quit his job if I could stop him from doing so. He had already been living in my house longer than I expected. I had once read that bachelors tend to develop odd little quirks from living alone. They develop very set ways of doing things and hate to have their routine messed with. I had been like that to start with thanks to my military upbringing and thankfully he hadn't created too much mess yet, but I was unhappy to be sharing my space with a person that did not come with a set of genitalia that complemented rather than matched mine and I was doing my best to keep a lid on it.

'Yeah, I suppose I will have to. They seemed fine about me taking the week off without warning. I have been there for years, and I like to think I am reliable.'

I considered broaching the subject of him going to live elsewhere, like maybe back with his wife but I had already had that conversation with him twice so when I next raised it, I would be much more forceful. The time did not feel right.

A loud and insistent knock at my door ended our conversation. The dogs, a moment ago asleep on the sofa, went whizzing in front of me as I turned and walked toward the door.

The shadow outside was indistinct as always but looked the right height and shape to be a lady. I opened the door and was almost bowled over by Hilary's wife, Anthea pushing by me as she came uninvited into my home.

'Good morning,' I called to her back as it disappeared into my kitchen. Over the top of her head, I could see Hilary frozen like a deer in headlights. His mouth hung open and his eyes were wide with what I assumed was fear.

I saw her arm come up and for a moment I thought she

was going to hit him. Violence was not her intention though; the arm became a finger to poke him with, and she started to screech. 'How dare you not come home grovelling for forgiveness?'

'Sorr…'

'Shut up!' she screamed. She opened her mouth to yell at him again and saw his black eye. 'What happened to your face? No, nevermind. I don't care, you worthless piece of meat. You pathetic man. What on earth have you been doing for the last four nights? Have you been shacked up here with your drinking buddy? Have you been out chasing women?'

'Well, I…'

'Shut up, Hilary,' she drew his nickname out mockingly, doing everything she could to make him feel less of a man. 'How apt that you would be known by a girl's name.' I had often wondered if she called him Brian or used his nickname like everyone else. I wanted to intervene. Had she attempted to hit him I would have been able to step in between them. However, I saw no easy method of halting the barrage of verbal abuse.

'I'm …' he started but was cut off again.

'You're what? You're sorry? You wish you had treated me with more respect? You wish you were more of a man?'

'That's enough,' I interrupted her flow, my voice louder and more insistent than hers. She turned her face to me, her head snapping around to fire back a retort that died on her lips when she saw my face. 'Brian sought refuge in my house. My house that I will eject you from, if necessary, Anthea. I encourage you to calm down and have an open and honest conversation with your husband. I will give you the space to do so, but I have listened to quite enough shouting for one day.'

She opened her mouth and looked like she was about to launch into another round of abuse based on the theme that all men should be castrated. I silenced her by getting in first. I softened my tone, 'Anthea this is my house. I ask only that you respect it.'

For a second, I thought the tactic had worked but her rage level was off the chart and reason was a spec in her rear-view mirror.

'To hell with the pair of you,' she announced as she spun on her heels and stomped in the direction of my front door. 'If you want to come home, I shall expect to find you on the doorstep on your knees begging.'

The door slammed hard behind her.

A moment of silence followed. 'Breakfast?' I asked. I was hungry, and I needed to distract Hilary or lose him in a terrible downward spiral as he spent the day trying to make sense of his life.

Thankfully he nodded, probably not trusting his voice to manage words.

Breakfast was conducted quietly. I left him to his thoughts when it became clear after numerous conversation starters that he did not wish to talk. I cleared the dishes away into the dishwasher and went upstairs for a shower.

When I came back downstairs, dressed and ready for work, Hilary was still where I left him - on his breakfast bar stool staring into a cup of coffee that was now cold. It was 0805hrs and time for me to walk the dogs. It was not raining, and it looked like there were hints of sky peeking through the clouds outside even though it was still dark.

I rapped my knuckles on the counter to get his attention. The dogs started barking, believing the noise was someone at the front door again. I ignored them, I needed them off the sofa anyway. 'Snap out of it, mate.' He looked up with nothing but misery and self-pity in his face. 'Let's focus on something we can control. If you don't want to go to work, I have a task to distract you.'

He nodded. Reset his face and stood up, pushing back his stool with some force as my words found some resonance. 'Yeah. Yes, you're right. I know it. I need to get a grip on my life.'

I put a comradely hand on his shoulder.

'Same task as yesterday?' he asked.

It was my turn to nod. We talked for a while about how yesterday had gone and what he had learned from it. Then I checked his equipment and wished him better luck today. He would call me if he had any success.

I left him in the house as I took the dogs out for a walk around the village. I put my things in the car, including a packed lunch as I was going to take the dogs to work with me. Hilary could lock the house when he left.

Kevin stayed on the windowsill in his tank.

Coffee, Crop Circles and Hopeless Adoration

Through muscle memory I parked behind my old office in the parking space I had been using for more than half a year and only realised my mistake when I got out of the car and my eye caught a piece of loose tarpaulin fluttering in the breeze above my head. The burnt-out structure was still surrounded with scaffolding and secured against the weather.

I slid back into my seat, almost squashing Bull in the process as he had already crossed into the driver's seat to follow me out of the car. With him now balanced on my lap, I reversed out of the space, took the car a further twenty metres and slipped it into the gap between James's Fiesta and Amanda's Mini Cooper.

I found them both in the main office at James's desk, or rather the dachshunds found them by zooming off ahead of me. By the time I arrived, Amanda and James were each scratching a dog belly while my idiot hounds rolled around on their backs with their paws in the air and their heads back in ecstasy.

'Good morning,' I hallooed as I came in.

James answered with his usual, 'Hey, boss.'

From Amanda, I got a smile. 'Good morning, Tempest.' She was radiant as always, but she seemed especially bright today like she had received great news or something. 'Have you got a moment?'

'Of course,' was the only reply I could come up with. She left Dozer on the carpet and led me to her office. Dozer stayed where he was for a second, then realised the attention had stopped, opened his eyes and flipped back onto his feet.

In her office, I thought for a moment she was going to shut the door and wondered what the conversation might entail. I kept quiet, so she could speak.

'Um,' she started.

'Alright. Out with it. What did I do?' My guess was I had done something she didn't like or been caught looking at her bum (not for the first time) and she was trying to form a sentence where she told her employer off.

'Wow. Okay. Did you call Brett?'

Oh. I'd been rumbled already. 'Not exactly,' I replied. I had sent Big Ben to speak with him. 'Essentially though, yes. Please accept my apologies if I overstepped. I felt there was a wrong to make right.'

'Yes.' Her answer came slowly, she was deep in thought. 'I would not normally tolerate interference in my relation-ships, but this time I feel I need to thank you.' Whatever she was thinking about, it was causing a smile to twitch at the corner of her mouth. Then I realised why she looked like a lottery winner this morning: She had gotten laid last night.

The exact details of her reunion with Brett would forever remain a secret, I was sure. However, I allowed myself to be convinced that I was guessing right, and I had lost her. It was a revelation as if my true feelings for her had only just coalesced and shown themselves. I was such a fool. An hour ago, I had been thinking positive thoughts about Natasha. Now they were tossed aside again.

I reached out and took her right hand in both of mine. She met my eyes, a surprised look on her face but she did not pull away. I was going to tell her how I felt. How I wasn't sure I could live without her and that I would do whatever it took to win her love.

'Anyone for coffee?' James yelled from the front of the office.

'Cor, yeah. I'm exhausted,' Amanda called back, leaning around me to focus on James then looking at me again with a cheeky grin. 'I didn't get much sleep last night.'

Any words I had in my head died before they reached my foolish lips.

'Was there something you wanted to say?' she asked.

I was still holding her hand. I gave it a squeeze. 'Just that I am happy for you. I'm glad it worked out.'

'Me too,' she said and gave a hopeful shrug that I translated to "Who Knows". She looked down at her captive hand. I followed her gaze, saw that I was still holding her hand and let it go wondering if I would ever get to touch her again.

I shook myself mentally. I had to change the subject. 'How did the crop circle case go?

Now that her hand was no longer trapped in mine she had moved behind her desk and was powering up her desktop. 'I have a case, that's for sure. Three farmers have joined together to hire us before they go out of business. They signed the contract and paid an advance yesterday, so I will be getting stuck in today.

James stuck his head through the office door next to me. He had his coat on ready to go outside. 'What's it to be?' We gave him our order for the coffee shop, and I handed over a twenty-pound note.

Amanda was unfolding a map on her desk as James went out the door. 'We need more maps. I bought this one yesterday as it shows the area of the farms in some detail.' It was an Ordnance Survey map of Cliffe Woods and the area around it. Amanda now had it held up in both hands looking for a place to stick it. 'Have we got any pins? Or some Blue-Tac?'

'Somewhere, yes.' There was a box of office stationery that had gone into the storage room in the back when we moved in. James had tided and organised since Tuesday though and the contents were now squirreled away wherever he had put them.

I found a roll of Sellotape and ripped off a couple of pieces which then stuck to each other and then my fingers as I tried to separate them. I tried again, this time taking only one piece and advancing toward the map holding it at each end. Amanda pointed to a wall, 'How about there?'

I nodded, and the map went up. More tape was applied, this time by Amanda's far more dextrous hands.

'So, the three farms are here, here and here.' Amanda drew three circles on the map. 'And the crop circles have appeared in these fields.' This time she drew clever concentric circles to represent where the phenomenon had occurred. She stood back. 'That's about it actually. I don't know any more yet.'

This was what I found all the time. I went into cases without the faintest idea how I was going to solve them, but it always seemed to work out. One just had to chip away at information and keep digging until something made sense. The witch case was proving to be just like that, although for once I felt certain that I already knew who the guilty people were, I just couldn't prove it yet.

'Oh, I forgot to mention. You might get a call from a TV show chap. I met him yesterday. He seemed to think I should know him and was doing his best to be charming while mostly making me want to vomit.'

'Sounds like a top bloke. Why will he be contacting me?'

'Well, he might not, but he's the star, his words not mine, of a cable TV show where they search for proof of extra-terrestrial life. It's called Alien Quest. He did tell me what channel it is on, but I wasn't really listening. Anyway, he's investigating the crop circles for his TV show and was at Brompton farm trying to do some filming.'

'How did you end up speaking to him?'

'He cornered me on my way back to my car. He thought maybe I worked at the farm and wanted to ask me some questions. Made a big show of telling me I was too beautiful to not be on camera. As I said, he was trying to be charming. I should have lied and told him I did work there but had to go. Instead, I said I was investigating the crop circles myself and suddenly he was asking question after question. One of his crew found me on the Blue Moon website and then he wanted to know about you. He might never call. I just wanted to warn you, in case he did.'

I pulled out my phone and googled the show. 'Jack Hammer?' I asked showing her the picture on my phone.

'That's him. Fancies himself as a lady's man. I have to believe that he changed his name too. Jack Hammer. He sounds like an adult film star.'

He certainly did.

'Coffee,' James announced coming back through the office front door. He had a tray in one hand and a bag in the other which undoubtedly contained one of the evil doughnuts he favoured.

Amanda and I both abandoned the map to fetch our coffee, then retreated to our respective offices. With Hilary despatched on his task, I was determined that I would find the coroner today and convince her to reopen the cases.

I called the number for the department where she worked. To my surprise, she answered the phone herself.

'Dr. Mallory.'

'Victoria, this is Tempest Michaels.' I made sure my voice had as much honey in it as I could muster. I wanted her to think I was calling to speak to her about personal business.

'Tempest,' she purred back at me. 'How good of you to call. I was just thinking about you.'

'Are you free today? I hoped I might visit you.' I was intentionally keeping my real motive unspoken.

'I have a cadaver they pulled from the river last night to examine, but I can make myself available. I have a private office with a bed in it for when I need to sleep here. We can pick up where we left off.' Her breathing had changed; she was practically panting with excitement.

I checked my watch and replied without committing to her plan. 'I can be with you for 1030hrs. Does that suit you?'

'Indeed, it does.' She made a growling noise like a tiger and laughed. 'Hurry up and get there, big boy. I need my medicine.'

We disconnected. She was a little scary. Were my love life not confusing enough already I would still run a mile despite her attractiveness.

I let Amanda and James know where I was going, called

the dogs and went out the back door. I would drop the dogs at home and go on from there to the hospital in Pembury.

Before I got to the door, a thought occurred to me. 'Did the signwriters come back with the new sign?' I asked James.

'Yes. Yes, they did. They were here yesterday afternoon. It only took them ten minutes to put it back up.'

Amanda was coming over. 'I haven't seen it,' she said as she went out the front door to stand in the street.

Soon all three of us were staring up at the bright new sign. It read Blue Moon Investigation Agency in large block capital letters and to the right was the logo blue moon I had found. I had made the selection quickly to get the job done with a plan that I could always change it later. There would be no need though – the sign was perfect.

Inside the office, Bull barked. I had left them on the other side of the door, a situation no dog is ever happy about. It jolted me from admiring the front façade of my office, so for the second time in a minute, I bid James and Amanda good day and went off to see the coroner.

What the Coroner Thinks

I arrived on time, but Victoria was not available. The lady on reception at the morgue assured me she was busy and asked what I wanted. Her attitude was dismissive as if whatever I wanted had to be insignificant compared to the other tasks she needed to perform, and she could barely find the time to listen to me say that it was a personal matter and to please let her know that I was waiting.

I sat down to wait on an uncomfortable plastic chair in the dingy room that housed the morgue reception. It was a depressingly drab space. I accepted that bright, happy colours would most likely be deemed inappropriate, but the decorator had picked a paint colour most likely labelled "hint of morose" and had then applied it to every wall and the ceiling.

I fiddled with my phone since there wasn't even a magazine to read.

After almost twenty minutes, the door to the side of reception opened and the coroner appeared. She was dressed in a fitted white blouse and straight-legged, grey trousers that met an ankle high boot. It looked expensive and well considered. Her hair was slightly mussed, and I could see a mark on her nose where a face mask had been.

'Sorry. The chap in the river appeared to have been murdered so my examination took far longer than I expected. Have you been here long?'

'No, no. Just a few minutes,' I assured her.

'Please follow me.' The unpleasant receptionist ignored us both as we left her behind. I followed behind as Victoria led me down a short corridor and into her office. On the door was written Dr. Victoria Mallory in a small panel.

She stopped in the doorway and held the door open, then grabbed my arm and stuck her tongue in my mouth as I tried to get through the small gap she had left.

Now I was on tricky ground. I had conned her because nothing was going to happen but if I told her that now, I would be kicked out and have wasted my morning.

'Whoa, slow down,' I laughed playfully as I ducked away to the other side of the room. I took my coat off aggressively and threw it into a chair to show I meant business.

Her eyes sparkled at me, and she started unbuttoning her blouse. She certainly knew what she wanted.

'I think we should play a game,' I announced.

That got her attention. 'What kind of game, you naughty boy?' Her blouse was undone and hanging off her arms to reveal her chest which she was very definitely thrusting at me. I noted again how strong her arms and shoulders looked.

'Let's pretend I'm *pumping* you for information.' I made the sentence all about the word pumping on purpose. 'I want you to answer some questions and my clothes will come off depending on whether you answer or not.'

She closed the distance between us. 'What about my clothes?'

'I promise to take those off once you have me naked. No touching though. Let's make the anticipation build.'

Her pupils dilated right in front of me.

'Question one.' I gripped the button on the right cuff of my shirt, ready to undo it when she answered. She was holding her breath, waiting for me to continue. 'Have you ever had sex in this room before?'

'Twice,' she replied.

'Do you think of yourself as a naughty girl?'

I think she might have actually had a small orgasm when she closed her eyes and breathed out that she was a very naughty girl that needed to be disciplined. One thing I had learned in my limited exploits was that women, even the most ladylike ones, wanted to think of themselves as sexually adventurous and most wanted to be dominated at times in the bedroom. Of course, I was forming my opinions from a small sample of the gender, but I had it right this time.

I untucked my shirt, glad that I had eliminated most of the bloating I had suffered recently and could see my abs again as I exposed my belly.

'Tell me, Victoria, you naughty girl. If Bernhard Myers wasn't killed by lightning, what else could have caused his death?'

Her eyes snapped open.

Too much too soon.

'What?'

I tried to steer back on course. 'Nevermind that. Tell me what you want me to do to you on that bed.'

'I don't believe this,' she snapped. 'You're still convinced they were murdered, and you didn't come here for this at all.' She said indicating her bulbous boobs and toned midriff.

I was trying to see a way of getting this back on track, but it was clear that we were done. I was failing my client though, a man that had been poisoned for his suspicions and was even now fighting for his life somewhere in this very hospital. I had to try something more direct.

'Victoria. You are right. My sole interest here is the case. My client has been poisoned with Anthrax for hiring me and the murderers are going to get away with it if you do not allow the verdicts to be questioned.' She had turned her back on me and was putting her blouse back on. The second time I had watched her do so without having gotten any further than seeing it taken off. Mr Wriggly was going to throw a strop, I could tell.

'Anthrax?' she asked as she turned back to face me. Her face was a mask of anger.

'He's upstairs somewhere being treated. I need your help to bring the people responsible to justice.'

'Because you cannot try a case for murder when the victim is deemed to have died of natural causes,' she finished my sentence.

'Exactly. I apologise for the subterfuge. It seemed necessary, and, though I doubt it makes a difference, I'm really attracted to you. I just cannot allow myself to be *that* guy.' That I had only been on one date with the woman I was talking about and was secretly in love with Amanda instead, I kept to myself.

'You seem like a very decent person, Tempest. But I don't play games. I made my feelings about the verdicts very clear when we first met. My verdicts stand and no court in the land would issue an order to have bodies exhumed and re-examined. I was also clear about my intentions in approaching you. That you have another woman and wish to be honourable is admirable, but ultimately also childish. Be gone, Tempest Michaels and do not come back.'

I felt defeated. I wanted to plead or threaten or do whatever was needed to get her to listen to reason. I saw the futility of it though. Grabbed my coat and without another word, I left.

At the revolving door that led outside, I stopped, turned around and went to visit Mick Cotton, my client. I wasn't certain that the hospital would contact me if he died. Now that I thought about it, they hadn't even taken my number, so I wanted to see if he was still breathing and if so if his condition had improved.

I went back to the main reception desk to wait patiently for one of the ladies there to become available. The elderly couple in front of me shuffled off, their matter dealt with and the lady behind the desk turned her attention to me.

I enquired about Mick Cotton and where I could find him. She tapped a few keys and gave me a ward and room number.

Entering the ward, I fetched upon another reception where yet again I had to introduce myself and explain why I was there. I was willing to believe the practice was necessary but couldn't imagine what they were trying to protect against with all the security hoops to jump through.

Mick was wired up to several machines that were monitoring heart rate, blood oxygen, temperature and other functions I couldn't identify. He had colour in his face though and looked rested. He was in a ward labelled special care which I assumed was one down from intensive care, for those not circling the drain of life.

He was also in a room by himself. I popped my head back out, looked around and caught the attention of a lady in uniform that was either a nurse or an orderly or something. Did they wear different uniforms for different roles? Big Ben would know. He liked a woman in uniform.

Or out of it for that matter.

It turned out that the lady was one of the doctors. I enquired about Mick's health and general condition, whether he had woken up yet and said that I was a friend, the lie once again more sensible than the truth.

He hadn't woken yet, was considered stable and had been taken out of the chemically induced coma early this morning. A full recovery was expected but a timescale couldn't be put on when he might wake up.

On my way back to my car my phone rang. Retrieving it from my pocket, I could see that the caller was Hilary. 'What have you got?' I asked.

'Movement.'

'Where are you?' On hearing his reply, I told him to follow at a distance, not be spotted and let me know what happened next.

My Spy

It was after lunch when I got back to my house. I didn't need to make lunch as I had been carrying it around since this morning. At this time of year, I could leave food in my car all day without concern that it might perish. Without the heating on, it was like a fridge inside.

The Tupperware box of chickpeas, boiled eggs, salad leaves, avocado, and seeds was tasty and filling if not entirely satisfying. I was craving a cheeseburger and doing what I could to ignore it.

My phone rang again. It was Hilary once more.

'She's here.' I could hear the nervousness in his voice.

'Have you got a good view?'

'Not really?'

'Can you move position, get to a better spot?'

'I'll try.'

I waited for his voice to return. There was a knock at my door. The dogs went nuts as usual.

'What the hell was that?' Hilary asked.

'Someone knocked on the door.' By the time I had

228

answered Hilary I had crossed to the front door and peeked outside.

Frank's odd little face was beaming back at me. 'Wotcha, Tempest. Care to let me in?' He was burdened with a heavy-looking armful of books. I pushed the door open and stepped out of the way to allow him passage. He came in, moving carefully because the dachshunds were dancing around in front of him and he couldn't see them with his armful of books.

'Hilary hold on a second.' I put the phone on a handy shelf and scooped the sausages. They wriggled in their excitement. There was someone to see and that meant being made a fuss of.

Frank made his way to the breakfast bar where he relieved himself of his burden with a loud thud that ejected a cloud of dust. Frank had some old books. He could see I was on the phone so held his left hand up and put the right hand over the top of it to form a tee shape.

I nodded and pointed to the kettle, so he knew to just crack on.

'What are they doing now?' I asked Hilary. He had moved as suggested and claimed to now have an uninterrupted view where he couldn't easily be seen watching.

'Erm, they are talking. They have a pot of tea between them and some cake.'

'Okay, buddy. As much detail as possible.'

'Oh. Yeah, okay. I think the cake is Battenberg. It's turned side on from where I am, but I should be able to tell when they cut it.'

I slapped my face with my spare hand. 'Not the cake, Hilary. More detail about the target.'

'Sorry. Sorry. That was obvious. I'm just nervous and not really thinking.'

'How about the bug. Remember the ruse we talked about. Just act that out and make sure you attach the bug to the underside of the table when you grip it.'

'Okay.' He swallowed, the nervous noise quite audible.

'It's no big deal. You just need to drop it, apologise and retrieve it. No big deal and you barely need to speak.'

Hilary had been set the task of tailing the four wives, sorry I should correct that, two wives and two not even slightly grieving widows. When he volunteered to help, I saw a simple task that I couldn't perform myself because they knew what I looked like. Hilary was so ordinary looking, so unremarkable, that he could follow them around without ever being noticed. Even his car was nondescript – a drab brown estate. Even so I sent him to watch their houses but advised him to move around rather than attract suspicion by staying in the same place all day. The end goal was to catch them meeting with the witch again. I wanted to find out who she was, where she lived and what the heck was going on.

Hilary was my spy.

If he got lucky, he would see them meet the witch and would be able to tail her home or to somewhere. If he was even luckier, he would have a chance to record their conversation and that was what he was about to try to do.

I had given him a small one-way listening device. It came with a very sticky pad on the back. He also had one of my cameras. Both were to be deployed if he got the chance. This was it. This morning, I had made him practice dropping his keys and kicking them with a swinging foot as he walked to make it look accidental. He was rubbish at it, but with fifty attempts he was close enough that he just looked clumsy and weird.

He hadn't spoken for more than a minute. 'Hilary are you still there?'

More silence.

'Hilary?'

More silence. I took the phone from my ear to stare at it accusingly.

'I did it,' Hilary's voice squeaked down the phone.

Frank had been listening quietly while making the tea. I gave him a thumbs up as he handed me a steaming mug. Then, with the phone in the crook of my neck, I flipped my laptop open. If the damned app worked, I would be able to listen in from my kitchen.

'I got the camera up as well,' he bragged, evidently proud of his achievements.

As the app opened, the view I had been hoping for popped up in a corner of the screen. I enlarged it but there was no volume. I could see the four women all squeezed in around one side of a table with the witch on the other side like they wanted to keep their distance from her.

'Hilary, are you sure you turned the bug on?'

'Err, no. Not entirely. I think I did what you said.' He really did sound unsure.

I spotted then that the volume was off on my laptop. As I pressed a key, their voices sprang to life to match the movement of their lips.

'... two sugars for me thanks.' It was Mabel speaking. Edna was playing host and pouring the tea.

'You can manage to do your own sugar, Mabel. You might be the first of us to get rich, but we won't be far behind.'

'I'm sure that's not what she meant, Edna,' chided Dorothy.

Edna cocked an eyebrow at them both, then swivelled in her chair to face the witch.

'What are we watching here, Tempest?' asked Frank.

'Frank. I'm sorry. I haven't so much as greeted you yet. Thank you for the tea. These are the four ladies that have colluded to murder their husbands. And that,' I pointed to the screen. 'Is the witch.'

'Huarrraagh!' Was the noise Frank made as he all but backflipped to get away from the laptop. In doing so, he dropped his mug of tea, which broke on impact with the floor.

The dachshunds skidded to a halt less than a second later having probably detected the noise of the cup falling through the air long before it hit the ground. They began lapping up the tea as I retrieved the broken bits of the mug. I made a point of turning the volume up so I could hear it over the bedlam in my kitchen.

'Anything for you, Rose?' Edna asked the witch. At last, I had a name or at least part of one.

'No, Edna. We need to get to business. I will call up the next storm this weekend and Barbara still hasn't supplied me with the necessary ingredients for my spell.'

'Can't Edna go next?' Barbara asked.

Frank had sidled back up to stand a pace behind me. I glanced at him. He was white as a sheet.

The witch was just staring at Barbara.

'I don't want to go next,' Barbara explained.

'You're next,' the witch insisted.

'But, but, I'm not sure I want to,' Barbara wailed. 'My Eddie has been really sweet to me lately. He thought I would be upset by Dorothy and Mabel losing their husbands so suddenly. He even bought me flowers.'

'Oh, go on, Barbara. Let Rose kill him. It's ever so good when they've gone.' chipped in Mabel helpfully.

'No,' she replied. 'I don't want to.'

The witch's arm flashed out to grab Barbara's arm in a bony vice-grip. 'I said you're next. We are committed now, or would you rather I changed it and said that *you* are next?'

'You wouldn't!' Barbara's horrified voice came back, but it was clear she wasn't at all sure that the witch wouldn't change her target. 'You said we were women banding together against the evil men in our lives, standing up to claim what is rightfully ours.'

This was solid gold, and I was recording it all.

'You will go through with it, little Barbara, or I will make you regret meeting me.' The witch was really quite scary.

I turned to Frank. 'You know that's just a scary old lady, right?'

He shook his head. 'No, it isn't, Tempest.'

Suddenly the conversation stopped. Or so I thought. When I looked at the screen they were still talking but I could no longer hear them. I turned the volume all the way up and could just about hear that they were speaking but making out the words was impossible.

Squinting at the screen I saw the problem. The bug had fallen to the floor. It was under the table but very visible. Either Hilary hadn't stuck it on very well, or he had inadvertently found a greasy mark. Either way, I was going to get nothing further.

Was what I had enough to convince the police to act? It was a great question. I downloaded and compressed the file.

'Frank I'm going to where they are in about sixty seconds. Right after I email this in fact. That old lady is killing men. My guess is that she's charging the ladies a cut of their insurance payouts, but you heard her plan to kill the next lady's husband, right?'

'Yeah, WITH MAGIC!' Frank shouted. He thought it was a valid point.

I could have argued with him, but I knew there was no point. 'I'm going now. I think you should come with me because I'm going to confront the woman and hopefully hold her there until the police arrive. If I am wrong, you can watch her turn me into a frog.'

I finished typing a note to accompany the video file and emailed the whole thing to Chief Inspector Quinn, his boss, his boss's boss and to the internal group cc that would get it into the inbox of every police officer in Maidstone. Having Amanda around had already proven useful, getting hold of email addresses was bonus material.

'Try ignoring that,' I said as I pressed send.

Behind me, caught in indecision, Frank didn't know what to do.

'It's not a witch, Frank.'

'Yes, it is!'

To Catch a Witch

I was pushing the speed limit on the back road that would get me to West Malling and the little tearoom they were in. In the passenger seat, Frank was doing what Frank does. He was being weird.

He had rosary beads wrapped around his right fist and was reading from the Bible while holding it upside down. I considered asking what he was doing but then I would have to listen to the answer. My hope in bringing him along was that he would see the witch in her true light as a frail old lady.

There was still a little voice at the back of my head reminding me that the frail old lady had found a way to make lightning rip men apart in their own homes.

I ignored it.

She had admitted her guilt and she was going down.

I had told Hilary to hang tight and that we would be there in fifteen minutes or less before disconnecting the call. Then I had called Maidstone police station from the car and asked for CI Quinn. The response I got was that he was unavailable. I couldn't tell if that meant he didn't want to talk to me or genuinely wasn't available.

I left a message for him to call me.

As we neared West Malling, I began to hope that there would be somewhere to park. Swooping in to confront the witch while she was still with the other ladies would be far harder if I had to circle for ten minutes looking for a spot.

I got lucky again though as a car was just pulling out of a spot in front of the pub they had been in a few days ago. The tea shop was just down the road, less than fifty yards from my car.

'Come on, Frank.' I nudged him as I took off my seat belt. I had no intention of hanging around to wait for him if he decided to dawdle. As I took off down the street, I heard the passenger's door thunk shut behind me and set of running footsteps keeping pace at my heels. A quick check over my shoulder confirmed he was following.

I had never been in the tearoom, so the orientation of the room itself was a mystery to me. Coming in through the front door, a young woman with some menus under her arm attempted to greet me, but I rudely rushed by her to find Hilary and the table of women.

Where were they? The building was an old one, so it had odd alcoves, but I believed I was seeing all of it. I stood in the middle of the room and spun in place. No Hilary, no table of witches. Then my heart sank as I recognised their table.

It was empty.

My listening device was still on the floor where it had fallen. I had missed them, but where was Hilary? Oh, my God! Had they taken him?

'Hi, Tempest,' Hilary said by my ear, making my heart stop. I swear a little bit of wee came out.

'You just missed them.' He was out of breath. 'I got them on camera though.' He held up his phone to show me.

'Where is the witch?' I begged him. She was the only one I needed.

'Oh, she went into the ladies toilet. Hasn't come out yet.'

'Where?'

He pointed, and I ran. She wasn't getting away for the third time. In the dimming light outside, blue flashing lights were filling the air. Someone had reacted to the email and my call, and it looked like they sent half the force.

I found the door to the ladies toilet, paused for a heart-beat and went in. Straight ahead of me was a mother bent down in front of a little girl who was sitting on a toilet with her knickers around her ankles. The stall door was open because mum didn't fit in it otherwise.

The little girl screamed in the wonderfully high-pitched tone that mostly only dogs can hear. I backed out of the room at speed, my ears assailed by the noise and my face flushing from the embarrassing scene.

The mum burst out after me though. 'Pervert!' she yelled accusingly.

My lips flapped a couple of times, but no words found their way out.

She turned to the small crowd inside the establishment. Most of them were already looking our way. 'Pervert!' she shouted and pointed. A man stood up. 'Dave, he was ogling our little girl in the toilets.'

'What?' The man looked rough. Even his tattoos had tattoos. 'Faye call the police.' He was clearly talking to the little girl's mother, and he was almost certainly the dad. I didn't need this hassle right now. Or ever for that matter, but definitely not now.

I started to protest my innocence but just as Dave came at me, his massive hands balling into fists, the backdoor to the tearoom opened behind me and uniformed police were coming in. It was a coordinated movement as they were coming through the door at the other end of the tearoom as well.

Dave froze, indecision etched on his face. I looked for a uniformed face I recognised and latched onto them. I was swept into the room with their passing, leaving Dave forgotten behind me.

The police were not armed, but their sudden presence had alarmed some of the customers quietly eating their tea and cake. I heard Quinn's voice before I saw him.

'Ladies and Gentlemen, please do not be alarmed. We will not take up more than a few moments of your time. It's imperative though that you remain seated while we conduct our operation. Thank you for your cooperation.'

He spotted me and crooked a finger at me, beckoning me over. I stood my ground and did the same back. When he didn't move either I shouted across the room to him instead.

'You missed them. We both did. You can round the ladies up at their houses. I gave you their addresses.' It had all been on the email. 'The fifth lady is still unidentified.'

'Don't tell me how to do my job, Mr Michaels,' he snapped. He sounded annoyed. I was getting to him.

Good. Pompous tit.

He whispered to the sergeant next to him, an action which elicited a reaction that took most of the police at that end of the building back out the front door. Now CI Quinn thought it acceptable to cross the room to speak with me.

'There'll be no press interview for you to crash this time, Michaels. No glory for you to snatch.'

I couldn't work the man out. I cared not for glory, nor much about publicity. They were clearly goals he cherished, but he acted as if I hadn't just presented him with a solved case. A day ago, he had turfed me out of his station for even suggesting I had a crime for him to investigate.

'You're a dick.' It seemed like the right thing to say, and I said it in front of half a dozen of his junior officers.

'What did you say?'

'Not an impressive, meaty dick though. Not one with some girth that some would consider worthy of applause. More like a tiny, insignificant dick. You know, hung like a baby carrot. That kind of dick. That's the kind of dick you are.' I was finished with the dick comparison. It had been something that Big Ben might have said and quite out of keeping with my usual manner of speaking. It felt right though. Like I had got something off my chest.

Quinn was tensing his body. He looked like he was going to hit me. I kind of wished he would.

I didn't give him the chance though. I looked across to make sure Frank and Hilary were there and turned my back to Quinn. He was insignificant.

Behind me were the toilets still and in the small passage that led to the back door were some of the police officers still. 'Has anyone come out of the ladies?' I asked them.

'The lady over there with the little girl,' a short blonde female office answered.

Where she was pointing Dave, Faye, and their daughter were watching the spectacle in front of them the same as everyone else in the room was.

'Sorry about earlier,' I offered the trio. 'I was trying to catch a bad person.' I worried that the little girl might be traumatised by my bursting in on her. Nothing I could do about it now though.

'The fifth woman, the murderer was last seen going into those toilets. She must be eighty years old so if she hasn't come out, she's still in there.'

'Let's go see,' the female officer said and pushed the door open for me.

It was empty. Quite utterly empty. Frank would be pleased and would have a theory to explain how she was vanishing into thin air.

I went to the end stall and stood on the toilet bowl. At head height was a window. I pushed it open and looked outside.

'I thought you said she was eighty?' the lady cop pointed out.

'I did.' I scratched my chin. There was nothing more to see so I climbed down and went back out to the tearoom. CI Quinn was already gone.

Only one officer remained beside the one that had come into the toilet with me. 'They are waiting outside,' she informed her colleague. They went out the back door and were gone.

The ladies would all be arrested and questioned. I was certain of that. The video and audio footage Hilary had captured was sufficient for prosecution. I had reason to feel good, but it was dark, and I had lost the witch again. She was out there somewhere and might do anything.

I shrugged to myself. There didn't seem to be anything I could do about it now and it was my mum's birthday party tonight.

Time to go home.

As we walked up the street, I put my arm around Hilary's shoulders. 'Do you have plans for tonight?'

Mum's Birthday Party

THURSDAY, NOVEMBER 10TH 1935HRS

I had elected to arrive late for mum's party to avoid some of the inevitable work involved in setting it up, but mostly because it would limit the time I would spend being shown around to her friends' unmarried daughters. I wondered if there would even be any men there. Surely some of her friends had husbands or sons.

I was right in that they did and there were men present, but they were outnumbered at least two to one. From the outside of the house, it was impossible to tell there was a party happening at all. The rhythmic thump of bass one might associate with a party was absent as was any other noise. Even when I opened the front door, very little sound escaped into the cool evening air outside.

'Are you sure this is alright?' asked Hilary. He was standing just behind me and looking uncomfortable.

'Of course,' I replied. 'They will be happy to have someone new to meet.'

I was a lying dog. I had invited Hilary along because a new man in the room would attract attention from the awful collection of single daughters and their mothers that formed the dominant party in my mother's friendship circle. Spending an evening talking to some of them and his wife would seem like a catch again. I was convinced I had seen the worst of her when she burst into my house this morning and that the two of them had enjoyed a loving marriage for the most part even if she did wear the trousers.

I steeled myself for the task ahead and let myself in.

Cliff Richard was crooning in the background, but not at a volume that would interfere with conversation. 'Hello, Tempest,' said a lady that I recognised but couldn't name. Mum had a lot of friends like that. Women that had known me since I was a baby, or at least a young child and talked to me as if we were old friends. That I had been absent, away somewhere with the Army for most of my adult life and thus had never spoken to them as an adult, or indeed at any point in the last two decades always seemed to escape them.

I replied anyway and asked her if she knew where my parents were. She pointed to the lounge. Mother was shorter than most of the people in the room, but then she cackled at something someone had said which made it easy to pinpoint her. As the lady in front of her moved, something caught the light and sparkled by my mother's face.

It was a giant ruby earring dangling from her left ear. It was swishing about under her hair as she talked. Pinned to her dress was the enormous brooch just above her left breast. No doubt her friends were all marvelling at the new jewellery and speculating about its origin or whether it was even real. Would any of them connect the short line of dots from their trip to Cornwall and the globally publicised treasure found there a few days ago? I might need to sow a few seeds of doubt this evening to throw people off the scent.

Especially since I didn't know how much of the treasure my dad had stuffed into his pockets.

'Uncle Tempest!' The cry came simultaneously from my nephew and niece, my sister's young children. They had spotted me from the place on the carpet where they were playing with my mother's crystal animal ornaments. I doubted they were allowed to touch them but would not be the one to stop them.

'Hi, kids,' I replied as I bent down to get a proper look at them.

'Where are the dogs?' asked Martha, looking around and beyond me for them.

'I left them at home, sweetie. Too many people here. They might get trodden on,' I explained.

It was not the answer she was looking for. 'Boring,' she replied, her attention turning back away from me, the excitement of my arrival forgotten.

'Hey, kid,' came my dad's voice from just behind me. I turned to find him carrying a tray of full wine glasses. 'Want one?' he asked.

'No thanks. I'm driving so will play it safe and have nothing. This is Brian.' I introduced the sorry-looking man standing behind me. 'Shall I distribute those for you? You look like you could do with a break.' He didn't actually. He looked like he was having fun and was using the need to perform tasks as a way to keep moving and thus avoid conversation with his wife's friends. But I had just intro-duced someone, so a shaking of hands was required.

'Sure,' he said as he handed over the tray. 'Pleased to meet you, Brian. Tell me, what keeps you busy?'

I left them to it and waded into the crowd in my parent's living room.

'Oh, Tempest. I'm so glad you are here. We were just

talking about you,' said my mother as I neared the group she was in. I already didn't like the sound of this. 'This is Madeline Munroe.' She said, swishing her arm like she was presenting a prize on a TV show.

Madeline was cast from the same mould as many of the women in the room and had what my mother would refer to as child-bearing hips. Madeline smiled at me and extended her hand.

I stared dumbly at it. I was using both hands to hold the tray of wine. 'Perhaps you could all unburden me of the drinks I am holding?' I prompted.

A chorus of, 'Oh, yes,' and 'Of course,' preceded the tray being empty about three seconds later.

Now that I could hold it with one hand, I shook Madeline's. 'Very pleased to meet you,' I said, not really meaning a word of it. Madeline was undoubtedly very nice but had a stern face that was neither warm nor welcoming. I placed her age at around thirty-two and her height at five feet eight inches. She was neither attractive nor repellent and was probably single and being subjected to the same indignity that my mother always put me through. The almost carbon copy next to her, similar in every aspect but age, was her mother..

Madeline smiled awkwardly at me, and I saw a chance to make the evening easier for us both.

'Could you spare me a minute?' I asked. I had failed to release her hand and was now tugging on it ever so gently and indicating we should move away from our mothers.

She came with me to a space in the corner of the room, passing between our mothers and the other women she had been with who were now all looking at each other and winking or exchanging knowing looks. They were exasperating.

'Madeline, am I right to assume that your mother drags you along to these events and parades you around like a prize to be won? My mother insists on trying to marry me off.'

'God, yes,' she replied, her shoulders slumping as the tension went out of them. 'She just won't stop going on about my biological clock.'

I laughed. 'That sounds very familiar. Mine is desperate for me to produce grandchildren. I worry sometimes that I will turn up to find she has a woman upstairs that she knows to be ovulating.'

Madeline's eyes widened at the thought. 'God, that's terrible. Mine wants me to be a virgin on my wedding night so disapproves of me dating – they won't buy the cow if they have already had the milk,' she said in a mocking parody of her mother's voice. 'So somehow I have to produce children without having sex and all the men I meet are so hopeless.'

I laughed again, this time because I now fell into the category of men that she had met, although I was certain that hadn't been the intention of her comment.

She changed the topic. 'So, this would normally be the bit where I start small talk and ask what you do for a living. I already know the answer to that one though.'

'Oh?'

'Everyone does. I don't think many of them can decide what to make of it, but they talk about it a lot. Your mother is always regaling them with your latest exploits.'

'I expect she makes it sound more exciting than it is.'

'Maybe, but it still looks pretty exciting. You were on TV last week having been involved in a dawn raid on a drug factory in Bearsted. I teach six-year-olds how to spell their name and add to twelve.'

She had me there. 'Have you been teaching long?'

We talked for a while. It was pleasant and kept our mothers off our backs but we both knew we would get grilled about the conversation later and be asked when we were seeing each other again. Thankfully she had also expressed that she was seeing someone.

Dad came by with a tray of sausage rolls. Madeline snagged one while I declined but a troubling thought occurred to me. 'Dad where is Hilary?'

'Hilary?'

'I mean Brian.'

Dad looked directly at me. 'Is he another cross-dresser that likes to pretend to be a lady at the weekends?' He was smiling with an evil smile. He had the same beliefs as me and didn't care what people did for the most part but knew that my mother's head had damned near rotated off its shoulders when she discovered I had employed an assistant that was gender neutral.

'No, dad. His last name is Clinton.'

'Gotcha.' He winked. 'As for his whereabouts, I don't actually know. I excused myself to deal with the food. Last I saw he was chatting with Debbie.'

Oh no.

'Won't you please excuse me?' I abandoned Madeline and went to look for him.

I couldn't see her anywhere. The house wasn't so big that she could easily hide, and in the end, I found her in the kitchen where she was pinning Hilary in place by blocking the doorway. She wasn't touching him that I could see, although he was cowering into the wall and might have been trying to claw his way through it as his hands were behind his back. Instead, she was standing in front of him with one arm up to lean on the wall, so she formed a diagonal barrier from the bottom corner of one wall to near the top corner of the other wall in the narrow galley kitchen.

'Hello, Debbie,' I announced my presence.

'Oh, hi, Tempest. Brian and I were just getting to know one another.'

'No, we weren't,' he squeaked.

'Yes, we were, silly. It seems we are both single currently.'

'No, I'm not.'

'Your wife kicked you out, darling. You said so yourself. No fun for *little* Brian down there, so your new friend Debbie is going to help you out with that, isn't she?'

Hilary locked eyes with me. 'Help,' he mouthed silently. It was a request I could understand. I had suffered a similar encounter myself one cold night when she came to my house wearing nothing but lingerie.

'Sorry, old boy. You're on your own with this one.' I backed out the door.

I heard him gasp as Debbie advanced on him.

I jumped back through the doorway. 'Only joking! Debbie, I apologise for denying you your prize. This one needs to go home to his wife. I worry that a night of passion with you might ruin him forever.'

I reached under Debbie's arm, snagged hold of Hilary's shirt, and yanked him out of harm's way.

'Everything alright?' my father asked on his way back to the kitchen with an empty tray.

'Peachy,' I called out as I turned a corner with Hilary still in tow.

Just coming out of the toilet with Martha at her side was my sister. I had spotted her and her husband a couple of times across the room but hadn't managed to speak to either yet.

'Hey, sis.' I pulled her into a hug. Her belly was seriously swollen now, making her look like a watermelon about her middle. 'How are you holding up?'

Rachael took my question as a cue to unload on me the long list of woes she was suffering in the late stages of pregnancy. I listened patiently.

Her husband Chris found us. 'Hi, Tempest.' I hadn't seen him or spoken to him in more than a year. There was no time for a catch up now either though as they were leaving. It was well after the children's bedtime, and he insisted that Rachael needed to go home and lie down. We shook hands and that was about it.

Mum's birthday party drew to a natural close as people started to drift away around 2200hrs. Some had work, although many of her friends were retired. Hilary had found some whisky and sunk a couple of neat ones to recover from his fright. He looked sleepy now.

I kissed my mother, shook my father's hand and pushed Hilary out the door.

Driving home, I planned out what I needed to do on Friday.

Just before setting off, I had received a phone call from a Sergeant Butterworth at Maidstone Police Station. Edna, Barbara, Mabel, and Dorothy had all been arrested yesterday evening and were being held for questioning regarding the deaths of Bernhard Myers and Andrew Cotton. I needed to come to the station to give a statement regarding my involvement.

I agreed to do so the next morning. It would eat up a chunk of my day but if a conviction was secured then everyone wins. Except the ladies of course, but, you know, don't go murdering.

The witch was still out there somewhere. A strange little

old lady that had eluded me every time I had tried to follow her. I was not going to label it as vanishing. Despite her age, she had somehow gone out the window at the tearoom this afternoon. Or she had never gone in there and Hilary was mistaken.

The case for my client was solved. He had asked me to prove that his stepmother had murdered his father. I wasn't content to leave it there though, nor was I certain that the witch would scarper. She had already been to my house once, I hadn't imagined seeing her in my garden. So, for me, the case was still running.

I would start working on a next case or cases, would see if Amanda needed any assistance with what she was working on and would continue to develop the business. However, I felt a need to find the old lady at the bottom of it all. The police might be able to obtain confessions from the ladies already in custody and from that might learn the old lady's name and address. I had a feeling though that none of them really knew who she was.

As I drifted off to sleep, my two dachshunds snoring quietly on the duvet next to me, it was the witch's face that I was picturing, framed in the flash of lightning outside my window.

Mick Cotton Lives

I had nightmares that night. This was not all that unusual, but mostly my dreams sucked me back into a time when I was in uniform and in combat, the horror of such events permanently etched into my brain in vivid detail.

My nightmare though had been all to do with the witch. I was still calling her that even though I now knew her first name. I had awoken to find her standing at the foot of my bed, lightning crackling from her fingers like a Sith Lord. She grinned at me as I sat up in bed startled, then blasted me with both hands. The resulting shock caused me to actually wake.

I left the bed to get a drink of water. When I returned, the dachshunds had retreated under the bed, something they rarely do so I must have been thrashing around for some time before I woke up.

Sleep found me again, this time blissfully peaceful until I woke to visit the gym at 0500hrs.

Sitting at my breakfast bar nearly three hours later, I was still playing the nightmare over in my head. The TV was on, the newscaster talking about an earthquake in Taiwan, but it washed over me. I was trying to distract myself by thinking about Natasha. Following our date on Wednesday I had asked her to let me know if she wanted to see me again and left it for her to text me. Thirty-six hours later I had heard nothing, so in typical Tempest Michaels style I was starting to assume that she wasn't going to text. I reminded myself that it had only been one day so far, and she might message me at any moment.

My phone rang. I snatched for it, hoping to see Natasha's name on the screen. When I didn't recognise the number, I acknowledged to myself that I had genuinely been keen to speak with her. This was a switch from constantly mooning over Amanda. I got on with the task of answering the call. 'Blue Moon Investigations, Tempest Michaels speaking. Good morning.'

'Mr Michaels, this is Mavis Cruet.' The voice was that of a late middle-aged woman. 'I work at Pembury Hospital in the Special Care unit. I have an instruction to call you if Mr Cotton wakes up.'

That brought my attention back to the now.

'He's awake?'

'He's eating some breakfast right now,' her voice bright with the good news.

'Thank you for letting me know. Will he be released today?'

'Oh, I shouldn't think so but that will be down to his doctors. Would you like to speak with him?'

It hadn't occurred to me to ask. 'Yes please.'

There was quiet for a moment while she carried the handset to his room. 'Hi, this is Mick Cotton.'

'Mick, good morning. This is Tempest. So glad to have you back among the living.'

He chuckled at the other end. 'I believe I have your fast reactions to thank for that.'

'I think the credit must go to the doctors and nurses. All I did was call them.' I hated being praised.

'That's very gracious of you, but without you I would have died at my house.'

'Think nothing of it. How are you feeling?' I asked to move the conversation on.

'As well as can be expected. They have said I will be weak for a while. Mostly I woke up hungry and thirsty, but they are looking after me.'

'Have they told you the news about your stepmother?'

'No.' Suddenly his interest was piqued.

I loved being able to call my clients with good news. 'She was arrested yesterday along with her three friends.'

At the other end of the phone, he whooped. 'Tempest you are brilliant. I'm so glad I called you. So glad I brought my suspicions to you. Has she been charged?'

'That I don't know. It's out of my hands now. The police will conduct the investigation and pursue a conviction if there is enough evidence. I have provided them with a video where the four ladies discuss the murder, so I doubt she will be able to wiggle free.'

'Good. I hope they hang the old bag.' I couldn't agree with his sentiment but then she hadn't murdered my father. I might feel entirely different if she had.

I thought of something to ask him. 'Mick have you any idea how the Anthrax got into your system?' I had assumed his poisoning was linked to the murders and perpetrated by the same old lady posing as a witch. He had runes on his house; a piece of evidence I would be asking the police to consider when I met with them later this morning.

Hilary walked into the kitchen, waving a hello as he

came. He saw that I was on the phone and kept quiet, though he did press the kettle into service.

It started to hiss as Mick gave me his answer. 'None at all. They said the reaction time to it entering my system and getting sick is measured in hours and I had been at home all morning. I had a guest at the house the previous night, so I cannot imagine where I picked up Anthrax.'

I thought about that for a moment. 'A house guest? You mean a woman, like a girlfriend?' He gave off a hetero-sexual vibe.

'Err, yes. Not a girlfriend though. I only met her yester-day.' He sounded a little boastful like he had picked up a hot girl by dint of being worthy.

I checked my watch. I needed to get moving. I wasn't sure, but the woman sounded suspicious. I also needed to learn more about Anthrax poisoning. 'Listen, Mick, I'm on my way to the police station this morning to give evidence regarding your stepmother. I don't know how long that will take but I'm coming to you afterwards. If they release you, please message me and if the woman contacts you again… Mick, have you got her number?'

'Yeah, in my phone. I don't know where that is though. I'll ask Mavis. Hold on…'

'No. I'll call you back. Just… It might be nothing.' I had a theory forming and I needed to let it simmer for a while. 'Just give me a few hours, okay? If the lady calls, please just say you will call her later and don't let her visit you.'

We disconnected. I drummed my fingers on the table and pursed my lips. There was something here that I wasn't seeing, only glimpsing.

I turned to face Hilary. 'What's your plan for the day?'

'I don't have one. I have a bit of a headache actually.'

'Okay. Feel free to keep the dogs company. I don't have

anything for you to do I'm afraid. No secret missions to deploy you on. Not yet at least. I have to go to the police station, so I might be late back for lunch. If you are still here then, can you take the dogs for a walk please?'

'Of course.'

'Righto. See you later then.' I grabbed my phone, checked my wallet and keys were in my pockets, slung my bag over my shoulder and stood up. In the living room I gave the dogs a quick pat and went out the door.

It was time to see the police.

Maidstone Police Station

It irked me that I had to pay for parking when I was at the station to assist them with their enquiries. That was how it would be recorded; I was assisting them. There was a general consensus to ignore the inconvenient fact that I had presented them with the case a day before they did anything and had pretty much solved the whole thing for them. I asked the desk sergeant, the same ignorant arsehole that had been there on Wednesday, about validating my parking ticket. He just made a derisory noise in my direction and walked away.

I wasn't made to wait too long for once. A different sergeant came through a door to escort me to an interview room. It was one I had been in before. A few weeks ago, a man that had attacked me while dressed as a Klown had tried to kill me again by throwing himself over the table I was now taking a seat at.

Having escorted me into the room, the sergeant left me there and closed the door as he went out. I leaned over, curious and tried the lock but I wasn't locked in, my paranoia about what tricks CI Quinn might play was unfounded.

I didn't even have to wait long, as less than a minute later CI Quinn himself together with the same Sergeant entered the room.

Warily we shook hands, but there were no words of animosity exchanged. CI Quinn's Sergeant, who I soon learned to be named Barraclough, went through the preliminaries such as setting up the tape-recording device and listing who was present.

'Shall we begin?' I asked when it seemed there was nothing else they needed to do.

CI Quinn leaned forward in his chair. The two of them had positioned themselves on the opposite side of the table to me. 'Mr Michaels. Please tell us in detail how you came to learn that Mabel Cotton, Dorothy Myers, Edna Hinkley, and Barbara Tremont were conspiring to kill their husbands.'

As he sat back into his chair I began talking, leading them through the initial contact with the client, the runes on the houses, the overheard conversation at the golf club and on to the stakeout that Hilary conducted at the tearoom in West Malling. I explained as best as I could about the old lady and her role in the murders and did so without ever referring to her as a witch. Quinn stopped me though when I started talking about the coroner.

'You think the coroner, Dr. Mallory is involved?' he asked.

'I cannot see how she could mistake a death by lightning for whatever it was that actually killed them. We have the wives on camera discussing the deaths and Rose, the old lady, stating that she's going to call up a storm this weekend to kill Edna Hinkley's husband. While I'm quite sure her witch act is all hokum, the wives have bought into it and are allowing Rose to murder them. They couldn't possibly hope to get away with it unless the coroner that would determine the cause of death was on the payroll.'

'Nonsense, Mr Michaels. I know Dr. Mallory socially. She isn't involved in any conspiracy to cover up a series of murders.' I wondered if socially meant they were sleeping together but didn't voice my question. 'Dr. Mallory will have given a death verdict based on the evidence she was presented with. You said yourself that you don't know how they are creating the lightning effect. When *we* find the old lady, the truth will be revealed.'

I pondered that statement for a while. Then I checked my watch. We had been going for more than two hours. I wanted to continue to argue that Dr. Mallory was involved but I saw the futility in it. CI Quinn was not one to listen. Certainly not to anything I had to say.

If I pushed the matter, he would continue to scoff at me. I cut my losses.

'Is there anything else that you remember that will be of interest to my investigation?' he asked.

I shook my head. We were done.

Coming out of the station I called Mick Cotton's mobile number. I hoped he would have found it by now.

He answered, but only after it had rung for an age and I thought it was about to go to voicemail. 'Hi, is that you, Tempest. I was asleep, sorry.'

'My apologies for waking you. I'm on my way to the hospital. You're not about to be released, are you?'

'No, they said I had to stay for at least another day.'

'I'll be there within the hour.'

I debated going home to walk the dogs, but this task was more pressing, plus Hilary was there. It was just after midday, a trip to Pembury and back, plus the time to chat with Mick would probably take up three hours or more. If I was unlucky, I would get caught in the school run traffic on the way back along the A25. It would double the time to get home.

No point delaying it then by going home now. I plipped the car open, gunned the engine and got going.

The Missing Piece

I found Mick propped up in his bed watching BBC1. Bargain Hunt was showing, but he switched it off when I came into the room.

'How did it go at the station?' he asked.

I didn't bother to regale him with anecdotes about CI Quinn. 'It was fine. They had already been able to obtain confessions from three of them.' Barbara was still denying any knowledge or involvement with the others and in the planned murder of her husband, a tactic that was unlikely to bring the result she wanted. 'My concern is with the whereabouts and identity of the witch and with who poisoned you.'

'You think Emma might be involved?'

'Emma is the girl you spent Wednesday night with?'

'Yes.'

'Do you have a picture?'

'No. taking pictures of girls you sleep with once is creepy, man.' A valid point. 'What do you want to see her picture for?'

I ignored the question. 'Can you describe her for me please?'

'Err, about five feet eight inches tall, blonde, stunning rack, slim waist.'

'More detail,' I prompted.

'Oh, err, really pretty blue eyes.'

'Her age?'

He hesitated, his cheeks coloured slightly. 'Somewhere around forty, I think.'

'Did you get her last name?'

'Stone.'

'Emma Stone? The famous Hollywood actress, Emma Stone.' That her name matched someone famous did not make it fake, but it hinted that she had given him a false name instead of her real one.

'Anything else? Anything else about her that you remember that might help give me an accurate picture?'

'Um, she had quite big biceps.'

And there it was.

I pulled out my phone, googled Victoria Mallory and showed him the picture.

'Hey, that's her! That's Emma Stone. Except it says Victoria Mallory on the picture.'

'Dr. Mallory is the coroner that examined your father's body and determined that his death was accidental.'

He looked stunned. He was adding it up.

'I think she's directly involved. Her verdicts are never questioned so she can write what she likes. The old lady...'

'The witch?'

'Yes, the witch is murdering people, I still don't know how, and the coroner is covering it up.'

'Why?'

'For money would be my first guess. I also think she poisoned you.'

His eyes widened. He hadn't connected the dots until then. 'How?'

'Anthrax can be dispensed in a powder form. It would have been easy for her to sprinkle it on something you ate or into a drink maybe. You can contract it by ingestion or inhalation, so it was probably easy for her.' I had looked up Anthrax poisoning while I was sitting in the police waiting room.

I looked about, twitching while I tried to make a decision. 'I need you to call the police. They need to come and take a statement from you.'

'Should I call them now?' he asked, his hand reaching for his phone.

I had already told the police that I thought she was involved somehow and had been dismissed. Mick would call from here and be able to report that I thought he knew who had poisoned him. 'Do it,' I said. There was grit in my voice now. I could sense the end of the case.

I hung around while he made the call. He spoke to one person, was passed to another and then another and the phone call got quite animated as suddenly the person he was talking to was quite interested in what he had to say. A poisoning in rural Kent was a rare occasion. I imagined at the other end of the phone was a detective that suddenly had a reason to take their feet off the desk.

When he hung up, he looked satisfied. 'They are on their way.'

I nodded and stood up. 'You don't need me anymore. I will be of no assistance with the police, I might actually cloud their involvement, so I will get going.'

'What about the witch?'

Good question. I didn't have an answer. That wasn't what one told the client though. 'I believe the police will soon have her in custody. Your stepmother and her friends will provide enough information for them to track her down.' I wasn't convinced that was true, but it sounded better than "Don't shut your eyes".

We said our goodbyes. I promised to send him a final bill, and he promised faithfully to honour it even though he worried that the ten grand he had received from his step-mother was now most likely forfeit and due to be paid back.

I left him with that quandary and headed for home.

Never Turn Your Back

I got home expecting to find Hilary on the sofa watching daytime TV or perhaps a movie, but when I called out to him as I closed the door behind me, I got no reply.

The dogs ran out to greet me though, so I went through my usual routine of making a fuss of them and letting them out into the garden. They trotted across the patio and onto the lawn where both lifted a leg. I left them outside to explore. It was trying to rain again. Spots were visible on my patio and there was another storm around. It wasn't visible, but I could hear it in the distance.

As I filled the kettle, I talked to Kevin the toad. 'You didn't prove to be of much use, did you? I was going to take you back to Frank, but he insists that he cannot keep you. So, what do I do with you? I don't want a pet toad.'

In response to my question, he farted. It made a high-pitched whistling noise as he had lifted his little toad bottom out of the water first.

'Lovely.' I moved away, electing to make tea later when

there wasn't so much toad fart in the air by my kettle. I would have to find a new home for him.

Another rumble of thunder as I was filling the kettle resulted in the dogs barking. They were not fans of the thunder and always barked at it. At night, when there was a storm, they would burrow right into me for protection, my closeness somehow comforting to them.

They wouldn't want to stay outside now so I went back to the patio door to let them in. I never got there though.

As I left the kitchen, I was drawn to a halt by the wet footprints on the tile in my lobby. Someone else had come into the house behind me. I rarely locked the door when I was in. I had only felt the need once or twice ever, like when the Klowns had been promising to kill me a few weeks ago and on Wednesday night when the scary witch was in my garden.

Now there was someone in my house. Bull barked, the familiar sound his particular bark to be let in. I had lived with them long enough to discern different barks.

I didn't go to him though. I turned slowly, looking for where the footprints had gone. They went toward the dining room/office.

With my heart beating in my chest, I stepped into the room. The witch was standing with her back to me. She was staring at the picture of her on the wall. The one I had taken with my phone.

'It's a good picture,' she said, her back still to me. Slowly she turned around. 'I have to commend you for your persistence and your ability. No one has ever tied anything to me before. No one ever got close.'

I was gritting my teeth, my face turning into an angry snarl. I was standing in front of a murderer. She hadn't the slightest remorse for her acts, nor did she show me the slightest fear and it was pissing me off.

I was a six-foot-tall muscular man facing down a hobbled old woman. She was shrunken with age and stooped. She might have been taller in her youth, but hunched over, she was only a little more than five feet now.

Then she produced a gun from her right sleeve. It was suddenly in her hand and pointed at me. I didn't recognise the make, my knowledge of weapons severely lacking, but if it was loaded the firm responsible for making it was hardly important.

'Kneel,' she spat out the instruction expecting me to comply.

'Not a chance.' I took a step toward her. Was she able to shoot me? Was that how she had killed the men? Was the whole heart bursting from the chest and all the burn marks a big act to cover the obvious bullet wound so the coroner could convincingly claim a different verdict?

She twitched the barrel slightly to the right and put a bullet hole in the wall next to me.

Okay, so she was quite able to pull the trigger. I halted my advance toward her.

'Kneel!'

If I knelt, she probably planned to move closer to me, maybe try to bind me or something. Her closeness would give me the opportunity to grab for the gun. I would need to grab its barrel, which would be too hot to touch even after firing only one shot, so I steeled myself for the pain I would need to endure. I sunk to my knees.

Thunder rumbled with intense volume. I hadn't seen the lightning, so it wasn't overhead but equally, it couldn't be that loud and be very far away. The dogs barked at the door again. They wanted to come in.

The witch looked up and out of the window toward the sky. 'Can you hear its power? I have called forth the most powerful of storms to dispatch you. Your pathetic police will not stop me.'

I lunged for her. She was not paying attention, but she moved with impossible speed for a woman her age, darting out of my grip and striking my right arm hard with the gun as it reached for her.

As I snatched my arm back, an involuntary reaction to the pain, she whipped out a set of handcuffs, slapped one over my right wrist before I could pull it back to my body and yanked me off balance.

She was impossibly strong as well!

Pitching forward, I started to worry, but she wasn't done yet. The cuff had instantly locked onto my wrist like it was supposed to, so using the bar that joined the two cuffs, she levered against my wrist to push me down.

I was flat to the carpet before I had time to react, and my wrist was twisted painfully against the joint. I knew I needed to break my wrist to get free so that was what I tried to do.

Because I am stupid.

Forcing my wrist against the direction it was designed to go sent a wave of pain through me that threatened my conscious state. It also gave her the momentary lack of resistance she needed to pull my arm behind my back and lock the cuffs to my other arm.

Then she knelt on the small of my back, her knee digging cruelly into my spine.

How on earth was I pinned by an eighty-year-old woman that couldn't even stand up straight?

'Wow,' she said coolly. 'That was easier than I expected.' Her voice had changed and now I recognised it.

She took her weight from my back. 'Hold still now, this is much easier if the victim is unconscious.'

I snapped my head around to see what she was doing but could do nothing when she landed on my shoulders and forced a rag over my face.

I had no idea what chloroform smelled of but as my senses went fuzzy, I felt certain it was what was on the rag.

As I drifted away, shaking my head to get her off as she held me in place, I thought about what I hadn't been able to see, what had just not occurred to me: The witch. The witch had never been what she seemed. She was…

End Game

I came around slowly, confused about what I was feeling, sensing. I was unable to move much but I was upright. I moved as much as I could, quickly arriving at the conclusion that I was strapped to a frame of some kind. I reached out with my fingers to touch it. It felt like plastic. I was also confused about what I could hear. It was quiet, but there was also a low, continuous hum, like a machine working. Enough of my sense returned that I realised I couldn't see because my eyes were closed.

I opened them.

'Hello, Tempest,' the witch said. She was sitting on one of my dining chairs.

I glanced about. 'Where are my dogs?' I demanded.

'Goodness, I wouldn't worry about them, dear boy. I locked them in the kitchen. They were making such a noise.'

I heard one of them, probably Bull, whine. The sound of my voice most likely the cause of his plaintive cry. At least they were inside and unharmed.

'I had to kill one of your friends,' she said it like she had changed the channel on the TV or turned down the thermostat. 'Big guy? Really pretty?'

Big Ben.

'He just let himself in. Terrible manners. He's lying on the floor by the door. I might have to cut him into pieces to get him out of here.'

He had probably phoned me to check I was going to the pub, got no answer and came looking for me.

'Nearly ready though. I should probably get ready too.'

She stood up. Stood up properly that is. No longer stooped, she was five feet eight inches tall and would have blonde hair under the witches cowl she still wore. She started to pull her black shawl-like robe open to take it off.

'Do you really think the police will not catch you, Victoria?'

She stopped her motion and stared directly at me. 'No one has ever worked it out before. Every time I have ever revealed myself to the ridiculous cheating husband, it was a complete surprise. It seems a shame to kill you now. I almost feel like I have met an equal.'

'What's making the noise?'

'Ah. Now that's an interesting question.' She continued to take off the witch's outfit. Beneath it, she had prosthetic skin over her arms and hands. I could see it now because it ended at her elbows and her top had much shorter sleeves. Her face and neck too were similarly covered, and a wig hid her blonde hair. I watched as she carefully took each piece of fake skin off and folded it into pouches before storing them in a case on my table. Then she took out a contact lens that made one of her eyes brown. The disguise was brilliant.

'You asked about the noise. This device,' with a flourish she pulled a black sheet off a squat lump on the carpet, 'is basically a giant capacitor with an electrode. When it's charged all the way up it can deliver a shock that will burn right through a person. I read about it in a medical journal more than ten years ago after a man had accidentally killed himself with one.'

The thing was half a metre in every direction and housed within a steel frame that formed a cube. It was dark in the room so making out details was hard, occasional flashes of lightning lit the room though to reveal a jumble of electrical cables connected here and there and circuit boards on one side. It was sitting on a sack barrow, the type with two wheels so that you leaned it back and wheeled it around at an angle. It looked heavy. On one side, a long, thick cable about three metres in length ended in a spike.

'They fit them in nuclear submarines. I couldn't tell you what purpose they were used for, but it was jolly hard to get hold of and modify. Apologies if I bore you with the details. It takes a while to charge up.'

'Oh, no problem.'

You complete psycho.

'This is where you beg for your life,' she prompted.

'Sorry to disappoint. I would rather know how many people you have killed.'

'Men.'

'Hmm?'

'Men. I only kill men. And the answer is seventy-three... I think. I lost count at one point, but I think it's seventy-three. Do you want to know why?'

'Let's circle back to that.' I was buying time. I didn't know what for, but it had to be a good idea. The lights were off in the house. At least they were in this room and the lobby. 'What was with the semen?'

'Oh, that. Well,' she grabbed a bag from the floor next

to the capacitor, unzipped it and pulled out something I couldn't make out. It looked like a large pile of cloth, 'the semen is something I collect. I get some from every man I kill as a reminder. I lost some a while back which is why I don't know what the true number is. I also used it to make the act more convincing. I can't let my sisters know who I am. They all believe the story of the spell. They like the runes bit, it's so mystical to them, makes it all so real and they collect for me the hair and the blood and the semen. I don't keep the blood or the hair, but the semen is a fun souvenir, don't you think?'

'What about me. You didn't get my semen.'

'Yes, I did.' She held up a test tube sized thing that had some liquid in it.

She had taken it while I was unconscious!

Unnerved and wanting desperately to check my junk, I watched as she unravelled the pile of cloth. It was a pair of rubber overalls with built-in boots.

'Are you sure you don't want to know why?' she asked.

'Oh, go on then,' I encouraged, faking my enthusiasm.

'Quite simply, all men are scum. The first one I killed was my husband. He cheated on me and had the audacity to tell me it was my fault. My father had cheated on my mother and bragged about it. I would have killed him too, but the bastard died before I had a chance. Killing my husband was so liberating, so rewarding. I knew I had to help my sisters out by freeing them from their cheating, lying bastard men.'

She moved to the device, checking something. 'Nearly there. I don't always use this, of course. It would leave a trail even I couldn't cover up. Sometimes it's poison. A few of them I drowned in the bath. A quick hit with the chloroform, hold them under for a bit. Easy. Then I turn up, do the autopsy and declare it accidental death. Fool proof.'

'All for a fee.'

'What? No! I never charge for my service. I do it for love. My sisters deserve my help. Have you not seen the joy I have brought?'

'What about my client? He was distraught at losing his father.'

She laughed at me. 'That loser? He bedded me without a second thought. Happily came in my mouth, so I could run to the toilet and pretend to spit it in the sink and then was generous enough to drink some Anthrax. You men make it all so easy. Except you. You turned me down. Twice. You are an odd character, Tempest Michaels. Anyone would think you were in love. Your client though? He's long dead.'

She started putting on the rubber overalls.

'He's not actually.'

'He's not what?' she asked the question without pausing her movements. The overalls were over her shoulder, and she was fiddling around behind her to catch the zip. 'Awfully dangerous this bit. Need to wear the right protective clothing.'

'He's not dead. Mick Cotton was rushed to the hospital and recovered from the poison.'

'Impossible.'

'I spoke with him earlier this afternoon. When I left, he was about to talk to the police. They have your picture.'

'Nonsense. You're making it up to delay your death.'

She reached back into the bag and pulled out a helmet with a visor.

'You told him your name was Emma Stone.'

That stopped her. Her face was showing anger for the

first time. She threw the helmet back down. 'You're lying!' she roared.

'How could I possibly know that if I hadn't spoken to him.'

She was trying to find an answer. Something she had missed.

'Then I'll have to kill him too,' she snapped at me.' You couldn't stop me, and you came closer than anyone. If I have to kill a few police officers, then so be it.' She picked the helmet up again. 'No. I have a better idea. I'll move again. I have moved plenty of times before. Maybe I'll go to America.'

She jammed the helmet on her head, then flicked a switch on top of the machine. Thunder clapped overhead as the noise from the machine changed pitch.

She picked up the electrode just as a loud noise came from the lobby the other side of the closed dining room door.

Her head snapped toward the noise. 'It looks like your big friend wasn't dead after all. He must have a tough skull. Do excuse me, I won't be but a minute.' She put the electrode back down on the floor, making sure the steel spike at the end was off the ground and resting on one of the insulated coils of the lead so it would not prematurely discharge and picked up the gun. She held it confidently in her right hand.

As she opened the door and stepped through it, I heard more noise. This time it was Hilary's voice!

He yelled, 'Take that, you psycho bitch!' And I could hear a struggle and the sound of the gun skittering across the tile. The umbrella stand next to the door went flying. I could tell because it was made of wicker. Nothing else makes a sound like that. I tried struggling free of my bonds but the frame I was tied to held me firm.

The fight between Hilary and Victoria was still going. I could hear Hilary losing though. A blow would land, and he would make a noise, an outrushing of air from his lungs as she hit his breadbasket or a gasp of pain as she grabbed or twisted or punched. I had been beaten by her in seconds and could testify to her ability. She had fight training, lots of it by my judgement.

'You pathetic sack.' Her voice carried through from the lobby before she came back through the door pushing Hilary ahead of her. She had his right arm by the wrist, and had it twisted up under his armpit It was folded against the joint and she was forcing it upward, so he had to walk on his toes. Her other hand was gripped around the back of his neck giving her control of his head.

She wheeled him around to face me. 'Another one of your friends, Tempest?' I said nothing. 'You really have let them down. I guess I'll just have to kill you all.'

At that precise moment, Hilary let all his weight go. He just folded his legs out and dropped. I heard a sickening crunch as his shoulder dislocated, but he caught her by surprise and dropped free.

In one smooth, fluid motion, he grabbed the electrode by its insulated sheath, came up to his knees and jammed it into her as she lunged for him.

In front of me, there was a blinding flash as the capacitor dumped its full charge through her body. She was propelled backward, hitting the window behind her with a sickening crunch. Hilary was blasted back to the opposite side of the room to fetch up against the patio doors.

Even I was shunted back, but the wall was mere inches behind me.

I was momentarily blind and deaf, but the terrible ringing in my ears was like sweet music because I was alive.

'Hilary?' I called. I could barely hear my voice. It was like my head was underwater. He might have answered but I couldn't tell.

'Hilary?' I called again.

'Here. I'm here, Tempest.' He was touching me. I couldn't see him but the big white nothing that was my vision was slowing fading in its intensity.

'Are you okay?'

He snorted with laughter. 'Never better.'

I wasn't sure what that meant but it sounded positive enough, so I left it alone. 'Did you see Big Ben? Is it true?' I didn't want him to be dead. It would leave too big of a hole in my life. Plus, I didn't want to go to his funeral and see eighteen thousand women turn up to mourn him.

'He's alive. I saw him moving. I think he's hurt though. There's blood coming from his head.' One of my feet came free. Hilary was untying me. 'Sorry, this is taking so long. My right arm doesn't seem to want to work.'

'It's dislocated.'

'How can you tell?'

'I watched it happen. The hold she had on your arm is designed to pop the shoulder out of its joint if the captive struggles.'

'What did I miss?' Big Ben's voice came from my left, over by the lobby door.

Improvised Pub O'Clock

FRIDAY, NOVEMBER 11TH 2012HRS

Twenty minutes later I slugged down a long draft of cold, crisp beer. Big Ben had placed a call to Jagjit who was sitting with Basic at The Dirty Habit pub around the corner wondering where on earth the rest of us had got to.

Jagjit had grabbed Basic and shouted to Natasha that there was trouble at my place, then the three of them ran to find Big Ben, Hilary and I all sat on the floor in the lobby with our backs to the wall and a very, very dead, attractive blonde lady lying in a heap in my dining room.

Natasha was incredibly sweet in her concern for me. I assured her I was the least injured of the three and was only still on the floor because my eyesight was still not fully returned, and my balance seemed a bit off. I told her that I was only alive due to Hilary's bravery and watched as she gave him a lip-to-lip reward. His chest and his very being seemed to swell as if his soul was glowing and growing.

We asked Basic to put the kettle on and sent Jagjit to buy beer from the village shop – to hell with my diet, I needed a beer. Only once those tasks were performed did I place a call to the police.

Jagjit got back before the police arrived so I was happily downing a can of Cobra lager when flashing blue lights started to reflect through the frosted pane of my door.

By then, we had moved through to the kitchen and had fetched chairs from the dining room for Big Ben and Hilary. We had fashioned a makeshift sling from a tea towel to support his arm and given him paracetamol and ibuprofen to take the edge off the pain. He was bearing it really well.

Big Ben had an egg-sized lump on the back of his skull that had split the skin and spilled a good amount of blood before the flow had stemmed itself. He acted as if he was already recovered in typical Big Ben style and was most likely considering who he could call upon to play naughty nurse.

The dogs tried to bark at everyone that came in to start with but as the procession of police, paramedics, coroners and then crime scene chaps kept coming, even they gave up.

'Reload,' I requested as I held my empty can above my head. I was sitting on the kitchen tile on a cushion with both dogs on my lap. I was comfortable enough and very glad to not only be alive but to be surrounded by people that I could trust.

While the police and paramedics and others buzzed around us, we chatted like we would on any other Friday night.

A female paramedic was dressing Big Ben's head wound and, as usual, she was not immune to his charm. As he blasted her with his best smoulder, Jagjit tapped him on the arm.

'Yes, mate?' he asked.

'Erm, just curious about whether there was an update on Bethany, Britney, and Bianca?' said Jagjit.

The smoulder faltered. 'I can report that I'm out of the mire with Britney. She messaged yesterday to let me know she was surfing the crimson tide.'

Natasha screwed her face up. 'Surfing the... Oh, my God, Ben. That's a horrible turn of phrase.'

'Not ambiguous though, is it?' he pressed on. 'I appear to still have an issue with Bethany and Bianca.' He sucked his bottom lip for a second, deep in thought. 'I honestly thought I would never get caught.'

The paramedic lady finished what she was doing and moved away, sensing that Big Ben was the player he looked to be.

'Having babies could really cramp my style. Girls will assume I'm married or at least involved monogamously with someone if they see me pushing a pram.'

'Two prams,' Jagjit added helpfully.

Big Ben scowled at him.

Hilary had something to say on the matter. 'I think you are coming at this from the wrong angle, Ben. Kids are great, and you are all getting older. If you don't start procreating soon, you may miss out on one of the best things in life.'

Unintentionally, I caught Natasha's eye. She gave me a smile that could have meant anything.

Big Ben looked to be considering Hilary's comment but hadn't been sold on the idea.

'Okay, how about we come at it from another angle?' Hilary tried. 'A few months from now you are presented with a son. What do you call him?'

'No idea,' he shot back, a trace of annoyance in his voice.

'How about Harry?' Natasha suggested.

'How about Ace?' asked Jagjit. Big Ben seemed to consider that one. However, before he could finish thinking and speak Jagjit continued. 'Middle name would have to be Hole though.'

There was a moment of silence as we all looked at each other, then simultaneously we all burst out laughing.

'Ace Hole,' spluttered Big Ben.

And so there followed a competition to come up with the best boy's name for Big Ben's son.

Chief Inspector Quinn arrived twenty minutes after the first uniforms had started coming through my door. I recognised his annoying voice giving orders.

I called out, 'In here, Quinn.' Then realised my error. I had shown an interest in him and thus opened a door for him to ignore me and pretend I was unimportant.

A paramedic knelt in front of me. They had spoken to me already and moved on to examine Hilary and Big Ben as the priority patients. Now he wanted to check out how I was doing. As he flashed a light into my eyes to see what they did, I asked him about the body in my dining room.

'I heard them say the spike had gone through the rubber to reach her skin. She died instantly from the charge.' He stopped talking and looked around. Big Ben, Jagjit, Hilary, and all the others were listening intently to what he had to say. 'Err, how much do you want me to say? It's a bit gory.'

'Tell us everything,' Hilary demanded.

'Was it you who got her?' he asked.

'Yup,' I replied before Hilary could decide how to answer. 'Bravest damned thing I ever saw. Dislocated his own arm to do it.'

The paramedic's face was filled with awe. He turned his head to find a colleague. 'Here, Wendy. Come listen to this.'

Wendy was in the lobby where she had been talking on the radio, most likely with their dispatcher or the hospital, but she did as asked and crossed the kitchen to join the man tending to me, drawing half a dozen other cops and random uniforms with her.

The paramedic, that had largely forgotten about my eyes, then regaled a growing crowd with Hilary's courage in facing down the crazed serial killer.

Encouraged to talk, Hilary launched hesitantly into a retelling of the tale from his perspective. He had gone to bed with a migraine in the middle of the afternoon and had awoken when Big Ben came in and called out for me. Hearing a scuffle downstairs, he slid out of bed and poked his head around the landing. What he saw was the witch standing over Big Ben as he lay on the tile in my lobby. Blood was creating a pool by his head and the witch had a steel bar in her hand.

Then he listened to her chatting as she performed unseen tasks in the dining room. She was addressing me by name, but I never answered or responded. Eventually, he concluded that I must also be unconscious.

He snuck carefully down the stairs, praying they would not squeak under his weight, then wracked with indecision, he waited and waited. His legs were going numb from standing still, but I had come around and was talking to her, talking about who she really was, and she was explaining that I was about to die. He heard her tell me all about the capacitor and what it would do.

To his great credit, Hilary didn't embellish his story at all. He described himself as terrified, the conviction of his tale drawing utter silence from the sea of faces now staring at him. When finally he could wait no longer, he had taken his keys from his pocket and thrown them hard at my front door to create a noise, then leaped at her when she emerged from the dining room with her back to him.

He admitted that he hadn't thought beyond tackling her and wasn't surprised when she proceeded to beat him half to death. He laughed at himself at that point, winning yet more appreciation from the crowd.

As he reached the end of the story, the crowd in front of us began to part. Someone was forcing their way to the front. As the paramedic that had completely forgotten about me and his colleague Wendy finally stepped aside, it was Anthea's form that they revealed.

'Hi, Anthea,' Hilary managed with a smile.

'Oh, baby. Baby, are you okay?' She had tears on her face. Her mascara now on her cheeks and making a bid for freedom.

Hilary shrugged, the foolish move rewarding him with a hard jolt of pain from his ruined shoulder. Anthea rushed to his side. 'I'll heal,' he replied. It was the exact right thing to say.

Wendy pulled out her phone and took a picture of the wounded hero and his loving wife. She was crying too. 'That's so beautiful,' she said. 'You are such a lucky lady.'

'I'm sorry, sweetie. I have been so wrong about you,' Anthea said. 'I have missed you so much.'

'That's okay, angel. Daddy's coming home now.' Everything about them seemed different. The whole dynamic had changed. I suspected that Daddy was, in fact, going to the hospital, but he would be home soon enough.

This was pleasing news to me. 'I'm glad you two have made up. Maybe I can have my house back now,' I joked.

Anthea snapped her head around, her face a scowl again. 'Why are you speaking? This is all your fault. How dare you bring my sweetie into harm's way?'

There was the Anthea I knew.

It was after midnight when I finally got them all out of my house. Both Big Ben and Hilary had gone to the hospital in ambulances. Hilary with his wife holding his hand the whole way. Jagjit and Basic had gone home at my insistence and though there was a part of me that wanted Natasha to stay when she offered to, I told her to go as well. I think her offer was just to help me out cleaning up and stuff rather than anything more fun. She kissed me before she went to the door. A slow, gentle, passionate kiss that I responded to in kind, but did so wondering if I should be participating. My emotions were still confused about what I wanted. Or rather they weren't because they knew what they wanted and were certain it was out of reach.

If I genuinely thought I was settling for Natasha, could I do so?

Finally alone, I let the dogs in the garden, made myself a rum and coke and went up to bed. Laying in the dark I thought back on the case. As a thought occurred to me, I leapt out of bed again and went downstairs to my mostly wrecked office.

The capacitor blast that had killed Victoria had gouged a hole in my wall and singed my curtains. There was blood in the carpet and basically the whole room needed to be redecorated. It was a task for another day.

At my laptop I pulled up the video footage I had taken on Monday of the ladies leaving the pub in West Malling. The witch had evaded me but watching now I saw Victoria leaving ten minutes after the rest of them had gone. It was just enough time for her to have changed out of her disguise in the toilets. I hadn't seen it because I had been looking for an old lady with black hair, not an attractive blonde half her age.

That Victoria and the witch were one also explained how she had gone out the window in the tearoom and how she had scaled the wall in my garden on Wednesday night. Impossible tasks for a stooped old lady and no trouble at all for a fit, athletic woman. It also explained how the witch had instantly known I was spying on them in the pub. She had met me the previous afternoon at Dorothy's house. Furthermore, I now knew why James's attempts with facial recognition software had yielded no results – the face of the witch didn't exist.

I closed the laptop down, the light from it extinguished to leave me in darkness. Trudging back up to bed I forced away thoughts of Victoria and how close she had come to killing me. I didn't want to dwell on her motivations or the lives she had taken.

It had been a taxing few days. Sleep did not evade me for long.

Postscript

THE PHONE CALL NO ONE WANTS

Sunday, November 20th 2143hrs

A week later, on the Sunday evening I was watching a cop show on TV. I had the dogs asleep either side of me, their warm heads on each thigh a comfort. Natasha had called to ask me out for lunch. I had declined, like a fool, telling her I still didn't feel right and needed a few more days.

It was an outright lie. Something I felt bad about, however, I doubted telling her I was besotted by another woman would do me any favours. I was still hoping I could clear my head from thoughts of Amanda and be able to move on before I ruined my chances with Natasha. I wondered if seeing Natasha naked would make me forget Amanda, but I knew it was unfair to invite Natasha to my bed just to see if I could find some interest in her.

I hadn't seen my parents today either which was relatively unusual, but I had spent the time repainting my dining room after having a chap in to resurface the walls earlier in the week. I still needed new carpet, but I was getting the room back to a liveable state. The carpet had already gone in the trash – it stank and there had been bits of Victoria's burned flesh in it.

DIY was not something I relished, nor was it something I hated so I knuckled down and got it done, missing out on roast dinner with mum and dad in the process. When I called to say I wasn't coming, mum revealed that I would have been disappointed anyway. Dad had taken an extra shift at the Royal Dockyard where he occasionally worked as a tour guide to show visitors around the warships they had there.

Anyway, my phone rang. The screen claiming that it was my mother calling. I answered, 'Good evening, mother.'

'Oh, Tempest, come quickly!' she wailed down the phone at me.

I was instantly alert, sitting upright to disturb the dogs. 'What is it? Is dad okay?'

'No!' she wailed again, her voice wobbling with emotion. 'I'm at the hospital.'

Dammit had he had a heart attack? I hoped it wasn't a stroke. Please don't let it be a stroke.

'They got him,' she said.

What? 'Who got who, Mother?'

She sniffed deeply, I imagined her usually stern face crinkled and snotty at the other end of the phone. 'At the dockyard. He kept going on about strange goings-on. Noises being heard by the night security guys, echoes of voices during the day coming from the rope room but no one there when they went to investigate.'

She fell silent. 'Go on,' I prompted. I was already out of my chair and moving toward the stairs. I was wearing slobby grey flannel gym gear which I had put on after a bath an hour ago following a session at the gym before that.

'He didn't come home on time this evening, which I thought was unusual but figured that maybe he had stayed to have a rum with one of the guys. Then I got a phone call from the police because he was found unconscious by a cleaner as they emptied the bins. They whacked him on the head and threw him in the trash!' She cried.

'You are in the Medway?'

'Yes.' Medway hospital was a twenty-minute drive from my house.

I promised to be there as soon as I could, disconnected and made the journey in under fifteen minutes by not bothering to stop at red lights or slow down for corners. Not a practice I would endorse but I felt motivated to arrive at my destination.

I wrapped Mum into a big hug and held onto her for a few minutes, kissing the top of her head and reassuring her. We were by his bed in A&E where there were doctors and nurses bustling about but no one currently attending to him.

There wasn't much they could do other than monitor him. He was still unconscious, but his vitals were all normal. He would most likely be transferred to a special care ward and tended to until he came around. An event that could not occur soon enough.

Sat by the bed was a man I didn't know. He looked to be slightly older than my father, his white hair little more than wisps on his nearly bald skull. As I let go of my mother I moved to shake his hand.

'Tempest Michaels,' I introduced myself.

'Alan Page,' he replied, shaking my hand with a firm grip. 'I worked with your father at the dockyard. I need to speak with you. In private, like.' He had an odd accent to complement an unusual pattern of speech. He had to be ex-Navy like my father, so chances were his original accent, from whatever region of England he had been born in, was long forgotten, washed away by leaving the area and the constant bombardment of other accents one gets in the forces.

I indicated with my head, and we moved to one side as my mother went to the head of the bed and held my father's hand.

Out of earshot, Alan still felt the need to check all around for anyone that might eavesdrop. When satisfied that we could talk, he turned his attention to me. 'There're rum goings-on at the yard, son. Your father and I were looking into it, but this has gotten a bit much for me now, I don't mind saying.'

'What kind of goings-on?' I asked, using the same unusual word.

'Whispers in the rigging room,' he replied, whispering the words with an ominous tone.

Next in the Blue Moon Investigations Series

vinci-books.com/crazyaliens

There are crop circles in the fields and unexplained lights in the sky at night. Does Amanda's latest case have aliens at its core?

Of course not, because there is no such thing! But when a farmer hires paranormal investigator Amanda Harper to look into his glowing milk, she doesn't sense how crazy things are about to get. Before she can even start investigating, a frozen body is found and the conspiracy theory nutters arrive to argue about the inner workings of an alien freeze ray.

Turn the page for a free preview…

Crop Circles, Cows and Crazy Aliens: Chapter One

A VISITATION

Tuesday, November 8th 2203hrs

In the darkness of the countryside, the creature crept forward. Through its visor, it could see the lights of the building ahead.

A light rain was falling. Drops hit the creature's protective suit but could not penetrate it. Underfoot the muddy soil squelched, the weight of the creature displacing the dirt as it walked.

It crept forward, the sound of its breathing loud in its ears inside the protective helmet. Nervously, it scanned about, hoping to make contact with the lifeforms that inhabited this place. It was not so bold as to dare to approach the dwelling it could see between the larger buildings. No, timidly it hoped it would be seen.

It had kept to the shadows as it approached, now though, to get any closer it would have to step into the light. It wanted to see inside the house. Light came from within, and noise too. Faint sounds of voices.

Crossing the expanse of moonlit yard, it could feel the unnatural surface of the concrete beneath its feet. It was nearing a window, planning to take a look inside when suddenly the door opened, pinning the creature in a shaft of light.

Frozen, it watched the new hole in the building. A human emerged. It was calling something, the voice high pitched, 'Here, Kitty. Puss, puss, puss.' A female of the species and clearly pregnant.

The woman was looking about but had not yet looked up. When finally, she did, her mouth was opening to call again. Like the creature, she froze, but it was momentary. As her eyes widened, she started to scream. The noise pierced the silence of the night, jolting the creature into motion. The protective suit it wore limited its range of motion, but it hurried away as fast as it could.

A second voice called after it, deeper than the first, but did not pursue. As it left the buildings behind, the creature inside the suit allowed itself a smile of elation. Seeing the inhabitants of the farm had been terrifying but exhilarating. It had been a necessary part of the plan – it needed to be seen, to be recognised for what it was.

It had no way of knowing what the inhabitants might now do, but it was confident it had set in motion a series of events that would enable it to achieve a glorious goal.

Crop Circles, Cows and Crazy Aliens: Chapter Two

RED LETTER DAY

Wednesday, 9th November 0745hrs

Waking up this morning, it felt like a big day. The 8th of November had been the last official day of my career in the Kent police service. That I had handed my uniform and ID card in more than a week ago, didn't change that this was the first day that I would not be paid for my service since I was twenty-one years old.

In the years that I had amassed in uniform, I had earned a pension. Not a big one, and it would be not until my fifty-fifth birthday that I saw any sign of it, but it was there tucked away, nevertheless.

I was scratching to find positives from the experience. It was a lot like attending ballet classes when I was four. I did it because I had seen it on TV and convinced myself that it would be glamorous and fun and then had tried really hard because I believed that success relied upon me giving it my all. In the end, I had given it up because I found it neither glamorous nor fun and the only reward I got was blisters. Being in the Police had been exactly the same.

It was behind me now though. My life had moved on. In some ways at least. I was still the same me; determined to be self-sufficient and capable while quivering inside half the time.

I caught myself in the act of self-doubt and berated myself out loud. 'Snap out of it, Amanda.' I sat up in bed and stared at the mirror.

My new job, working for Tempest Michaels at the Blue Moon Investigation Agency, was different every day. I was telling myself that this was a positive thing, even though I was not entirely certain it was. There was a part of me that wondered if maybe I should learn accountancy because it would be mundane and safe. Safe sounded good because in the few cases I had already pursued in my new job, I had been threatened, tasered, stripped naked and almost killed. Some of those on more than one occasion.

My adrenalin was getting employed more often than I had anticipated. My boss kept assuring me that this was not normal and that most of the cases he'd investigated since opening the business had involved hours of research and careful deduction, rather than chases, fights and stitching wounds closed.

That was not my experience thus far.

I swung my legs out of bed, then propelled myself up and into the cool air. My first task was to shut the window as my skin was already goose-pimpling from the November temperature coming through it. I found I had to have the window open at night – it was too warm otherwise, even with the heating off. Once up though and without the sanctuary of my duvet to maintain my warmth, it needed to close.

In the living room, I turned on the TV, powered up a news channel and flicked on the kettle for coffee. I had elected sleep over gym but forced myself to perform some basic stretches and exercises. Yoga poses, and some calisthenics would do for today.

At twenty past eight, with coffee, a pint of water and a blueberry bagel in my belly, I set off for work. I needed a new case so this morning would involve reviewing enquiries, calling a few clients and determining which case or cases held the most merit. Case selection was more complex than solving the case itself according to Tempest. As a firm that investigated the paranormal, most of the enquiries we got were from complete whackos.

Just yesterday, James, the office assistant, had read me an enquiry from a man that claimed to be in possession of a demonic banana. Tempest had taken the time to email the man back with instruction to throw it away.

There was all too much opportunity to rip people off. Tempest could have sold the man a story about the dangers of demonic fruit, taken some tap water labelled as holy water and charged the idiot five hundred pounds for an exorcism. Of course, if that had been something Tempest might have entertained, I would never have taken the job with him. He was all about integrity, charging an honest fee and making sure we felt decent about the service we provided.

The service itself was often about picking up where police investigations could not continue. Some crimes did defy explanation, but more regularly there was no crime occurring, there was just a mysterious event that the client wanted unravelled. We had one such case on the books now – crop circles.

The client had first emailed us a few weeks ago. It was a

something or nothing enquiry where they had something mysterious happening but didn't really know what they wanted us to do about it. Now it seemed to have escalated with additional odd occurrences. Yesterday, in the filtered emails that James sent Tempest and me, was a further email from the same client in which he claimed the cows' milk at the dairy farm he owned had turned luminous. This now was more serious for him than the loss of some wheat because his income stream had been shut off.

Thinking about my next case options in the car as I drove to the office, this one came out as a forerunner. Thankfully, the journey from my apartment to the office each day only takes a few minutes because I know the backroads to get there and avoid almost all of the early morning traffic. The main arteries leading into and out of Maidstone, where I live, and the surrounding Medway towns, all clog terribly at peak times. If I had an office-based job, I would most likely buy myself a pedal bike and cycle to work rather than fight the endless traffic.

My job though was far from office based. Instead, I spent more than half my time out doing investigative work. There was research to do, but it was mostly performed by James because he was not only good at it but of the three of us, he was permanently in the office, so that we always had someone there to receive enquiries in person. The new office, which we only moved into two days ago, occupied a prominent position on Rochester High Street. Its prominence generated drop-ins where people walking by would stick their head through the door and make their enquiry in person.

The percentage of genuine enquiries to crazy ones actually seemed to be higher when made in person although we only had two days' worth of data to go by thus far.

I pulled into my parking spot a few minutes after eight thirty. I was the first one to arrive this morning. More usually James beat me and often Tempest too. I liked that I was the keen one today.

Inside, I powered up the lights and the coffee machine and turned on my computer before I heard footsteps echoing along the passage that connects the carpark with the main office.

'Morning,' called James as he swished in through the back door. It opened next to my office, so he was instantly outside my door.

'Hi, James.' I had to look up to check what James was wearing. He liked to cross-dress. He was gay and mostly gender-neutral, but in the short time that I had known him, he'd been dressed as a girl more often than not. Only in the last few days had the balance swung to boys' clothes. Today he wore black skinny jeans, a white shirt, black tie and black leather jacket with a pair of four-inch red stiletto heels that really complimented the whole ensemble. His hair was getting long and voluminous. The style this morning was swept from a side parting on the left to create a low hanging flick over his right eye. It was stuck in place with product. He also wore more make-up than me, which when you consider that he was trying to look like a girl and wasn't, came as no great surprise.

'You're in early,' he observed. 'Want some coffee?'

'I set the machine already,' I called after him. My computer had finished its boot up which allowed me to get started. I was surprised at how excited I was to get stuck into a new case.

About the Author

When Steve Higgs wrote his debut novel, *Paranormal Nonsense*, he was a captain in the British Army. He would like to pretend that he had one of those careers that must be blacked out and generally denied by the government, and that he has to change his name and move constantly because he is still on the watch list in several countries. In truth, though, he started out as a mechanic - not like Jason Statham in the film by that name, sneaking around as a hitman, but more like one of those sleazy guys who charges a fortune and keeps your car for a week even though the only thing you went in for was a squeaky door hinge.

At school, he was largely disinterested in all subjects except creative writing, for which he won his first prize at the age of ten. However, calling it the first prize he won suggests that there were other prizes, which is not the case. Awards may yet come, but in the meantime, he enjoys writing mystery and thriller novels and claims to have more than a hundred books forming a restless queue in his mind because they are desperate to be written.

Now retired from the military, he lives in southeast England with a duo of lazy sausage dogs. Surrounded by rolling hills, brooding castles, and vineyards, he doubts he'll ever leave, the beer is just too good.